ght ©2023 by Nannette Potter

ly Publishing
nnewawa, #274
CA 93613

ition: May 2023

79-8-9873547-0-4 (paperback)
79-8-9873547-1-1 (hardcover)
79-8-9873547-2-8 (ebook)

esign by Cherie Foxley at www.cheriefox.com

in the United States of America

PIERCE THE DARKI

NANNETTE POTTER

Copy

Thank
copyri
witho

Grayl
655 M
Clovi

First F

ISBN
ISBN
ISBN

Cover

Printe

For my parents, Frank and Mamie Dias,
and to the loves of my life,
Mark, Phillip, Monica, Jeff, Alexandra, Kaylee,
Ayden, Noah, and Devyn

God decided in advance to adopt us into his own family by bringing us to himself through Jesus Christ. This is what he wanted to do, and it gave him great pleasure.

CHAPTER
ONE

November 14, 7:55 p.m.
London, England

Sir Edward Dunn adjusted his tie in the elevator and basked in his good fortune. He intended to celebrate his divorce from wife number three—finally. Even with a prenuptial agreement, the damn woman still left with millions of his hard-earned money. Tonight he'd get roaring drunk and bed a beautiful woman, and not necessarily in that order. His palatial home in the country paled against the robust distractions of London. A stay at the Park Lane Regent never disappointed. Although the last time his bit of fun at the hotel cost him his marriage.

He would rather be horse-whipped than spend one more evening at the nearby Royal Opera House in Covent Garden. Or take an evening stroll to London's West End, with its cacophony of theatregoers, as wife number three had insisted upon every damn visit. No, his tastes ran to more private entertainment.

The Regent's Boulevardier Bar afforded him this luxury. The dim lighting and dramatic black and burnished gold décor served seduction on a silver platter. Music from the adjoining foyer wafted through the open double doors. The atmosphere oozed romance, but with three ex-wives and no children, Sir Edward lived for his own pleasures. While it was true that making lucrative arms deals as chairman of the Maritime Defense Corporation could be better than sex, he sometimes needed reminding that the activities were not mutually exclusive. He richly deserved a night out.

A waiter escorted him to a seat at one of the intimate golden coves that lined the interior. After ordering one of the rare whiskies off the menu, he scanned the room. Dozens of patrons sat around dark wooden tables. All the barstools were occupied. Three attractive women appeared to be alone or waiting for someone. In orbit around them he counted seven overeager men shifting about like hyenas circling prey.

Sir Edward dealt with reality, facts, numbers. And he never lied to himself. Women did not find him attractive. Never had. At sixty-one, he shaved his head rather than deal with the tufts of hair that remained around his ears. His lack of exercise showed in both physique and waxen pallor. But his wealth more than compensated for his lack of appeal.

His competitors learned by hard experience not to underestimate him. Just last week he had crushed a hostile takeover attempt by his leadership and adept maneuvering. He refused to be put out to pasture like an old gelding or to allow a simpering foreigner to steal his company.

One of the circling men, perhaps in his thirties, made his move on the stunning blonde at the end of the bar. Amused, Sir Edward grinned as the man's charming demeanor turned to dismay, stepping back as if the woman were going to literally bite him.

Time to show these pups how a real man made a conquest.

The blonde took a sip of her martini. Her mane of long hair beckoned to be mussed and fondled. He fantasized about running his hands through the silky mass. She wore a scarlet sleeveless dress, a perfect shade for her pale complexion, with a plunging neckline that accentuated her firm breasts. Based on his experience, a woman dressed provocatively, sitting at a bar alone, signaled a green light to a bit of fun. She could be here on a first date. Or perhaps her tastes ran to someone more mature—someone with more to offer.

He motioned for a waiter and ordered another drink for himself and one for the blonde. Five minutes later her gaze lingered on him as she raised her fresh martini in a toast. After taking a few sips, she stood, straightening her dress. She needn't have bothered. The short dress hugged the curve of her body, and she damn well knew it. The sway of her hips mesmerized Sir Edward as she covered the twenty-five feet between them.

"Why, aren't you the gentleman," the blonde said in a lilting Southern drawl. She slid next to him on the settee, crossing one long leg over the other.

"She's making her move."

Vivienne Martel spoke softly into a wireless security microphone from one of the far tables with a direct sightline to Sir Edward. For the most part, surveillance bored her, except for the rare occasions when she assumed a role and played dress-up. Today she'd created a role to blend into the atmosphere of elegance and sophistication.

Vivienne had begun trailing Sir Edward in the morning, changing her appearance once to avoid detection. But she needn't have bothered. He was oblivious to anyone not wearing a short skirt. She could almost feel sorry for the blonde.

After several rounds of drinks, Sir Edward and the blonde stood to make their exit. She hugged his proffered arm to her breast and leaned into him, careful to keep the small, pearl-encrusted evening bag in her left hand.

"They're on the move."

Vivienne left fifty pounds on the table and followed the pair. For this leg of surveillance, she'd chosen a frumpy, floral dress and a gray wig that reminded her of Queen Elizabeth II's coiffure. The handle on her cane bore a carved wooden lion, and inside its shaft hid a rapier-pointed blade. A Walther PPQ semi-automatic pistol lay snug in her handbag.

"Moving to the lift."

People milled about the lobby, making it difficult to stay in the guise of an infirm elderly woman. At this pace, she would never reach the lift in time. As a young man carrying an ice bucket hustled past her, Vivienne called, "Young man," in a loud, tremulous voice. "Please be a dear and hold the elevator door."

Anxious to please, the young man smiled, ran to the lift and, juggling the ice bucket, held the door open. Sir Edward and the blonde, alone in the elevator, glared at the old woman, clearly annoyed at the interruption.

Unperturbed, Vivienne entered and turned her back on the couple. An hour earlier, she had poured Annick Goutal Gardenia Passion eau de parfum on her dress. The aroma of gardenias filled the elevator. An overpowering aroma of perfume to dull other senses.

The lift slowly climbed. Sir Edward, ever the optimist, had reserved a suite at eleven thousand pounds a night. A pittance for a man with his annual income.

Her heart hammering in her chest, Vivienne removed the glove from her right hand. In situations like this, it was advantageous to grip a rapier or gun bare-handed. Sometimes her work could be quite thrilling. She could hear fabric rubbing against fabric behind her. The blonde wasted no time.

The doors opened onto the sixth floor. To her left, Vivienne saw her partner pushing a room service cart toward them. She sidled to the right, allowing the couple to pass in front of her.

Sir Edward and the blonde were trapped between them.

Without hesitation, the blonde drew a semi-automatic from her clutch and drew down on the waiter.

"Chase!" Vivienne cried out.

Her partner dove behind a side table, the bullet grazing his upper arm.

The blonde fired again. Chase hurled himself at the nearest doorway, giving him only inches of cover.

Vivienne saw the muzzle of his Glock clear the wall. Afraid of possible crossfire, she pulled on the lion's head, exposing the rapier, and lunged at her opponent. The slit in the red dress allowed the blonde to move without restraint. She dodged, the rapier only shearing the red fabric.

As Vivienne recovered, ready to strike again, the blonde drove her elbow into Sir Edward's nose, blood quickly soaking the front of his shirt. Chase emerged from the doorway and drew his gun, but the blonde grabbed Sir Edward by the scruff of his suit and hauled him up, using him as a human shield, a gun to his head.

"Darlin'," she said to Chase, "it seems we're deadlocked." Flicking her gaze to Vivienne, she addressed them both. "I propose y'all allow me to leave on this elevator, and I leave you this pile of excrement," she drawled, her face awash with exhilaration. "Sir Edward, be a sugar and press the button."

Sir Edward complied, and within seconds the elevator doors opened. The blonde backed one careful step, then another into the elevator, dragging Sir Edward with her.

Chase locked eyes with her over Sir Edward's shoulder. "I don't trust you."

The blonde smiled. "Smart *and* handsome."

Just as the doors began to close, Chase and Vivienne moved forward in concert. They halted as she kicked Sir Edward out of the elevator to sprawl at their feet.

And took one parting shot.

Directly into Sir Edward's head.

Chase fired his weapon into the closing doors, though Vivienne could tell by the flash of the blonde's smile that he'd failed to hit her. He ran for the stairs, leaving Vivienne with a lifeless Sir Edward Dunn.

The assassin was intuitive, cunning, and ruthless. Vivienne should have known her brother would only hire the best.

Her vendetta against her brother was like an open sore—perpetually bleeding, never healing, the pain a constant irritant—but there was much more to her mission than mere revenge, however richly deserved. René must be stopped before more innocent lives were lost.

CHAPTER
TWO

November 14, 9:06 p.m.
New Orleans, Louisiana

Genevieve "Blade" Broussard adjusted the push-up bra she wore under the black leather jumpsuit, exposing an almost indecent amount of cleavage. In this part of the French Quarter, a little skin sold tickets, and this gig barely covered her living expenses.

"Damn bikers are here again," Xavier muttered, peeking around the edge of the shabby red velvet curtains that concealed the stage.

I can't catch a break.

Six weeks ago, illusionist Nikki Flynn had come flying into The Rising Sun like a genie on a magic carpet, offering Blade the one thing she desired most: validation from a *somebody* that her impalement act was good enough to be on the world stage. Or at least on the Las Vegas Strip. But her big break as an opening act for the hottest new magic show on the Strip had turned into imminent unemployment.

Tonight was her last performance and she had no one to blame but herself. Trusting Mickey Gillespie, her dirtbag manager, to finalize the Las Vegas deal was foolish. If that wasn't bad enough, she'd given Madam Toussaint two weeks' notice without a signed contract in hand.

As a final insult, Blade had learned Nikki Flynn had chosen a damn *mind reader* to be her opening act.

Blade clenched and unclenched her fists in an effort to relax. "We're on in one minute."

Xavier stretched one leg and then the other, his skintight leather pants molded to his thighs. Razor-edged abs glistened with posing oil. Her assistant popped his pecs and grinned. "*Laissez les bons temps rouler.*" Let the good times roll.

She nodded. "Let's give them a show they won't forget."

"Welcome to the Jungle" blared over the sound system as the curtains opened. Blade and Xavier appeared in a perfectly choreographed routine to the standing-room-only crowd. The noise of the audience and music made her head throb, but she kept her practiced smile plastered on her face. She knew the stage lighting she'd chosen transformed her chestnut-colored hair into a lake of molten lava running over her shoulders. Twin bursts of faux fire rose eight feet in the air above them, drawing the eye to the Wheel of Death.

"What you are about to witness," she said into her wireless headset mic, "can be dangerous and result in death. The impalement arts—"

"Hey Red, impale *this*," a biker hollered, clutching his crotch in one hand and a Coors in the other.

Typical. The guy was straight out of Central Casting in his black skull cap, black wife-beater tank, and black leather vest with patches above each breast pocket. His whole crew wore black. They were a clichéd blight on the sea of people who had paid the cover charge to see this performance.

Ignore him. Just get through tonight and move on.

"This seems innocent enough," she began again, brandishing her knife, allowing the light to catch the glint of steel. "But all is not what it appears to be. This blade can cut, or stab, or cleave. It can penetrate a beating heart or save one. Tonight, I will use this simple tool to *blow —your—mind.*"

Lights flickered as thunder rolled overhead, barely audible over the music. The crowd, clearly hammered, surged closer to the stage. Blade was fine with unpredictable crowds—she expected them, and used them to her advantage. That's what made each performance unique. But this crowd felt different, like one breathing, volatile entity. One slip, one wrong word, and the performance could turn disastrous. *Which might not be so bad*, she reminded herself, considering this was her last performance at this dive.

She silently groaned as Skull Cap and five of his pack forged their way to the front of the crowd.

"How about you and me taking this outside," he boomed. "You can show me how well you can *blow*"—he leered—"*my—mind*."

The crowd responded with clapping and catcalls.

She envisioned plunging the knife straight into the moron's heart. But in truth, her fury was directed at herself, for being blinded by the *illusion* of Nikki Flynn who was all hype and no substance.

Blade paraded the length of the stage, buying time, holding the knife in her left hand. Audiences were fickle, and these bikers threatened to turn her performance into a free-for-all. She needed to distract the audience, to lure them back to the performance rather than side with the bikers.

Skull Cap bawled out something blessedly unintelligible, but it still earned him laughs.

A trickle of sweat traveled along her spine. She knew how to handle hecklers. Never let them get under your skin. She noted Xavier shaking his head, willing her to ignore the biker.

Nope. Not tonight.

She wheeled on him. "Okay, hot stuff," she said. "Are you man enough to ride the Wheel of Death?"

"Ride you, sweetheart? Anytime," the biker slurred.

"How many of you want to see him take the ride of a lifetime?" Blade called to the crowd.

The audience burst into cheers and whistles. One of his pack shoved him, causing him to momentarily lose his balance.

Blade gave the audience a mischievous grin and winked. *This is going to be fun.*

The lights went out, the music exploded, the twin pillars of fire danced on cue—and Xavier stomped offstage, refusing to participate. He stood among the audience, arms crossed, disapproval etched on his handsome face.

I'm gonna bring this house to its knees. She grasped the biker's hand and led him to the Wheel of Death. Just a little over six-feet in diameter, the black wheel dominated center stage. Skull Cap peered back over his shoulder, nodding to the audience. He tried to grab her, but Blade deftly side-stepped him and positioned him in front of the device. In a matter of seconds, she'd bound his wrists and ankles to the soft pine wood with leather straps.

The high-octane music throttled into overdrive as Blade primed the audience for the one and only act of the night. "In 1938 the Gibsons thrilled audiences when they introduced the Wheel of Death at Madison Square Garden," she said into her headset. "The Veiled Wheel of Death has only been performed by four artists to date. But tonight, not only will I perform this feat, but I'll do it using *both hands simultaneously.* Are you ready to see history made?"

"Hell yeah!" someone called out.

"Blade! Blade! Blade!" someone began to chant. Instantly the crowd fell into the same rhythm.

"Any last words?" she asked the biker through her mic.

"You're not the first woman to handcuff me," he snickered.

Okay, pal. You asked for it.

She secured white silk paper over the target area. Now the biker was completely concealed, although Blade knew precisely where every limb was positioned.

She walked to the black onyx table that held her equipment. She strapped on the custom-made holster that held two sheaths that belted around each thigh. There were four knives in each sheath. Resembling a futuristic gunslinger in her costume, she stretched out her arms, shaking them slightly to loosen her shoulders, then sashayed to the wheel and, with one hard pull, started the wheel in motion.

The beat of the bass drum pulsated through her body as she removed two knives and gauged their weight, their perfect balance in each hand. In one choreographed move, she flipped the knives into the air, catching each by its blade before rearing back, lunging forward, and letting the knives fly.

Thwack. Thwack.

In less than one second she drew out another two knives. In less than

9

five seconds all eight knives were thrown, and the bright, white paper showed no stain of blood.

The audience erupted in shouts and applause. When she removed the thin veil of paper, the biker had passed out, with his tank front covered in thick, yellow vomit.

CHAPTER
THREE

November 15, 12:30 a.m.
Andratx, Mallorca, Spain

The Spaniard drew deeply on his cigarette, then pitched it over the retaining wall. A stiff breeze caught a few dying embers before they disappeared into the night. He leaned his knuckles on the stone wall, and stared at the Tower of Souls in the distance.

For centuries, that strong sentinel had withstood punishing storms and attacks from pirates and invaders. In the twenty-first century *he* would be the watchtower, protecting the planet and mankind from itself. Even if it meant sacrificing a few hundred million souls in the process.

His ancestors had long been wealthy landowners, loyal to the Spanish crown, each generation holding powerful government positions. His grandfather, a renowned bullfighter, appeared on the cover of Time magazine in America, bringing prestige and honor to his family and country. Even his own father served as Secretary of State for International Cooperation—until he died in a car crash with his wife when the Spaniard was twelve years old.

Sent to live with his aunt and uncle, his *Abuela* insisted he be groomed to follow family tradition, and the Spaniard was sent to a military boarding school in England. Intelligent and glib, he thrived in the all-male environment where manipulation and coercion reigned supreme. He excelled in history and found the military campaigns of Alexander the Great, Julius Caesar, and Sun Tzu fascinating. But what captured his curiosity and focus were the dictatorships of Hitler, Stalin, and Mao Zedong. How did these men rule millions of people? Through fear? Propaganda? Starvation?

Seeds of his future began to form.

Post-graduate studies at Oxford earned him high praise from professors, many urging him into politics, but his passions went well beyond that of being a politician. A profession of vast wealth and privilege was required; and so he founded Martel Unlimited, a fashion retail company that would eventually earn him billions and open opportunities for his global campaign.

For years, he cultivated relationships within the power elite of a dozen countries, invested and expanded his interests in international trade and media ownership, and kept his illegal activities hidden behind the mask of the Spaniard. Every business decision, every relationship, every Euro spent was to fulfill one goal: to birth an authoritarian world government ruled by him.

During the past five years, the Spaniard had doggedly acquired twenty-five percent of the world's arms-producing and military-services companies, primarily in Europe and the Middle East. Like any military campaign, he strategized and used appropriate force when necessary. But that wasn't enough. The United States, China, and Great Britain would soon be begging on their knees. Tonight's operation in London must succeed.

He who controls the weapons controls the world.

The Spaniard's hostile takeover attempt for Maritime Defense Corporation had failed, due in large part to Sir Edward Dunn, who had proven to be a worthy opponent. Dunn's elimination could not attract undue attention, yet a clear and definite message must be conveyed to the other board members—sign over the company or suffer the consequences.

To that end, Ellis Stephens had been dispatched to London two days ago, her orders simple: assassinate Sir Edward Dunn with finesse. An accident, a suicide, it made no difference. A master at her craft, she eliminated the enemy with precision, like a scalpel in a surgeon's hand.

By now, Dunn should be a blip in history. He checked his smartphone for the third time in the past thirty minutes. No message, no call.

The Spaniard paced the length of the terrace in his silk robe, bare feet brushing against the cold travertine tiles. At fifty-one, he looked a decade younger with his wavy salt and pepper hair combed back, and trim athletic build thanks to an exercise regimen that twenty-somethings would envy. Tabloids often compared the charismatic fashion magnate to his grandfather, the matador who amazed crowds with his showmanship.

Why hasn't Ellis reported in?

He paused at the patio bar and poured himself a generous amount of 1762 Gautier Cognac into a crystal tumbler. At least the French could do this right. He brought the glass to his lips and swallowed, savoring the liquid gold as it warmed his throat. Heat settled low.

Phase One of his ambitious plan to disrupt predetermined governments and appoint puppet regional rulers would take a deep reservoir of wealth. Martel Unlimited, over the decades, had generated billions, which the Spaniard tapped to multiply his riches by drug-running, engaging in human trafficking, and backing certain pornographic enterprises. These were necessary evils. Sacrifices must be made.

His phone rang in his pocket. "Ellis, *qué sucede?*" he asked after the fourth ring. "Did all go as planned?"

"Yes," she said. "But we've been compromised."

That word...*compromised*. It evoked weakness, vulnerability.

"Be here in two hours. I'll expect a full report when you arrive." He ended the call and jammed the phone back into his pocket.

"*Mierda!*" he screamed.

He took another swig of cognac, then dashed the empty tumbler against the tile floor. Glass flew in all directions, the sound reverberating in the stillness.

A security guard hotfooted around the corner of the villa, gun drawn. The guard took one look at his employer, turned on his heel, and returned to his post.

The Spaniard balled his hand into a fist. A traitor roamed among his ranks. This Judas was getting sloppy—or desperate. Two failed operations in the past four months. Many millions lost. And he knew at the heart of his failures beat his sister—Vivienne.

Was his organization so easily penetrated? The traitor would die, slowly and painfully.

Copper fire bowls adorned the four corners of the pool. Flames illuminated the approach of a young, naked woman along its decking, hips gently swaying, a smile playing at her lips. The nineteen-year-old reminded him of a tiger, both in and out of bed. The scratches she'd left on his back hours before still stung.

She wrapped her arms around him and kissed his neck, biting the flesh along his jugular vein. "Join me for a swim," she cooed. Her hands strayed to his chest until he shoved her away.

"Go back to bed," he growled.

Hope stretched languorously in front of him, defying him, before diving into the water without a splash. Water vapor rose from the eighty-four-degree water. The Spaniard studied the former swimming champion as she glided over the water's surface, one fluid stroke after another, her long blond hair flowing behind her.

Business before pleasure.

"Quinn!" he bellowed, dropping into one of the patio chairs.

Alec Quinn emerged from the villa, taking long strides to the terrace, wearing jeans and a Manchester United sweatshirt. The Spaniard's second-in-command slept little, a lesson well-learned from his youth on the streets of London.

"Is Sir Edward Dunn neutralized?" Quinn asked.

The Spaniard considered the question and the younger man. He remembered the sly teenager lifting his wallet in London without fear. Even then, the Spaniard had recognized Quinn's cunning and resourcefulness. Raw talent and promise. Rather than hire trusted staff, the Spaniard decided to cultivate one. Educated at the University of Manchester and trained by a paramilitary organization, Quinn's brain and brawn could handle any situation. At thirty-one, he managed the illegal day-to-day operations of Daystar LLC, a shell company with no apparent ties to Martel Unlimited.

"The London operation was successful. Ellis should be here within hours."

Quinn nodded. "Your orders?"

"I read the dossier you prepared on Genevieve Broussard. Her DNA is a match. It appears my sister kept secrets from me before her disappearance."

"Genevieve is definitely your niece," Quinn said.

"Take the jet to New Orleans and bring her here. I don't care how you do it. I want her in my possession within ten days. If my sister is behind these setbacks, this should even the playing field."

Quinn nodded and turned on his heel.

The Spaniard often thought of Quinn as a ghost. The younger man was adept in any situation, but most importantly, his lieutenant never left a trail that could lead anyone back to himself or his enterprise. Genevieve would soon be under his control, bait to capture his sister.

The Spaniard tilted his head back, watching the storm clouds roil over the island. Insignificant compared to the tsunami he intended to unleash on the world in fifteen days.

Shucking his robe, he waded into the warm water, hip deep, allowing the sensual contact to arouse him. He stood in Hope's path and caught her by the waist as she rose up. "Change your mind?" she asked, wrapping her arms around his neck.

His hands ran across her stomach and over her breasts, then snaked around her neck and slowly squeezed. Hope tried to pry his fingers free, but he tightened his hold. Panicked, she began to struggle, but the Spaniard fully submerged her into the water. She tried to get her footing, to raise her tall frame for leverage, but her body eventually surrendered as she slowly lost consciousness. He loved this part of taking a life, to see the sheer terror when they realized only seconds remained to them on this earth.

He closed his eyes, imagining it was Vivienne he held underwater. His sister had betrayed him once. She would not have the opportunity to do so again.

Once, his grandfather spoke of *El extasis*, the ecstasy, after killing a courageous bull in the ring. Hope had come to know too much to live. Her lifeless body, yellow hair cascading around her, was beautiful. He shook his head, reliving the last day with her. She would be missed, but as in bullfighting, there were other women to tame, fight, and conquer.

Nothing excited him more than the hunt.

CHAPTER
FOUR

November 17, 4:31 p.m.
Florence, Italy

Vivienne Martel considered how best to plead her case.

Rain pelted against the windows of a converted farmhouse above *Piazzale Michelangelo,* the home of Thomas Kazir, the present *Soldati di Cristo* Commander. Once every quarter, Thomas opened his home for an evening meal and planning session that sometimes lasted well past the stroke of twelve. Tonight, five senior staff, including herself, sat around the barn table laden with pasta dishes, fried chicken, sautéed vegetables, and warm bread. Lively banter and exaggerated exploits buzzed among the group, and for the first time since being promoted to second-in-command, she felt disconnected from her comrades. The secret she kept felt like a betrayal to her mission and friends.

She rose from the table to crack open a window with a view of the backyard. The soft patter of rain and the fresh damp pungency of earth soothed the ghosts that always hovered just out of reach. A string of outdoor party lights illuminated the patio, making the shrubs and flowers glisten. The sight of a runnel traveling down the sloping yard transported her to another rain swept scene across the globe eight months before.

Heavy rainfall and the possibility of landslides through the forested terrain of the Chittagong Hill Tracts in Bangladesh had made the trek to the small village treacherous. The keening cries of women could be heard before her party arrived at the clearing. All that remained of the village were smoldering mounds of wood, old people huddled together under the canopy of trees, and bodies of dead men. The young women, gone.

Missionaries assigned to the area reported widespread attacks on the Jumma people, routinely targeted by the military and Bengalis settlers. The Ecumenical Council of Churches had contacted the Soldati to ask them to investigate the allegations and take action—if necessary. Vivienne led a few of her team to search the area for any other survivors.

One disfigured young girl lay curled, hidden among the foliage. Vivienne did not attempt to hold the traumatized girl. Instead, she fell to her knees, bowed her head, and prayed. The forest stilled, as if it too grieved for the dead and missing.

Above pristine lakes, the green, forested mountains hid the uglier truth of a government intent on ethnically cleansing the beautiful Chittagong Hill Tracts for economic gain. The terrified elders were questioned, but they remained mute. Her team packed what they could and led the twenty-two survivors to safety. Upon boarding boats that awaited them at the Karnaphuli River, the young girl grabbed her hand and whispered, "*Spyāniyārḍa.*" The Spaniard.

Vivienne reeled, an icy spike of cold piercing her soul. She recalled those two words from her childhood. Memories flooded back of her grandfather's estate in Andalusia, his performances in the bullring, and her twin brother's nickname for her—*La Española*—as she mimicked her grandfather with a red *muleta* and sword. Happier days, before life changed irrevocably.

As she leaned against the bow of the boat, foreboding clawed at her. If the Spaniard and René were the same person...she had to be sure. No matter the time or cost.

During a three-month leave of absence, she had chased leads, hopscotching third world countries to eventually uncover the truth. The Spaniard hid in plain sight behind wealth and respectability. Proof was another matter.

To underestimate the Spaniard meant a multitude would suffer the consequences if she could not convince her comrades around the table that her brother must be stopped. If given a chance, she would kill the bastard and not feel one ounce of remorse.

Vivienne spun around, her action interrupting the meal. "We are this close to exposing the Spaniard," she said, holding her thumb and forefinger an inch apart. "Three days ago, we failed our mission to save Sir Edward Dunn. One woman upended our operation."

"We had our asses handed to us," Chase corrected. "I have the stitches to prove it."

Undeterred, Vivienne said with renewed vigor, "But, based on actionable intel, we have thwarted two attacks on munitions plants in Great Britain and Germany. Millions of lives have been spared."

She began pacing around the table, unable to sit still.

"My informant tells me there is an operation in play to kidnap an American. The target is unknown, but the Spaniard has made it a top priority. Which makes it ours. We can't stop now."

"First," Thomas countered, "you can't possibly know if our interference has saved millions of lives, although I'm sure it has hurt his bottom line." He paused to sip from his caffè. The Nigerian looked more like an accountant than a commander, with his crisp white shirt sleeves rolled to his elbows. He gave the impression of someone relaxed, enjoying a coffee and croissant at a bistro with a friend. No one made that mistake twice. He led the organization with a steel will and resolve that would rival the Apostle Paul's.

"Vivienne," he went on, "I appreciate how passionately you believe this Spaniard is your twin brother. But I fear your judgment, my friend, is clouded." Thomas placed his porcelain cup on the table. "Our intelligence shows no ties between René Martel and any illegal activity. You expect us to risk our lives and compromise our mission based on one source whom you refuse to identify."

She paused and took a deep breath before taking her seat at the table. The Soldati utilized the cover of darkness and an incredibly expansive and sophisticated intelligence-gathering network to minimize casualties and maximize results.

"I'm as utterly devoted to our mission as anyone here, but there won't be any Christians to save if René isn't stopped." It was all Vivienne could do to maintain her composure. "This isn't hyperbole, Thomas. This is a twenty-first century Hitler with incredible resources at his disposal and few, if any, constraints. He doesn't need to go to the trouble of conquering countries one at a time. It's all there for him—wholesale domination, in a single stroke. Unless he's stopped."

Thomas steepled his fingers before him. "May I remind everyone sitting around this table that even after two millennia, radicals still burn Christians at the stake. It is our sole mission to protect and save those who are at risk. We don't single out one person or entity and put our soldiers in harm's way." Thomas' gaze circled the other five people around the table before settling on Chase. "One of our own could have been killed during the London fiasco. Thankfully, Chase only sustained a minor injury. And yet, Vivienne, this informant tells you the Spaniard has plans to kidnap an American. Care to speculate on why you're being supplied this intel?"

Vivienne refused to take the bait. "We can't ignore a person in imminent danger. I propose we investigate the claim and have a rescue team on standby."

"This isn't our fight," Thomas reasoned.

She slowly scanned the room, then glared at her superior. "I want to hear from the rest of the team."

"This isn't a democracy," Thomas snapped. "There is a chain of command, and you aren't Commander—yet. But, feedback from the team might clear the air. Xiu, you're the IT genius, what have you learned so far?"

The young woman hesitated, clearly uncomfortable with reporting first. "There is no doubt that René Martel has amassed a considerable fortune. Maybe a staggering one. According to *Forbes*, his net worth is $43 billion. But"—she wagged two fingers in the air—"he has two offshore accounts that have received an influx of money in the past two months totaling another $20 billion. My team is continuing to unravel his significant holdings until you order otherwise."

"That is more than enough to buy a nuclear bomb," Vivienne said under her breath.

"Luc, as our chief strategist, do you think this Spaniard poses an immediate threat?" Thomas asked.

Luciano Conti shifted uncomfortably as Vivienne turned her attention to him. After a decade of working together, she depended upon his ability to stay resolute under pressure and somewhat detached from the rigors of field operations. This placidity also drove her positively nuts.

"Between the time we stopped the destruction of the two munition plants and our failed London operation, forty-eight Christians have died in North Korea, India, and China. Why not discreetly give our intel about the Spaniard to MI6 or the CIA? Let the Brits or Americans do something about him."

Vivienne snatched her mug of instant coffee from the table, stood, and walked back to the window. She winced. *Nothing more appalling than cold instant coffee or Luc living up to my expectations.*

"Finn, your thoughts?" Thomas asked.

The Irishman had joined the Ireland Defense Forces after the death of his sister in a bombing in Northern Ireland. There he learned how to dispose of bombs and other ordnance. Vivienne could never read Finn. He was fearless in a fight, contemplative in strategy meetings, and kept to himself in his downtime.

Finn winked at the group. "Let's give the bugger a kick in the arse."

Vivienne exhaled slowly, relieved that at least one person was on her side. The streetlights below appeared like apparitions, one by one, like all the ghosts she could still see and hear on her failed missions. She would take the fight to René, no matter the outcome of this meeting—for the lost. For the forgotten.

Two to one and only Chase left to give his opinion. Despite their age difference, Vivienne understood the younger man's battle with an unreconciled past. Regret and remorse, twin specters in their psyche.

"Vivienne is right. We've seen Gaddafi, Hussein, and the Ayatollah Khamenei. The Spaniard is one nuclear weapon away from causing mass destruction. If this is a vote, I'd vote with Vivienne. He could strike anywhere, anytime."

Thomas stood, leaning his arms against the table. "Thank you for your candor. Until I make a final decision, Xiu, you and your team will continue to drill into Martel's business affairs. Chase and Finn, you're on standby for a rescue operation if we hear of an American taken captive. Luc, monitor and coordinate our efforts." Thomas walked to the sideboard and poured two glasses of red wine, making it clear the meeting was over—early. "Vivienne, please stay."

The four Soldati filed out, leaving a cold silence in the room.

"Join me in a drink?" Thomas said, taking a seat next to her.

Vivienne could never stay angry at the man who rescued her from the streets of Paris. She took his hand in hers, absorbing his warmth as she rubbed her thumb against the soft skin of his palm. It had been years since he fought in the field, but she knew he remembered every operation, every casualty the Soldati di Cristo suffered.

"Do you know anything about this American?" he asked gently.

"I would tell you if I did," Vivienne said, not meeting his eyes.

"You are not a good liar." Taking hold of her chin, he turned her to face him. "It's Genevieve, isn't it?"

"The bastard has found my daughter."

CHAPTER
FIVE

November 23, 5:55 p.m.
New Orleans, Louisiana

Blade rode the red Ducati Streetfighter V4S as if the devil himself were on her tail. The bike's engine screamed as she weaved in and out of heavy commuter traffic. Adrenaline coursed through her, the cold wind hitting her body like a solid sheet of ice. She revved the engine, cutting in front of a diesel truck, missing its grill by inches.

Taking the exit, she approached a hard right turn. Like throwing knives, muscle memory kicked in: in one fluid motion, she slid back in her seat, locked her left leg into the scallops on the tank, and leaned. She fought the urge to brush her hand against the asphalt as if she were a speed skater on ice. After righting the bike, and with a twist of her wrist, she accelerated.

Until she hit the end of the road.

The Gators watering hole reminded Blade of a bayou swamp house in serious need of a new roof and a fresh coat of paint. Old rusted trucks hunkered near the front door. This bartending gig was just a pit stop, she reminded herself. Nothing more.

Roughnecks gathered outside, smoking cigarettes and shooting the breeze after their fourteen-day shift on an oil platform. Blade parked her bike next to a classic 1975 El Camino. She removed her helmet, leaned over, and shook her long hair free, aware of the men checking her out. One of them let out a low whistle. Her last performance at the Rising Sun had been nine days ago. This job paid minimum wage plus tips. Desperate to make rent next week, she couldn't afford to squander any opportunity. She winked at the group as she went inside.

Three hours later, sweat beaded her forehead as she poured one beer after another from the tap. Splattered grease clung to her black tank top from po'boys filled with alligator sausage and dripping hot gravy. She could just make out the clack of billiard balls above raucous laughter and deafening rock 'n' roll.

"Karaoke starts in five," Gloria shouted over the din, flipping a near-empty bottle of gin to finish a bottle trick. "Great night for your initiation."

Karaoke? Shoot me now.

Precisely on time, the music started, and the first singer grabbed a microphone.

Sounds of all kinds—except anything that passed for musical—careened off the cavernous room's cinder block walls as a hefty middle-aged woman launched into a determined rendition of "Man! I Feel Like a Woman!" It would be funny if it weren't so excruciating. Blade drew and released a deep breath, then steeled herself for another mind-numbing four hours of pouring beers and blending margaritas.

The crowd's drinking only amped up as the night wore on. Her tip jar overflowed with tens and twenties, thanks to a few lessons from Gloria. The customers appreciated nothing more than an ample pour and a little cleavage. And there was nothing stingy about roughnecks. They worked hard and played hard.

"Hey, I'm talkin' to you," a bleary-eyed redhead shouted to Blade, rising off her barstool to grab a bottle of tequila and only just managing to keep her ample breasts from spilling entirely free of her low-cut cheetah sweater.

A dull ache throbbed behind Blade's eyes. Obnoxious drunks haunted her wherever she worked.

"Wassa girl gotta do 'round here to get a drink?" the redhead slurred to her brunette companion before sloshing tequila all over the bar in her attempt to fill two shot glasses. Blade itched to take the shot glasses and ram them down her throat. But before she could snatch the bottle from her, a ball-capped roughneck yanked the bottle from her hand. The name patch on his work shirt read "Holt."

For a second, Blade thought she'd lucked into an ally—until she saw his feral grin.

"Pretty lady like you shouldn't have to pour her own drink, right, fellas?" he brayed. Within seconds, three of his coworkers crowded in tight around the two women, wolves on the scent.

Clearly thrilled by the attention, the redhead shouted, "This is what I call service!" Both women snickered after polishing off two shots.

After retrieving the bottle, Blade dismissed the women, who were well past the point of no return. The men around them appeared ravenous and thirsty. Before Blade could take their drink order, the brunette wrenched around on her stool, "Whoa, take a look at the eye candy, Evie. We best slow our roll."

Blade tracked her gaze to see an attractive man standing just inside the front door. The brunette might be drunk on her ass, but her observation was on the money. Broad-shouldered, tall, almost absurdly well-dressed in a navy blue pinstriped suit, his hazel eyes seemed to inhale the room. There was not one single element of this guy's appearance that suggested he belonged in, or anywhere *near*, Gators.

Much as Blade welcomed the diversion, this stone-cold handsome stranger spelled nothing but trouble if he didn't turn around and leave.

"Those *shoulders*," the brunette said, licking her plumped lips like a bloodthirsty cannibal. "Yummy."

"Sugar," the redhead said, gingerly slipping off the barstool, "we're taking him home with us tonight. I'll bet he tastes better than beignets." It took her a moment to gain her footing, but then she made straight for the blue-suited newcomer—until she was brought up short.

"Hey, hold up!" Holt groused. He'd seized her by the arm. "Where the hell do you think you're going?"

"You're hurting me," she said, trying to pry his hand off.

Blade rounded the bar to defuse the situation, but by the time she joined the pair, the newcomer had already crossed the floor and complicated matters.

Crap.

"She's pissed, mate," Blue Suit said to Holt. "Leave off."

Holt outstared Blue Suit, unimpressed by the British accent or tailored suit. "Mind your own business, *mate.*"

What was it about men and damsels in distress? *Crazy Brit.* She should just go back behind the bar and wait for the inevitable brawl. But four drunken roughnecks against one swanky Brit wasn't fair.

She shifted in front of Blue Suit and served Holt and his boys a smile. "Hey guys, how about a round of drinks on the house?"

Bleary-eyed, Holt sized up Blue Suit. Apparently willing to accept the offer of a free beer rather than escalate the altercation over a woman, he crowed, "Can't turn down a free drink."

Blade expelled a rush of air, relieved a fight had been averted. But before she could return to her place behind the bar, the redhead teetered on her three-inch heels and toppled into Holt's arms, causing him to lose his balance. He tried to catch himself, but instead caught empty air. They both fell to the floor, a tangle of arms and legs. The crash caught the attention of bored customers. A good old-fashioned fight trumped mediocre karaoke any day of the week.

As Blade leaned over to help disentangle the couple, one of the pack shoved her out of the way.

"This is your fault," a man wearing a red flannel shirt accused, jabbing a finger into Blue Suit's chest.

Here we go.

"That's no way to treat a lady," Blue Suit said, punctuated by a swift uppercut to the chin that dropped the man neatly to his knees.

Blade crab-walked backwards, trying to extricate herself from the skirmish. She spotted Gloria on the phone, most likely calling the cops. The customers had already converged around them, allowing little space to maneuver.

One of the pack held Blue Suit's arms behind him while Red Flannel Shirt hammered blows into his midsection. Without any thought for her own safety, Blade reached past the brunette and grabbed the attacker's shirt. Enraged, he reacted by taking a swing at her. Blade dodged a fist to the face, but the blow caught the brunette on the shoulder, propelling her back into the crowd. Blade reacted by driving a direct punch to his groin. He screamed an obscenity as he crumpled to the floor in obvious pain.

"Make for the door!" Blade yelled to the Brit above the din.

The Brit freed himself from the man holding his arms and kneed him in the midsection, then drove a fist to his jaw.

Blade rocketed over the bar, grabbed her jacket, helmet, and tip money, then bolted for the front door. On the way, she grabbed the Brit's hand, pulling him with her.

Once outside, the still, cold air carried the wail of sirens. Blade hurried them to the Ducati and hooked a leg over the seat. With the flick of a switch, the machine growled to life. She revved the engine. "Coming?"

The Brit grinned as he hopped on back. "Brilliant."

As the first police car rounded the corner, Blade opened the throttle, and the Ducati disappeared into the night.

To hell with second chances.

Woldenberg Park was deserted except for a homeless man digging through an overflowing trash can. Once a stretch of warehouses and industrial docks, the revamped, pedestrian-friendly area now boasted bricked walkways and public art. The mighty Mississippi River, awash with reflective light from the Crescent City Connection bridge, looked inviting in the moonlight.

The mild breeze that came off the river caught tendrils of Blade's long hair, lifting it away from her shoulders. What had possessed her to bring the Brit to this place? She didn't even know his name. As a bit of insurance, she carried her helmet as the two stretched their legs near the water.

"Thanks for saving my hide back there," the Brit said, gingerly working his jaw. "Although it was a bit of a rough ride."

Blade laughed. "You didn't need my help. But if I'm honest, I haven't had so much fun in months."

"You probably won't have a job tomorrow."

"No. Probably not." Even after a brawl, the Brit still rocked the English gentleman vibe.

He cast a sidelong glance at her. Embarrassed at being caught scoping him out, she took a direct approach.

"Why were you at Gators? Obviously, you weren't there for a drink or a hook-up."

"Alec Quinn," he said, holding out a hand. "Just flew in from London this morning. And you're just the woman I've traveled half the world to meet."

She'd expected more than a weak pickup line from the Brit. His words stung.

What an ass.

"I'm tired," she said. "I think you can find your way back to your hotel from here." Helmet swinging from her right hand, she headed to her bike.

"Wait," he said, running after her. "I'm not exaggerating. I traveled from London to meet with you—Blade Broussard, the spectacularly talented impalement artist. At least, that's what *Maxim* expressed in their story about you."

She stopped in her tracks.

"I'm here to offer you a million dollars—American." He pulled out a business card from his suit pocket and handed it to her.

She examined the card by the weak glow of a nearby streetlight. *Alec Quinn, Solicitor, London, England.* "You don't fight like a lawyer. I could order business cards with the same information. It wouldn't make it true."

"My employer is quite particular and demands the best. You *are* the best impalement artist in the world, aren't you?"

"Damn straight I am. What would this employer expect for a million dollars?"

"Nothing illegal or illicit. One performance as part of a marketing campaign at his villa on Mallorca with a few influential guests for added exposure. Very exclusive. If you accept, Xavier will also be invited. He would be paid $200,000 for his time and trouble."

Blade could still feel the warmth of his hands on her waist as they had ridden through the streets. Ridiculous to feel a connection to a man she'd met only an hour earlier. She looked straight into his hazel eyes. They didn't waver.

Alec looked at his wristwatch. "It's late. Think about the offer. You have my contact information. I'll be staying at the Ritz for the next two days."

"Who would I be working for?"

Alec shook his head. "I'm afraid a nondisclosure agreement will need to be signed before I can reveal his name. Once you sign the agreement, I'm authorized to pay you half of the agreed price."

"Five hundred thousand dollars?" Blade croaked.

"Five hundred thousand, and no strings attached."

"And Xavier?"

"Same deal. Once he signs, he'll get half the agreed price. Or we can hire another assistant for you once we arrive at the villa."

"This seems very cloak-and-dagger," she said.

"Nondisclosure agreements are common with high profile clients." He took a few paces back, appraising her. "Maybe my employer has made a mistake."

One million dollars. This would give me a fresh start. High-end digital effects, sophisticated lighting, dramatic pyrotechnics. Maybe even finance a gig in Las Vegas.

She studied the business card and carefully worked through her immediate opportunities. It didn't take long. And each second that ticked away moved her further from her goal of becoming a headliner.

"I'll sign."

"You won't regret it."

CHAPTER
SIX

November 24, 10:07 p.m.
Aboard the *Sol y Luna*, off the coast of Mallorca

The Spaniard scrutinized the five people from the floor-to-ceiling observation window on the *Sol y Luna* as they disembarked the corporate helicopter. He stood, hands folded behind his back, satisfied to monitor his security force escorting his investment group to the conference room.

Time to cull the herd.

With the LED underwater lights and pool lights turned off, the yacht floated miles from shore like a remote resort in open water. Occasional flashes of lightning illuminated the undulating sea, exposing their vulnerability—no one could leave the yacht unless he sanctioned their departure. In the Spaniard's experience, people who felt isolated and intimidated were more apt to acquiesce.

The Spaniard flung the door open to the dimly lit conference room. Five heads swiveled toward him, mannequins in perfect unison. Each came from diverse backgrounds, but all lived by the same rules of greed, ambition, arrogance, and deception. Normally, these were traits he respected, and they were vital for the inception of his new world order, but one among them thought him impotent, weak.

Narrow-beam accent lighting illuminated his grandfather's *Traje de Luces,* leaving no doubt as to his pride and heritage. His grandfather, a *Matador de Toros,* wore this particular Suit of Lights at his last performance. Francisco Martel had commanded the bullring with an iron will and charisma. No one disrespected the Spaniard's *abuelo*—at least, no one who lived. The Spaniard had learned much from his grandfather.

Dmitry Andropov, one of the five investors, jumped in his chair when the Spaniard threw open the door, but quickly collected himself. Tanned and fit, the Russian oligarch scum was exceptionally wealthy and known for his adroitness in maneuvering among the powerful. A case in point: his recent purchase of a resort from the current President of the United States, bought at an insanely inflated price, had earned Andropov access to many key figures in the American government.

The Spaniard despised cowardice and Andropov was a prime example of a man who never stood on any principles other than his own greed. If he cringed in alarm at the mere opening of a door, he would surely soil his pants before the meeting was over.

Before settling into his chair, the Spaniard poured himself a glass of Tempranillo from the sidebar, allowing the silence to stretch.

"You've kept us waiting," said Muhammed Faheem, a Saudi businessman with ties to the Royal family. The narcissistic, corpulent Saudi wore the traditional *thobe* and *ghutra* to hide how far he had strayed from the Islamic faith. His excessive nature had made it easy to turn the Saudi from a respectable businessman to a cocaine addict with a penchant for prostitutes. Although the Spaniard controlled the man, Faheem still retained a false sense of entitlement and protection from the Saudi prince. *No importa,* he would soon be obsolete.

"When I recruited each one of you," the Spaniard said once he'd taken his seat, "I took you into my confidence and shared my vision for our future. I've doubled your initial investment. Yet one of you has put my operations at risk." He pounded the table with his fist. Crystal water glasses rattled in the wake of his fury. "There are consequences for disloyalty."

"Your vision is implausible," Andropov blurted, beads of sweat forming on his bald head. "It sets us up for not only failure but retaliation from the West's largest superpower. And I, for one, refuse to lose my investment."

The room held its collective breath.

Teresa Escobar shifted in her chair, crossed and re-crossed her shapely legs. The Spaniard recognized the young, attractive Venezuelan banker as a kindred spirit, willing to do anything to further her ambition. In this case, to further his interests by laundering billions through her bank, as did the South American drug cartels she did business with.

Her dark eyes met the Spaniard's, bold and unapologetic. "Dmitry is an overstuffed fool," she said, eliciting an outraged squeak from the man, "but he does make a point. When you first approached us, your ten-year plan made sense. Weaken the superpowers while clandestinely taking control of the global defense engine, leaving each of us to take a regional approach to govern. But you've sliced that timeline in half, and we think it too ambitious to ensure a lucrative outcome."

Jack Han, China's equivalent to Bill Gates, nervously patted his brow with a handkerchief. Pak Yong-Chun, with direct access to North Korea's Supreme Leader, listened to the wrangling. Both diminutive men, often reticent, delivered results no matter the human cost.

The Spaniard considered the two. "Are you in agreement with Teresa?"

In perfect synchrony, they nodded.

He pressed a button on his armrest, and within seconds Ellis glided in, wearing a smart white pantsuit. She made her way to a workstation in the corner of the conference room.

Andropov loosened his tie, perspiration dripping freely down his cheeks onto the lapels of his navy blue suit. The other four looked uneasy as the blonde smiled sweetly from her chair.

The Spaniard drummed his fingers on the mahogany table. "I've arranged for a small demonstration of the power I wield. Ellis?"

A screen lowered into position from the ceiling. With a few keystrokes, an offshore bank account came into view.

"As y'all can see," Ellis said in her honeyed Southern drawl, "Mr. Andropov has $21,385,650 in his account. Pay attention. I just love this part." Her long red fingernails tapped the keyboard. Within seconds Andropov's account displayed a zero balance.

"*HET,*" Andropov sputtered, knocking his chair over in his haste to stand. "You cannot take my money!"

"Ah, Dmitry," the Spaniard said, relaxing in his chair. "You still think you have value." He shook his head almost fondly, as though the Russian were an adorable child. "Those funds are not lost, I assure you. I've merely transferred them to your replacement."

The pale skin around Andropov's full lips turned gray. "You are *sumasshedshiy.* You are *all* crazy. Keep the money. I demand to go home."

"You are in no position to make demands. I told you," the Spaniard said, considering them one by one, "all of you. Once you agreed to be part of my unique investment group, there would be no turning back."

The stifling air felt as charged with imminent threat as a bullring. Andropov's eyes roamed restlessly about, and he couldn't seem to catch his breath, almost hyperventilating. The others averted their eyes. It reminded the Spaniard of the squeamish spectators who failed to appreciate the *estocada*—the final symphony between the matador and bull.

In desperation, Andropov made a run for the door. With catlike grace, Ellis closed the distance between them before he made it halfway. "Please," he whined, attempting to shrink from her. "I have a wife, children."

Humming low, her red nails danced across his suit until she draped one arm around his neck as if they were old friends going out for a drink. He attempted to break free, his breath coming in heaving gasps, but she held him close with no apparent effort. Smiling, Ellis hugged Andropov closer, her body perpendicular to his. Lovingly, she cradled his chin in her hand, caressing his cheek. With one merciless upward thrust, his neck snapped. Ellis gently guided his limp body to the floor. She looked up, a smile still on her lips.

With a slight nod from her employer, Ellis leaned over, closing Andropov's bulging eyes before exiting the stateroom, her pumps muted on the white carpet.

Muhammed Faheem could be heard gagging into a napkin. The others sat in stunned silence.

The Spaniard rose and poured himself another glass of Tempranillo, remembering his grandfather's *estocada*, the final act of thrusting the sword through the bull's neck and piercing its heart. He raised his glass. "To our rekindled partnership."

CHAPTER
SEVEN

November 26, 8:25 p.m.
Somewhere over the Atlantic Ocean

The sleek Gulfstream G650 tore through monochrome clouds backlit by moonlight. From the oval window of the front cabin, Blade watched the play of shadow and light for inspiration. She dropped her pencil to the table and sat back in the soft leather seat, her frustration mounting as she sketched possible costume designs. Not for the first time, Blade wondered if the one million dollar price tag for her impalement act was too low.

This could be how I live for the rest of my life.

Her affluent employer turned out to be the billionaire fashion icon, René Martel. Blade recalled his picture on the cover of a glamour magazine as she waited in the grocery line. Liquid amber eyes, much like her own, jumped off the page and captured her attention. A life of wealth and privilege—the stuff of dreams. This opportunity could open doors to the entertainment industry that up till now remained welded shut.

Celebrated for being a nonconformist, René Martel planned to unveil his re-envisioned line of menswear in December rather than during the typical Men's Fashion Week in January. Only eleven days to plan and execute a performance that would generate buzz within the fashion industry. Among the invitees were magazine editors, top designers, and celebrities. This gig demanded more than the form-fitting black leather jumpsuit she wore in New Orleans. She'd dreamed of a big break and unlimited resources, but here she sat with her sketchbook filled with a sea of swirls and lines that showed no imagination. At this rate, she would be labeled a laughingstock by them all.

Alec stepped from the galley brandishing a champagne bottle and two flutes. He had taken off his suit jacket and rolled his shirt sleeves up to his elbows, exposing a black rose tattoo on his forearm.

"Nice tat," she said. "Clearly the work of an artist. Living in New Orleans for six years kind of makes me an expert."

He grinned, obviously pleased. "In ancient Rome, the black rose symbolized power and strength." Alec pressed a bottle of Dom Pérignon against his thigh as he unscrewed the wire tab. "I just thought it looked cool."

"What are we celebrating?" Blade said, laying her sketchbook aside and appreciating Alec's natural grace as he moved about the cabin before taking the seat opposite her.

"To new beginnings," he toasted.

"To new beginnings," she repeated, taking an offered flute.

His cologne filled the cabin, reminding her of a forest after a rainfall —heady and masculine. Just being near this man made her body respond in ways it hadn't for years. Warmth spread throughout her body. It wasn't the altitude, the champagne, or the excitement of creating a new act.

It was Alec Quinn.

"You're not having any regrets, are you?" Alec said.

Blade took a deep breath. "Of course not." She smiled, hoping he couldn't read her thoughts. "Flying in a private jet will ruin me. I'll never sit in coach again."

Alec chuckled. "I remember my first time. And now look at me," he said, holding out his arms. "What were you working on?"

Blade reached for her sketchbook and held it up. "Creative block. My costume designs are nonexistent. How can I tie my performance into your marketing campaign when I know nothing about the menswear line? My career is riding on this gig."

"Don't worry about the launch. That's our area of expertise. Your job is to entertain our guests."

His blunt answer didn't sit well, nor did the prospect of giving a mediocre performance. Even at a young age, she had understood that success came with hard work and determination. At fifteen, the youngest challenger at the World Championship Knife-Throwing competition in England, she'd spent the night before the final round throwing knives well into the early morning hours. Tired and sore during the competition, she had miscalculated a crucial throw. Her mother had stood on the side-lines, hands clenched at her sides, eyes fixed on her daughter. Blade's youth and ranking were no excuse for missing the throw.

Between events, her mother had taken one of Blade's hands in hers, tracing calluses with delicate fingers. "Fight with everything you have… in here," she said, pointing to Blade's heart. "Only you control your destiny."

Blade didn't win the competition. Though that misstep had been a hard lesson for a teenager to learn. As she stood on the podium, a sharp biting wind cut through the spectators. She searched until she found her mother, tendrils of ash-blonde hair whipping about her face—and found a woman still fiercely proud of her daughter. Nine months later, a drunk driver crashed into her mother's car, killing her instantly and leaving Blade without her north star. She was left bereft with a disinterested father who believed she should direct her energy on academics rather than waste hours throwing knives and axes in their backyard.

Alec topped off her flute. "A penny for your thoughts?"

"You never told me how René Martel heard about me."

Alec's green eyes twinkled. "Ah, but I did. It was the cover of *Maxim*. Martel couldn't take his eyes off you, luv. You looked smashing in your black leather and windblown hair."

"Glad to know the article gave me some exposure—no pun intended."

Alec burst out laughing, and she joined him. It hadn't been *that* funny, but the two of them laughed until her stomach ached. It felt good, cathartic, to share a good belly laugh.

Over the next hour, he told her about his upbringing in Liverpool, so different from hers. No father, and a mother with little interest in raising a child. He lived rough, moving from flat to flat.

"My mates taught me to fight, among other life lessons," he said, regarding her intently.

"How did you start working for a man like René Martel?"

"Ah, that's a story for another day, luv. Unfortunately, work calls before we touch down in Mallorca. You'll find René Martel a generous employer, but also a demanding one. Get some sleep. I'll be in the aft cabin. We should arrive in a few hours."

After dimming the light over her seat, she mulled over what she'd learned about Alec. A classic rags-to-riches life story. An orphaned teen who'd survived by his wits. This only added to her attraction to the man. She knew relationships required time and effort. Both nonexistent in her chosen profession, except for the occasional dinner/movie date, but the chemistry had never been *right*.

Until now. The possibility made her smile.

Rather than sleep, she allowed herself to fantasize about a life of packed crowds and endless opportunities to further develop and show-case her talent. When sudden turbulence shook the plane, Blade snatched the bottle of champagne before it could spill and buckled her seat belt. With a swig directly from the bottle, she picked up her sketch pad and started to work. With a suddenly ample bank account, failure was impossible.

Blade slipped on her sunglasses as the bright noon sun shot daggers through her eyeballs. *Damned champagne.* But the air was crisp and fresh after a morning rain. From the top of the airstairs, she could see puddles of water gathered on the runway, as if sand dollars were scattered over a wash of black sand.

"Better late than never," Alec muttered under his breath as a silver Mercedes sedan rolled to a stop below them. Today he was once again the quintessential English gentleman, all perfect planes and angles in a tidy charcoal suit, obviously tailor-made. He'd been aloof this morning—preoccupied with work, she hoped, not suddenly bored by her.

Before leaving New Orleans, she'd rewarded herself with a shopping spree, spending thousands on a new wardrobe. Alec had made no comment on her clothing choice of designer jeans, white silk shirt, leather jacket, and boots. But compared to him, she felt shoddy and unsophisticated.

Her head throbbed from too much champagne and not enough prudence. Alec, ever the gentleman, gestured for her to go before him. The sight from the top of the stairs made her stomach churn but she simply had to power through it. Blade needed to be at the top of her A-game when she met René Martel—not undone by a hangover.

The pilot pulled Alec aside at the base of the stairs, while a uniformed chauffeur rushed around the Mercedes and held the door open for her. "Genevieve Broussard?"

Odd that the driver used her name, she thought, as she settled into the back seat. He wore aviator sunglasses and a black hat pulled low on his brow. His erect posture, compressed movements, and general wariness reminded her of some military personnel from Barksdale Air Force Base and Camp Beauregard, who had often frequented the Rising Sun.

The man slid into the driver's seat and pulled the door shut—but instead of waiting for Alec with the engine idling, he looked at her in the rearview mirror, then punched the accelerator. The sedan shimmied slightly before shooting away from the jet.

"What the hell are you doing?" Blade demanded, twisting around to see Alec running after the car, cell phone to his ear.

"Saving your life," the chauffeur said as he maneuvered past a taxiing jet.

American. "My life isn't in danger. You've got the wrong person. I'm an entertainer." The Mercedes swerved onto an empty runway. At this speed, she couldn't risk flinging herself out of the car.

"René Martel isn't who he appears to be."

The driver made a hard left turn. She could smell the acrid smell of rubber as the tires screamed in protest. The Mercedes fishtailed but straightened out. He floored the gas pedal. Finding police cars blocking the east exit, he hooked the car into a 180-degree turn only to be intercepted by police cars swarming through the west exit. Rather than stop and give himself up, he drove straight into the nearest hangar.

Once inside, he slammed on the brakes. "Follow me," he said, unbuckling his seat belt before scrambling out.

She wasn't going anywhere.

The man opened the back door, grabbed her wrist, and yanked.

Get him off the centerline.

She grabbed the lapels of his suit and pulled, planting her feet firmly against his chest then driving him back with her legs, sending him bouncing off the door. Pressing the offensive, she delivered a piston-like *chassé bas* to the head that brought the driver to his knees.

Stunned, he said, "Don't say we didn't warn you." With that, he stumbled farther into the hangar, disappearing behind another jet.

Within seconds, Alec ran up to her. "Are you all right?" he murmured as he enveloped her into his arms.

Now that the threat had receded, fear choked her, making it all but impossible to breathe. Early in her career, she'd been stalked by an overzealous fan. When the stalking turned physical, she found herself alone with a man holding a six-inch hunting knife at her throat outside of her apartment. It had been easy to immobilize her. Thanks to a neighbor who heard her screams and called the police, the assailant had been arrested. The aftermath had left her with a scar along her jawline and a fear that clung to her like cigarette smoke in an unventilated room. The following week, she'd enrolled in Savate, attaining her silver glove after four years in the sport. Today, her training could very well have saved her life.

Before leaving New Orleans, Xavier had pleaded with her to stay home. Who would pay a million dollars for one performance without a catch? The kidnapper had known her real name, where to find her, and who she worked for. Xavier was right. Blind ambition can kill just as surely as a gator in the swamp.

CHAPTER
EIGHT

November 27, 2:07 p.m.
Palma, Mallorca

As Vivienne walked into the Cathedral of Santa Maria of Palma, the air cooled significantly. She envisioned the God of the universe providing a cool respite for penitent believers, with bent knees, to confess in His loving embrace. This was holy ground, whether you believed in God or not. She dipped her forefinger in holy water, crossed herself, and prayed to God she wouldn't scream to the rafters in bitter disappointment.

Vivienne scanned the nave. Tourists milled about, snapping the occasional picture. A group of teenagers giggled, trying to separate themselves from an elderly couple. A low drone of incessant chatter from a local tour guide disturbed the solitude. This lack of piety chafed against her strict Catholic upbringing. Few understood the sacrifice Christ had made on the world's behalf. If they did, she doubted they would be taking selfies with his mother, the Virgin Mary.

When Chase had failed to meet at the rendezvous point near the harbor, Vivienne knew she'd made a grave error. As second-in-command of the Soldati di Cristo, she insisted on meticulously planned operations. All team members thoroughly briefed. Every contingency analyzed with protective measures in place. At the outset, she knew this extraction was a high-risk operation with a low rate of success. Chase had tried to warn her, but she'd refused to listen.

Rather than seeing the massive crown-of-thorns canopy illuminating the altar before her, she replayed the unsanctioned operation. She'd purposely kept Thomas in the dark. And she'd compromised her integrity by manipulating Chase to gain his cooperation. Thankfully, he had escaped without harm.

As she walked down the center aisle, she thought of Christ's sacrifice on the cross for all mankind. Through his death, those who believed in him would be redeemed, bought back by his blood. Anyone at any time could be spiritually saved. Was there any greater love than this? Vivienne wondered to what depths she would plummet to save Genevieve from the monster she called brother.

She found Chase in the front pew, gazing at the rose window high on the east wall above the altar. Its beauty dominated the space with a composition of yellows, greens, reds, and blues.

"Did you know there are one thousand two hundred and thirty-six pieces of stained glass in the rose window?" Chase asked, without turning in Vivienne's direction.

"No, I didn't," she whispered as she joined him.

"There are sixty-one stained glass windows here. Cheyenne would have loved this church," he said.

Even after six years, Chase still grieved for his murdered wife. Vivienne knew all too well about grief and its hold on a soul.

"I should never have put you at risk. I'm sorry," she blurted out in a hushed whisper.

Chase's silence stretched as he clenched and unclenched his hands. The tour guide led his group for a closer look at the altar. Vivienne's icy stare made its point. The group moved farther away, allowing the two some level of privacy.

Eventually, Chase turned to confront her, his anguish tangible. "Sorry doesn't cut it. Why didn't you tell me the truth?"

"What truth?"

"Genevieve Broussard is your daughter. It's obvious to anyone with half a brain."

Vivienne leaned back, the wooden pew hard against her shoulder blades, her chest tight from the aroma of frankincense hanging in the air. Of course, he would discern the truth. As a former Navy SEAL, he was trained to detect small details. She forced herself to breathe. His friendship and loyalty deserved better than deception.

"I held my daughter for six straight hours before I placed her in the arms of another woman," she said, eyes closed as she relived the moment. "There's not a night that the shame of that moment doesn't whisper in my ear. What kind of woman gives her child away?"

She halted, then carried on, needing Chase to understand. "The kind of mother who is desperate and terrified. The worst kind of animal on earth."

"Does Thomas know?" Chase said through gritted teeth.

Vivienne remembered that day in Paris when Thomas had found her, hungry and pregnant. Light snow covering the ground. Her thin coat not keeping her nearly warm enough. "Thomas has a knack for helping lost people," she said. "He noticed a very pregnant woman looking through a bakery window. He offered to buy me a chocolate éclair. By the end of the day, I was safely ensconced in the home of an elderly couple until I delivered Genevieve. After...afterward"—she choked, brushing away tears—"he introduced me to the Soldati di Cristo. The work gave me purpose, a chance to redeem myself. To eventually be part of a new family."

"That's right. A *family*." His voice rose. The tour guide and several people in his group turned. Chase lowered his voice. "When we're in the field, our survival depends upon mutual trust. You have my back. I have yours. It's a simple concept. But you sent me to extract her, on my own, without backup, for a personal reason. The oath we swore before God means something. We can't compromise that, or we're *nothing*."

Vivienne rose to leave, but Chase grabbed her forearm, forcing her back. "The team isn't here because you've kept this operation a secret. Right?"

"I couldn't risk his order to stand down."

"When I put my life on the line, I need all the facts—not just ones you're willing to share." Chase leaned forward, clasping his hands together. "I *trusted* you."

The words stung. His anger was palpable. Every Soldati swore to protect the weak, the persecuted, the defenseless. Her abuse of power and placing her daughter's life above his was inexcusable.

"What are you going to do?" Vivienne asked, afraid to voice her fear.

"This isn't what *we* do, Viv. You understand this better than anyone," he hissed.

"My daughter is in the hands of a psychopathic murderer." She touched his shoulder, willing him to hear her. "I gave Genevieve away once. I won't lose her again."

Chase squeezed his eyes shut and drew and released a deep breath. He rubbed his bruised jaw. "Your daughter packs a mean kick. Lucky for me she wasn't wearing a three-inch stiletto."

Vivienne allowed herself a smile. "Does this mean you will help me?"

"If we have any chance of a rescue operation, we need the team."

She nodded.

Chase stood, his game-face on. "Thomas saved you, Vivienne. And you saved *me*. In more ways than one. It's payback time."

CHAPTER
NINE

November 27, 2:35 p.m.
Palma, Mallorca

After giving a cursory description of the would-be kidnapper to the *Guardia Civil*, Alec bundled Blade into a taxi and drove directly to the villa. Still shaken, conflicting thoughts of the driver's warning and Alec's concern troubled her. *René Martel isn't who he appears to be.* What had stopped her from conveying that to the authorities? The impostor's urgency and sense of purpose, or his sincere cobalt-blue eyes?

Wariness replaced anticipation.

She examined Alec as he thumbed a text message on his cell phone. He exuded genuineness, as did the five hundred thousand dollar retainer and private jet, tangible things that confirmed the legitimacy of the job offer. But the kidnapping attempt had unsettled her. Maybe she should back off, stay in a hotel, think about what just happened, investigate René Martel's job offer with a detached eye rather than an emotional response to Alec.

"We're here," he said, tucking his phone into his suit pocket as the car slowed. "You'll feel better once you settle in."

Wrought iron gates slowly opened, revealing a massive two-story Italian villa. The hatchback rolled slowly around a circular drive that stopped just shy of a walkway leading to an arched front door. Italian cypress trees, meticulously trimmed shrubs, and palm trees created a sense of symmetry to the grounds. As a teenager, Blade often rode her bicycle to La Jolla, where homes like this existed with views of the Pacific Ocean. With her parents financially supporting her pursuit of becoming a world champion, this lavish lifestyle could never be attainable. Ten miles separated her childhood home from La Jolla, but it may as well have been a million.

Two armed guards approached the taxi, their automatic rifles visible. The driver cringed behind the wheel, refusing to exit the hatchback. Alec threw bills onto the front seat, while Blade opened her door and stepped out. Rather than provide a sense of security, the men and their weapons instilled a feeling of foreboding.

Alec joined her on the front walkway as the taxi rattled through the gates. He gently touched her elbow, steering her to the front door. Involuntarily, she recoiled, second-guessing her decision to accept this proposal. He gave her a quizzical look, withdrawing his hand.

Blade inhaled deeply, taking in the familiar tang of the sea. She'd often take her Ducati to Biloxi Beach to escape the stench of stale cigarette smoke, unwashed bodies, and urine that could rise from the streets of New Orleans just before a storm. She lifted her chin, *willing* the soft sea breeze to allay her apprehension.

A faint shadow passed behind the leaded glass window adjacent to the door before being thrown open by a young woman wearing a coral silk pantsuit and crystal-studded sandals. Brazen confidence oozed from the dark-haired beauty, lustrous silky hair cascading over bare shoulders. Black almond-shaped eyes raked over Blade.

"*Bienvenido,* Genevieve. I am Señor Martel's assistant, Graciela." Her smile was anything but warm. "He has talked of nothing except you. I've never met a professional knife-thrower."

Blade, still reeling from the kidnapping attempt, was confused by the woman's hostile tone. Unsure of the dynamics at play, she couldn't resist answering the provocation. "And I've never met a *professional assistant* before."

"Let's get you settled then," Alec said lightly as he ushered her through the foyer and up the carpeted serpentine staircase leading to the second story.

From the landing, Blade glimpsed Graciela marching to another room, her heels clicking on the terracotta tile floor.

"Is Graciela René's daughter?" Blade asked, although the answer was obvious. But she wondered how Alec would respond.

"Hardly," he said with an awkward smile.

Three doors to the right of the staircase, Alec opened the door with a flourish. "This will be your temporary home. *Mi casa, su casa*, as the Spanish say. René won't be available until this evening. The two of you can talk about his expectations then. But I am afraid I will need to confiscate your phone for the next twenty-four hours."

"My phone?" Blade gripped the straps of her new designer backpack. "That wasn't part of the deal."

"I'm afraid I do need it. And your knives. We can't have you disclose your location, even inadvertently. Nor can we have you in possession of weapons. Hand them over."

Blade stood her ground. His tone of voice pissed her off. One million dollars didn't give anyone the right to confiscate her property. This deal was appearing shadier by the minute.

But, then again, this gig would change her life forever.

"You can have my phone," she conceded, "but not my knives. I need them for practice." She removed the phone from the backpack and placed it in his opened palm. "I'm going to take a hot shower and rest. It's been a long day. Where will you be?"

"In the study to the right of the stairs. I'll be back in two hours to take you on the grand tour," he said, his tone conciliatory as he closed the bedroom door behind him.

Blade's inner alarms continued exploding like Fourth of July fireworks. The hot shower had done nothing to alleviate her fear and uneasiness. She had signed a nondisclosure agreement, so why take her phone and isolate her?

She threw open the curtains, allowing the bright sunlight to penetrate the room. The intricate filigree grills obstructing her view of the Mediterranean were lovely, but all she could see was how effectively they caged her. While the beautifully appointed bedroom, with its cream walls and canary yellow accents, did little to immediately calm her, the soothing environment couldn't help but have its effect as the minutes ticked by. A bucket of bottled waters, a platter of assorted cheese and fruit, and a carafe of wine had been left for her on a side table. Absently, she opened a bottle of water and nibbled on cheese as she sank into an overstuffed chair...and within moments, the alarms were ringing again.

The demand for her phone and knives especially spiked her paranoia. Did they think she planned to impale René Martel to the wall when she met him and post selfies with her trophy on social media? It was ludicrous.

From her chair, she could see armed guards patrolling the perimeter of the villa. Who could be coming to the performance to warrant such security? Or was René Martel just a neurotic, pretentious billionaire?

To hell with being relegated to her room.

She threw on jeans and a T-shirt and quickly wrapped her long hair into a messy bun. Before leaving her bedroom, she picked up a pair of sandals. Forget about waiting for a guided tour. She'd rely on her own assessment of the situation.

Soundlessly, she moved down the curved staircase in bare feet. Once she reached the first floor, muffled voices came from her right. Most likely the study. She passed through an arched hallway and stopped just short of closed French doors.

"So then the meeting went as expected?" This was Alec, she knew.

"They are under control," said another man, with a Spanish accent. Martel, no doubt. "The attack on the UN will be executed as planned. Is TNA1 ready?"

"We're on schedule. Ellis and Vega are in Geneva, as you ordered."

"And the girl?"

"Upstairs. Spooked, after the kidnapping attempt. How the hell did anyone know she was coming in on the jet?"

"Vivienne should not be underestimated. A lesson I hope you've learned. This could have ruined my plans."

"I've got Genevieve well in hand."

"Make certain it stays that way. Vivienne will make her move to rescue her. And when she does, I will take her prisoner."

Blade retreated and slipped on her sandals. Questions flooded and overspilled in her mind. Could she have heard correctly? Could they possibly be planning an attack on the United Nations? Could the chauffeur/kidnapper have been telling the truth? And who was this Vivienne?

Heart hammering, she raced in the opposite direction, through a deserted kitchen area, to a marbled terrace overlooking the Mediterranean Sea.

She tripped over the three travertine steps to the pool area. Fountains burbled, giving the impression of utter peace and tranquility, in extreme counterpoint to her own emotional upheaval.

She'd heard Martel clearly, which meant Alec was part of an elaborate deception. They could not allow her to leave the island alive.

Sailboats gracefully skimmed along the surface of the water. A pair of jet skis circled a yacht anchored in the distance. There must be a dock somewhere on the estate. She searched for a path to the water and spotted a break in the bougainvillea near the edge of the property.

"How do you like my home?"

Blade spun around to find herself face-to-face with René Martel. According to the tabloids, he'd just celebrated his fiftieth birthday in Monte Carlo. His smooth skin and healthy tan made him look years younger. He wore white cotton trousers with a navy blue polo shirt and white loafers. The yacht she'd seen was probably his.

Somehow, the sum of all these appealing parts chilled her. Most disturbing were the amber eyes that so mirrored her own.

"You startled me," she said with a smile, assuming her stage persona. "I needed fresh air. My day, as I'm sure you've heard, has been...challenging." Mastering her expression as well as her emotions, she extended a hand to her new employer. "I'm Blade Broussard. And you are René Martel."

"You have done your homework. I like people who are prepared. Who are professional," he said in a velvety Spanish accent. He lifted her hand to his lips.

She repressed an urge to pull her hand away. "You've been very generous, and I intend to deliver a performance you'll never forget."

"I have no doubt. You caught me on my way to a business meeting. Tonight we will dine together."

"Palma is only a few kilometers away. Would Graciela be available to drive me into the city? Or perhaps I could borrow a vehicle?"

"Sadly, that will not be possible. I will explain this evening."

As he turned to leave, three armed security guards materialized and formed a triangle around him. *Sneaky bastards*. Even if she'd tried to run, they or their unseen comrades would have stopped her within seconds.

The four men stood waiting at the edge of the patio area. Martel reddened, obviously displeased at being kept waiting, as Graciela made a grand entrance as if she were royalty. She wore a diaphanous orange dress that swirled around her long, tanned legs, and a floppy straw hat that lifted in the wind. She slid into position beside him, linked her arm through his, and nodded back at Blade as the group made their way to the dock.

Having made note of their route, Blade waited a few moments before wandering to the edge of the patio area. This gave her a clear view of a ten-foot drop to a service road and a wooden dock. Moored to the dock were several powerful-looking jet skis and a speedboat that carried Martel and his entourage to the yacht she'd seen earlier.

As if on cue, Alec drew near, shaking a finger at her. "I told you I'd personally take you on a tour. What have you been up to, luv?"

"Just becoming familiar with the property—and meeting René Martel."

"What did you think of him?"

"Charming, attractive, polite, and rich," she said, nodding at the yacht.

"Bloody hell, you're a good judge of character," he said, chuckling. "He's also charitable with his money and time."

"A real philanthropist. Good to know." Blade cupped her hand over her eyes to block the bright sunlight. "I will need a practice area for knife throwing. Can that be arranged?"

"We can set something out here if that's agreeable."

"Who wouldn't want to practice with this scenery? I assumed I'd be performing here, but I haven't seen a space large enough. But you've already planned for this."

He nodded. "You will be performing in Palma. Would you like a real tour of the villa?"

"I'd like nothing better."

I need to find a way off this island to warn the authorities about the attack on the UN.

As Alec ushered her from one room to another, Blade tried to mark the location of security cameras and guards. Before leaving, she would need to find proof of the planned attack on the United Nations. Without that, no one would believe some random knife-thrower. René Martel was a reputable international businessman. In truth, she wouldn't have believed it herself.

CHAPTER
TEN

November 27, 7:58 p.m.
Palma, Mallorca

Blade mentally prepared for dinner as she would for any performance—by focusing on the details and visualizing the audience, or in this case the actors in play.

The Great Joe Mancini, her friend and mentor, had taught her some of his trade secrets after catching one of her first performances at the Rising Sun. "You need pizazz, kid," he joked. "You can only throw so many knives and axes before boring the audience to death." As a result, she had incorporated the art of misdirection, costuming or lack thereof, and special effects. Valuable lessons learned, yet she'd allowed herself to be duped.

Hiring her had been the work of a master manipulator and Alec his confederate, a plant to entice her to the island.

Her kidnappers would rue this day.

With a critical eye, she examined her reflection in the full-length mirror. The black halter cocktail dress left little to the imagination. Given what she now knew about Alec Quinn and his subterfuge, she felt foolish for purchasing the dress with the intent of impressing him. Pathetic.

The expensive dress, tailored to hug every curve, was not ideal for defending herself in a fight—if it came to that. Taking a fighting stance, she practiced a few uppercuts and jabs, noting her response time. Not bad, considering her three-inch heels and plunging neckline. If given a chance, she would like nothing more than to slam her fist into Alec's face for his duplicity.

Play the part.

People's lives depended on her.

Blade entered the dining room precisely at eight o'clock. Martel presided at the head of the table, wearing a leopard-flock dinner jacket over a black shirt open at the neck. Not many men would feel comfortable wearing animal print, at least the men she knew in New Orleans. The conversation seemed tense between Alec and Graciela, but abruptly stopped, which made her think she had been the topic of discussion.

"I haven't kept you waiting, have I?" Blade said, careful to keep her tone light.

All eyes turned to her.

"You look bloody beautiful," Alec said, rising to offer his seat to her.

Lying bastard. She'd been conned, but there was no one to blame but herself. Alec had exploited her vulnerability, but she'd allowed the attraction she felt for him to cloud her judgment. Ever since she'd started knife-throwing competitions, her peers had misjudged her. Alec and René Martel were making the same mistake. She couldn't wait to prove them wrong.

"What do you think of the island?" Martel asked, draping his napkin over his lap.

"From what I've seen, it's beautiful. I've arranged to rent a car tomorrow," she lied. Nothing like sparring to identify an opponent's strengths —and weaknesses.

"What have you done?"

"I called a local rental company. I find distractions help with my creativity. I rarely travel, and this is a chance I don't want to waste."

Martel's gaze shifted to Alec, then back to Blade. "I'm afraid I didn't explain myself. You can't leave the villa."

"Because of the kidnapping attempt at the airport? As Alec told the police, the attack was probably a random act by a mentally ill individual." This sounded so lame, she wondered how the police could've written this up in their report.

Martel stilled, his shark-like eyes resting on her.

"Leave us," he commanded the others.

Alec and Graciela left quickly without a glance in her direction, closing the double doors behind them.

The air stilled. Hairs bristled at the nape of her neck. She caught the cloying scent of the stargazer lilies that filled a crystal vase on a corner table, an odor that brought to mind her mother's funeral and the obligatory condolences from people who knew nothing of the woman who had championed her dream. Blade couldn't help but feel this memory was a harbinger of events to come. For the past few hours, she kept thinking about the significant resources expended to bring her here. Why would a billionaire bother with a little-known impalement artist?

As though reading her mind, he said, "Surely you don't think you're worth a million dollars for one performance." He gazed intently at her for a long moment before continuing. "It is true you intrigue me. When I first saw your picture, my breath left me. You looked so much like my twin sister. I read the article and learned you were adopted. My curiosity got the better of me. Your eyes give you away. Your bright, intelligent, amber eyes. Unfortunately, there is no performance or marketing campaign. I brought you here as bait to trap my sister—your biological mother. You are *mi sobrina*, my niece."

Stunned, she abruptly got to her feet, knocking over a glass of wine. The red liquid spread over the white table cloth, like blood traveling in the rivers of her palm when she mishandled a knife.

Although yes, she'd been adopted at birth, Dominique and Marie Broussard were simply her parents. Even with the burgeoning convenience of genealogy websites, she'd never had any interest in locating any biological relatives. The only mother she'd ever cared about died ten years ago.

"Sit," Martel commanded. "I assure you, I have gone to great lengths to validate its truth." He pulled a picture from his suit pocket and slid it to her. "I always wondered why Vivienne disappeared from my life—she was pregnant with you."

For the first time since entering the room, Blade noticed there were no knives on the table. *Damn.* Even without a weapon and using her Savate training, it would be easy to incapacitate him.

As she sat, her eyes were drawn to the photograph before her. Her emotions swelling despite herself, she grabbed the picture and brought it close. The image showed a young Martel and what had to be his twin sister smiling at the camera, the two obviously comfortable with having their photo taken. "We were celebrating our twenty-first birthday," he said.

Even then, Martel exuded cool in his white double-breasted suit, dimples framing a brilliant smile, aviator sunglasses perched on his head. Vivienne wore a heavy rosary around her neck, her messy black hair caught up in a scarf. Of course Martel would have recognized Blade's uncanny resemblance to his sister. Blade forced herself to recognize that she and this despicable man shared many of the same features—a strong jawline, high cheekbones, and the same accursed amber eyes.

"This doesn't prove anything," Blade said without much conviction as she laid the picture face down on the table, away from the red stain.

"True. But you cannot argue with science," Martel said as he pulled another piece of paper from his breast pocket and held it out for her. "Here is a copy of the DNA test. We are *familia.*"

"That could easily be forged."

He nodded, throwing the DNA results on the table. The white paper soaked up the red wine, turning it a ghostly shade of pink. "If the DNA results are forged, then that would make me a fool for bringing you here at great cost. I am no fool. In fact, I consider you an investment."

"I don't understand."

"You don't need to understand."

He snapped his fingers, and the double doors reopened to Alec and Graciela. Had they been listening? "Lock Genevieve in her room, Alec. We will be hearing from Vivienne soon, and I wouldn't want our captive to get away."

Blade rubbed at her skinned knuckles. It had felt good to knock Alec to a knee with a right cross. He had played her, used what she'd most wanted against her. There was nothing lamer than being an easy mark. Except a dead one.

She paced the length of her bedroom—her cage, for all intents and purposes—fighting to keep control. Breathe in, slowly, deeply. Breathe out. She sat cross-legged in the middle of the room, clearing her mind. Then refocusing. Her breathing grew shallower.

Measured.

Precise.

Martel's scheme to lure his sister to the villa paled in comparison to the ramifications of an attack on the UN. It pierced through her, just as surely as a knife hitting its target. What twisted reason could Martel have to risk thousands of lives?

Fury replaced fear.

She could not, would not let that happen.

Escape was her only choice. But first, she needed proof of Martel's planned attack before making her way to the dock. If none of the jet skis had keys in its ignition, she would hike the shore to Palma.

After turning over the evidence to the police, the threat to the UN and Vivienne would be quashed. Nothing would give her more satisfaction than seeing René Martel and Alec arrested and behind iron bars.

CHAPTER
ELEVEN

November 28, 1:38 a.m.
Palma, Mallorca

Blade's body vibrated like a tuning fork pitched to a high frequency. She splashed cold water on her face to slow her thundering heart. Earlier, while she confronted Martel during dinner, someone had entered the bedroom and taken her knives and passport. No one knew her location, and with no phone or Internet access, she was as good as dead.

She dressed quickly in black running tights and long-sleeve running shirt by a sliver of moonlight through a slit in the curtains. Cash, a change of clothes, and a hoodie were stuffed into the overpriced back-pack that leaned against the wall near the door. She estimated a three-hour window before anyone discovered her missing. Evading the security guards would be the major obstacle to her getaway.

"Thanks, Joe," Blade whispered as she inspected her set of lock picks. As a magician, picking locks was a required skill. While he tutored her, he would joke that every woman needed to know how to pick her way out of a jam. On her last birthday, he gave her this personalized set.

Reluctant to turn on a lamp, she improvised by clenching a lighted compact mirror in her teeth as she commanded her shaking hands to still. Carefully, she inserted the tension wrench into the lock. She leaned her forehead on the doorknob. *Calm yourself. You can do this.* Remembering the crusty friend who had wrapped her birthday gift in newspaper and blushed when she planted a kiss on his weathered cheek, she held the doorknob in her left hand and inserted the ball rig into the lock with her right, lifting the pins up, pin by pin. After forty seconds and two tries, the door unlocked.

Time to get out of here.

Noiselessly, she opened the door a few inches and peered out.

No guards.

Blade slung the backpack over her shoulder and opened the door. She descended the stairs, senses on high alert. Once on the first floor, she turned right in the direction of the study. Crouching low and keeping to the shadows, she listened intently, expecting to run into a security guard. She spied the doors to the study and inched forward—until she saw a pair of legs near a piano bench. She froze. Until a hand clamped over her mouth. A body rolled atop her, pinning her to the floor.

The backpack dug into her back and unbalanced her. Struggling under his weight, she freed her left arm. She tried to gouge his eye, but the man smoothly countered, clutching her throat in one hand and pinning her arm with his body.

"*Listen to me.* I'm Chase Maserati. I'm here to rescue—"

"Get off me!" she hissed. Whoever this man was, in the gloom, wore a neoprene diving suit and a diver's hoodie, making it nearly impossible to see his features.

"Lock it up," Chase whispered. "I've got to get you out of here."

Blade recognized the voice. It was the chauffeur who'd warned her about Martel. She stopped resisting, and he eased himself warily off of her.

"Don't make any sudden movements and follow me."

"I need to get in there," she whispered, pointing to the study.

"Your mother sent me," he said, grabbing her forearm—hard.

Blade yanked her arm back and sat back on her haunches. "My mother is dead. And I'll only be a few seconds."

"We're wasting precious time," he said through clenched teeth. "Security is tight. No time for a detour."

She shook her head and pointed once again to the study.

His eyes narrowed, then he ducked low and headed for the patio doors, using furniture as cover.

No time to argue with him. She stood and ran to the study, pulling her backpack off and unzipping it as she went. Once there, she knelt behind the desk and opened the middle drawer. An alarm blared.

Damn.

Blade scooped up the contents of the drawer and desktop, stuffed them into the backpack, and made for the patio. She found Chase waiting for her just outside before bolting for the pool. Gunfire erupted in the darkness. Blade hesitated before following behind Chase. He stayed in the shadows, well away from the lit copper fire bowls. If those gunshots were aimed at them, the glimmer would only make them easy targets.

As they rounded the corner by the pool, taking the path to the access road, a security guard blocked them, holding a handgun leveled at Chase's chest. Rather than stop, her would-be rescuer kept running straight at the guard. A shot fired, and the security guard toppled over.

There were others in the darkness on their side.

She jumped over the body and kept running toward the dock, muscles pumping hard. The dock was only twenty seconds away. Blade couldn't see a boat or jet ski.

Bullets hit the wooden dock, sending pieces of wood flying. No time to think, only react.

"Hope you know how to swim!" Chase yelled over his shoulder.

Glancing behind her, she saw two men dressed in black gear aim their weapons at them. Running at full speed, she overtook two defenders who knelt to return fire with automatic rifles, giving them precious seconds to escape. One of the men's heads exploded, sending a shower of blood and gore flying through the air.

What have I done?

This isn't happening.

Bile rose up and out, the acidity burning her throat. Chase grabbed her arm and pulled her after him. They plunged into the sea just before the dock convulsed by an explosion.

Someone had just been killed.

To rescue her.

Inky blackness smothered her. In a moment of déjà vu, she clawed at the water, just as her friend had thrashed in the Merced River years ago, unable to catch his breath as he struggled against the current. Panic seized her as the sea's drag pulled her underneath the water until she felt a hand pull on the strap of the backpack. Jolted into action, she twisted and kicked hard, propelling herself upward.

"Swim!" Chase roared as she spluttered a mouthful of seawater.

Automatic gunfire cracked the darkness, strafing the water only a few feet from her. Blind terror kept her arms moving, one stroke, then two. She'd never been a strong swimmer, and the backpack made it difficult to stay afloat, much less make progress in Chase's churning wake. Three lengths separated them. The thought of drowning terrified her. Swallowing water, the blackness closed around her. Would anyone even care if she went under?

Then he was beside her. He'd slowed to come parallel with her. "I won't let anything happen to you. We're almost there. Let me take your pack."

"No," she sputtered. "I've got it." Despite the cold and exertion, she couldn't risk losing any proof of the planned attack on the UN.

About fifty feet ahead, she recognized a round object—a submersible. National Geographic used these in their underwater specials. A tall man in black tactical gear stood on its meager platform, balancing what looked like a rocket launcher on his shoulder. Looked like, and *was* a rocket launcher, as a second later, a flat tail of fire and smoke streaked straight to the villa. In another few seconds, the entire estate turned into an inferno.

"Keep moving!" Chase ordered.

Mercifully, Blade reached the sub's platform and clung to the slick hull. Almost safe. She tried to pull the backpack off with one hand, afraid to let go of the sub. Strong hands hauled her up. She rested on all fours, gasping for air.

"I'm Luc," said the man who'd plucked her out of the water. "A friend of your mother's. Get inside. There is a blanket to keep you warm."

That phrase again...*your mother*. Who were these people, and how did Vivienne fit into the picture?

"What the hell happened?" Luc said.

He couldn't be talking to her, since it had to be obvious she hadn't the slightest idea.

"Shen's gone. Finn should be right behind us."

"Help Genevieve get below," Luc growled. "I'll wait for Finn."

Before anyone could move, someone who had to be Finn effortlessly heaved himself up on the platform, tearing off his balaclava.

"Where is she?" he yelled, upon her in a millisecond. He didn't touch her, only leaned in close, inches from her face. "I could *kill* you." His spittle sprayed over her, but she refused to avert her eyes. "My best friend is *dead*, thanks to you."

Blade shoved him with both hands. "I didn't ask for your help. Everything was under control before you came."

"*Under con*—You gobshite! Shen would still be alive if you had just followed Chase's orders," Finn shouted, ready to spring at her again. "We took out the guards leading to the dock, without casualties. No one should have died. But you tripped the alarm."

"Leave off, Finn," Chase said, placing his body between them. "We were ambushed. She didn't know."

"Everyone in the Triton," Luc ordered.

Finn shoved past them, easily vaulting through the top hatch. Luc followed, throwing the spent rocket launcher into the sea.

Blade could not resist the pull of the inferno. The spectacle reminded her of a painting she'd admired months before at an exhibition in the French Quarter. Silly to appreciate the depiction of London's Great Fire, with people streaming from gates within the city wall. The artist had blended variant shades of orange to depict the monster that consumed without morality or intention. Witnessing the devastation was far more horrific. She imagined Alec cornered by the flames, burning alive. No one could survive an explosion like that.

Following them through the hatch into the sub's tight, dank quarters, Blade settled, chilled to the bone, into a corner seat in the front row and drew a blanket over and around herself. The meager warmth did nothing to dispel the images of the man's—Shen's—head exploding, or the firestorm that had incinerated anyone still breathing. Finn's furious accusations hit her like bucket after bucket of ice water. Already, guilt gnawed at her for her part in the destruction and carnage.

Death had found her—again.

The hatch secured, Chase grabbed the joystick and piloted the submersible. Luc sat pressed next to her, scrutinizing her in the dim light. Only Finn appeared to react to his friend's death as he sat, expressionless, staring out through the transparent hull. She closed her eyes as the Triton made its descent. There were worse ways to die than drowning.

CHAPTER
TWELVE

November 28, 1:44 a.m.
Palma, Mallorca

Martel casually sipped espresso while he stood in his security command center in Palma with Alec Quinn and Graciela. Two women sat behind a bank of twelve monitors, manipulating camera angles for the best views. Security cameras covered every inch of real estate, including the dock and the street leading to the villa.

They watched as three black-clad men slipped past a perimeter guard wearing night-vision goggles mounted on their helmets and carrying M4 rifles. Martel felt a stab of disappointment. Vivienne was not among them.

Quinn had found this abandoned warehouse several miles from the city limits of Palma. The isolation this building afforded was ideal when dealing with competition and the more distasteful aspects of this business. Similar outposts were located in several countries worldwide.

The LED display cast harsh shadows across Graciela's profile. She turned and withdrew, presumably to sit in another room. Not everyone could stomach combat and the damage one human being could inflict on another.

Did Vivienne really think she could get the drop on him?

The day before, Martel had swapped his elite squad with a local security team hired by Ellis. The Spaniard, always confident, did not doubt his security force. But why take risks with the lives of a competent workforce if he didn't need to? His main objective was to capture Vivienne—alive. If she showed, he could send in his elite force within minutes by helicopter. If she didn't show, the idiots for hire were expendable.

He studied the bank of security monitors with detached interest. His niece showed remarkable innate talent as she made her escape. Instincts could not be taught. What a waste. He could have been a mentor to the girl. One more betrayal to hold Vivienne accountable for.

Like a proud father, he pointed to the monitor. "Genevieve sensed the intruder before he made his move." He laughed and took another sip. "The girl is a natural. A second quicker, and she might have inflicted real damage."

"She's going into the study," Quinn said over Martel's shoulder.

"*Mierda*," Martel muttered under his breath as he saw her scoop all the contents from his desk drawer and stuff them into a bag. Not that he had any incriminating records at the villa. But no one took anything from the Spaniard without repercussions. "Give the order," he snarled.

Quinn spoke into his headset. "Take them out."

Martel and Quinn stood transfixed as the action evolved in real-time on the monitors before them. Several of his security team fell over as Genevieve and her companion made a run for the dock. Two of the intruders knelt, shoulder to shoulder, and returned the security team's fire at the mouth of the dock. No boat or other vehicle could be seen on the monitors, although Genevieve and her companion kept running the length of the dock. All four were effectively trapped.

"Finally," Martel muttered.

A bullet met its mark, one of the intruders reeling back. "Play that back in slow motion."

The technician obeyed without a word. The grainy image came into focus, displaying the point of impact, the intruder reeling backward, brain and gore flying from the skull into the night air. Another monitor caught the remaining intruder throwing a flash bang up the incline. An explosion, then the bloom of a smokescreen. The remaining security force made their way through the haze and fired their automatic weapons into the water.

"Incompetent bastards!" Martel grabbed an empty chair and smashed it against the concrete floor, again and again. Metal legs tore from its frame. A two-bit circus performer and a few men had bested the Spaniard. Spent, he wiped the spittle from his chin with a shaking hand. His best chance at capturing Vivienne had just vanished underwater.

Minutes later, the villa exploded into a wanton burst of light in the blackness. Stunned, the Spaniard stood, emasculated by the total devastation. This fiasco must be contained, his reputation kept intact. Or he would be a laughingstock among his investors.

"I want Vivienne found," he said, his voice a low rumble, "and Genevieve dead."

Quinn turned to leave, his cell phone already to his ear.

"Take care of this, personally," Martel ordered. "No excuses, no mistakes. You have twenty-four hours. *Comprendes?*"

The realization that this could not be contained hit him squarely. He had made no secret of his stay at the villa. The media would be on this story like a shoal of piranha feasting on hapless prey. This could be a public relations nightmare—or a goldmine, if spun properly.

"Wait," he shouted after Quinn, who turned in the doorway. "Call Ellis back from Geneva and have her meet us in Barcelona. All hands on deck," Martel said. "Call a press conference. This was an attack on me and I barely made it out alive. Tell Vega to stay in Geneva, as planned."

Quinn nodded.

Lessons could be learned from every failure. Vivienne had managed to survive and thrive with the help of mysterious allies determined to thwart his quest for a new world order. Not even the threat to Genevieve would bring her into the light. His twin was more ruthless than he ever thought possible. He, too, would never put himself at risk if there were other alternatives.

But she could not possibly know of his plans without help. Someone who knew about Genevieve, the proposed attacks on munitions plants, and his plan to permanently remove Sir Edward Dunn. Only three people fit the bill: Quinn, Graciela, and Ellis.

Daystar, LLC invested heavily into research and development in the defense industry. Besides creating the killing agent TNA1, the R & D team had produced a digestible tracking device that proved exceedingly useful in dealing with nomadic terrorists such as ISIL or the Taliban. Put a small quantity in their drinking water, and people could be tracked for approximately thirty hours. Normally it takes between two to three hours for a person to expel their intake of fluids. With nanotechnology, minute fibers the size of a grain of sand would adhere to the stomach lining before the natural digestive process would render them useless.

Alec had withdrawn to a nearby hotel for calm. Martel's outbursts could last for hours, and straight off he needed to concentrate.

The first rays of dawn appeared over the horizon, but he sat in the dark, pondering his next move. This was the ultimate chess game, with no margin for error. He could repossess Blade well within the twenty-four-hour deadline. But would he? She excited him like no other woman he could recall—vulnerable, beautiful, and tough. Women who fit her physical description could be found in any city and be finessed into the sack with no attachments. Yet, his thoughts in the last few days strayed, over and over, to this knife-thrower. He'd always thought only tossers believed in chemistry between two people, but he couldn't deny the connection between them. He'd learned to be callous, but perhaps he could save Blade from Martel and still get what he wanted.

Alec opened the tracking app on his phone. A red dot pulsed near Ibiza. The ice bucket of Pellegrino in Blade's room for her refreshment had been spiked with the tracking fluid. *Cover all the bases*. His years on the street and subsequent employment with Martel had taught him to cover his arse, to never drop his guard. Martel wasn't privy to this particular bit of intel, and it allowed Quinn a small window of opportunity. But the timing must be perfect.

CHAPTER
THIRTEEN

November 28 - 2:23 a.m.
Mediterranean Sea

The Triton made its descent.

The six-person submersible allowed for generous amounts of head, elbow, and leg room—except for Chase, who piloted from behind the passenger seats. Blade felt lightheaded as she absorbed the vast emptiness through the nearly 360 degree view. No one guessed the enveloping blackness made her feel as if she were in an underwater coffin. Beads of sweat dotted her forehead, despite the cold wet clothes clinging to her body.

She ventured to tap the acrylic hull with her fingernail. It felt no denser than the acrylic top on her desk at home, and that didn't seem nearly thick enough to protect them from the water's pressure. The design made it perfect for underwater exploration, allowing for panoramic views of underwater sea life. The headlights startled a school of silver fish, causing them to disperse into the void as the submersible moved on.

Claustrophobia had always kept her from any enclosed space with no possible means of escape. Yet here she was. Sealed into this tin can with three other humans like sardines. Without warning, her vision blurred and dark spots floated within her vision. *I can't faint now.* She put her head between her knees and took deep breaths.

"If you're going to be sick, use this," Luc said from her left, pressing a plastic bag into her hand. She slapped his hand away as Finn gave a derisive snort.

Blade drew the blanket around her, trying to focus on surviving these moments and making it to land. The pitch-black views to either side and below her were no help, but every time she closed her eyes, images of Shen's last moments on earth bloomed. She fought against the raw emotions of guilt and remorse, certain her actions had caused the man's death. Today's tragedy was just one more burden to carry. Could death be attracted to those already familiar with the devastation it left behind? That would at least be an explanation for why it kept seeking her out.

Her eyelids grew heavy. Jet lag, lack of sleep, an attempted kidnapping, a botched rescue operation—it wasn't as if she had no reason to be exhausted. Worse, she was a prisoner. Thirty minutes or four hours could have passed in this underwater dungeon.

Who *were* these people? Rationally, Vivienne Martel could be her biological mother. René Martel's scheme to snare his sister by involving Blade seemed insane, but plausible. But for complete strangers to risk their lives for her? That was inconceivable.

Imperceptibly, the submarine began its ascent. The men around her broke their silence as the Triton bobbed to the surface. The sky, a somber gray, gave her a sense of grounding, of home. Every morning, she'd wake just before dawn, to run and think, with just enough visibility to see obstacles but dark enough to bask in the cool morning and avoid the torrent of people in the French Quarter.

Silhouetted against the predawn light was an enormous yacht, at least half a football field in length. She'd sometimes seen ships in and around New Orleans, but not a one compared to this.

"You'll be breathing fresh air in a few minutes," Chase offered as he piloted the sub to the yacht's stern.

Can't be soon enough.

When Chase finally opened the hatch, she took a step, but Finn cut her off. He leaned in tight to her ear and said, "Have a care. Accidents happen in our line of business."

Chase watched him stalk off as Blade joined him. "He's just letting off some steam," he said to her. "The man is a ticking time bomb. I think he needs a few days to cool off."

"I'll talk with him," Luc said. "We've all been affected by Shen's death. At present, we need to extend our friend grace. He lost his sister in an explosion. Most likely, he's on his way to break the news to Xiu or knock back a glass of Jameson's. We're all tired. Genevieve, I suggest you rest before we leave. Chase, show her to one of the cabins while I debrief our commander."

"Who's Xiu?" Blade asked through chattering teeth after Luc had left them. A cold wind skipped off the Mediterranean. Miserable and chilled, she just wanted this nightmare to end.

"Shen's sister," Chase said. "Come on. I'll find dry clothes for you. Maybe a hot shower will warm you."

"Where are we going, once we've regrouped?"

He shook his head. "Sorry, but that's privileged information. You'll be told the basics and nothing more."

The bedroom suite was tight but functional, with a stocked refrigerator, coffeemaker, and snacks. Blade sat on the edge of the bed, cocooned in a plush robe. The hot shower had indeed warmed her. She tore into a package of chocolate chip cookies, washing it down with a hot cup of hazelnut coffee. The caffeine should revive her for a few hours. The wet clothes lying in a sodden heap on the floor were another matter.

With renewed resolve and assessing her plight—at the mercy of strangers and with no idea where they were taking her—she turned to formulating a course of action that would move her, *fast*, to stopping the attack on the UN. That meant getting to the mainland and locating the nearest police station or American Embassy. But would anyone believe her story? Would anyone really buy that billionaire mogul René Martel planned to destroy the United Nations?

No, not without proof.

She grabbed her soaked backpack from the carpeted floor and unzipped it. As she'd expected, the papers were drenched. But they were still legible. Flinging the white comforter to the foot of the bed, she set to carefully separate each piece of paper on the sheet—household bills, brochures for yachts, travel information to Thailand. And a lone business card: Aebischer-Graf Properties in Gstaad, Switzerland.

Gstaad could be near Geneva. If only she had her iPhone to pull up a map. There must be a laptop or other device where she could access the Internet.

The knock on her door startled her. Hastily, she threw the comforter over the wet papers. She opened the door to see Chase standing there with a bundle of clothes in his arms.

"I thought you could use these," he said, handing her a stack of folded clothes. "You're taller than Vivienne, but they should do."

"Thanks."

Freshly showered and shaved, he looked less intimidating in jeans and a blue turtleneck pullover. Fine lines crinkled the corners of his eyes, most likely from years in military operations in the Middle East. Many a woman had no doubt fallen for those sapphire-blue eyes and dimpled chin.

She took the clothes and started to close the door, but Chase stayed it with his hand.

"I realize the last few hours have been rough. It's been tough for all of us. But we're the good guys, whether you realize it or not."

"I just want to go home. Can you make that happen?"

Chase nodded. "But we have one stop before we fly you home. Vivienne is waiting for you at headquarters."

"And if I don't want to meet Vivienne?"

He shrugged. "I'm just following orders."

"Good to know you're a rule follower," she said before slamming the door in his face.

Blade sat on the bed and threw the borrowed clothes across the room.

For years, she had rarely thought of her adoption. Marie and Dominique Broussard were her parents—plain and simple. With the possibility of Vivienne Martel as her biological mother, Blade acknowledged a morbid curiosity about the circumstances surrounding her adoption. But being forced to meet with Vivienne rankled her.

As did Alec Quinn's betrayal. That hit bone-deep. A mistake that could have cost her life. It also left her second-guessing her judgment. Chase seemed sincere. But in her current situation, living by her emotions was a weakness she couldn't afford. The lives of hundreds, possibly thousands, depended upon her.

CHAPTER
FOURTEEN

November 28, 8:45 a.m.
Florence, Italy

Chase maneuvered the Land Rover through traffic along the Arno River. Luc rode shotgun, intent on sending a text message on his phone. Blade ignored both men as she absorbed the beauty of Florence, an oasis of earthy pigments—mustard, umber, and sienna. She felt transported back in time to the Renaissance, where Leonardo da Vinci and Michelangelo created works that would ultimately endure for centuries. A shame she would not be here long enough to partake of the city's history and culinary delights.

Being safely on the ground did not dispel her fear or mistrust of the people who held her. If anything, it made her a static target. Something she was familiar with.

Minutes ticked by. She did not have time to waste sitting in the back of an SUV crawling through morning traffic. Not to mention being forced to meet Vivienne.

All I need is one chance, one second to bust out of here.

After a few cursory orders at a private airstrip in Spain, neither man deemed it necessary to speak to her. Except for the occasional glance from Chase in the rearview mirror, she might have been invisible. She

72

preferred the quiet. Admittedly, being a professional impalement artist didn't seem the best choice for an introvert.

As they drew nearer to city center, the lure of freshly baked pastries and cappuccinos brought scores of tourists from their hotel rooms. The windshield glistened in the morning sunlight. A new day, a bright beginning for most people. For Blade, it was another chance to stick René Martel to the wall, while at the same time stopping a plot to kill hundreds at the UN. Although she had no tangible evidence against Martel, it would be a relief to report what she knew. With a clear conscience, life would go back to normal.

The car slowed to a near stop as pedestrians crossed the street. This was the break she'd been waiting for. Blade pulled on the door handle.

Damn child safety locks.

"We'll be at our headquarters in a few minutes," Luc said. "Here, put this on." He threw something black in her direction.

Blade held it out before her. A black hood, suitable for a kidnap victim. Enough with this crap. "I'm not putting this on. Unlock the door, I'm getting out here," she ordered.

A blue and white Lamborghini with the Polizia insignia rolled past. Desperate, she pounded against the window, trying to gain the attention of the officer behind the wheel.

Luc twisted around, locking his hand around her forearm, and attempted to pull her away from the unwelcome stares of onlookers.

"Don't touch me," she said, whipping her fist up and around, catching him on the cheek.

"Help!" she screamed against the closed window.

"*Stai zitto*," Luc said, half his body now in the back seat. "Shut up, or I will knock you out."

Chase accelerated, honking the horn at the stragglers who still blocked the street. He turned left as Blade grappled with the older man. Two blocks away, he braked—hard.

"Enough!" Chase shouted.

They froze, and his laser-like eyes bored into hers. "We've lost a good man on our mission to rescue you. Whether you like it or not, you are going to meet with Vivienne. I strongly suggest you play nice for a few more hours."

The car moved back into traffic. Vivienne may be her biological mother, but she didn't owe the woman anything. The fabric of her life was slowly unraveling because of her purported relationship with this stranger. She would meet the woman and leave. With any luck—and, she reminded herself, with plenty of money in her bank account—she'd be on a plane to New Orleans by midnight.

Vivienne slid the cell phone back in her jeans' back pocket and resumed pacing the length of the conference room. Genevieve would be here within minutes. Her chest constricted, a dull pressure that reminded her of loss—and excitement.

Marie had sent periodic reports and pictures of the girl through the years, but when she died, Dom stopped all communication. Vivienne nonetheless managed to keep track of the rising star, and was proud when Genevieve captured the International Knife-Throwing Championship. She'd even bought a plane ticket to New Orleans, but canceled it the next day.

According to Luc, Genevieve was combative and angry. Of course, who wouldn't be? She could have been killed. As a senior member of the Soldati who had pressed the team into attempting the rescue, Vivienne accepted full responsibility for Shen's death.

She pounded the wall with a fist. Her brother was a bastard. Fear had dictated her choices nearly thirty years ago. Not anymore. René fed on the innocent and vulnerable like a parasite. *Spyāniyārḍa.* That one word had set her soul on fire. Unwittingly, from that moment, Vivienne had set into motion this particle of time. Somehow, in the midst of her desire for revenge, he had uncovered her most coveted secret. She should have known he would find Genevieve.

She leaned her forehead against the cold window overlooking the city. A tear, like a drop of rain, lazily rolled down her cheek. Vivienne closed her eyes and remembered the most important day of her life. Heavy rain had pelted the hospital window as she pushed Genevieve into the light. She held her daughter close and inhaled the sweetness of her newborn baby. Entrusting her delicate little girl to someone else to raise tore her soul into shreds. It was as if heaven itself were spilling the tears that she could not. Reason had forced her to give Genevieve away, the only and best protection for her daughter. But on rainy days, she allowed herself the luxury of fantasizing about her daughter. In her reverie, they would meet at her recently purchased villa in Tuscany, sipping sangria under a waning afternoon sun, sharing stories of their separate lives.

She shook her head. *Not like this.* Not under an umbrella of coercion and death. What could she possibly say to her daughter? *I'm sorry I gave you up for adoption, but that was the only way I could protect you.* This sounded trite. Focus on the motivating fact before them: *My brother is a psychopath who will stop at nothing to destroy me.* Genevieve had already experienced his insatiable need for control…and revenge.

A hand fell gently on her shoulder.

"It will all work out, Vivienne," Thomas said. "God is in control."

"Is he, Thomas? Sometimes I wonder," she said, squeezing his hand. "I never wanted to involve Genevieve in my life. I should have sent René to hell years ago, before meeting you, before the adoption. I could have led an ordinary life."

"You're not a murderer," Thomas said, standing shoulder to shoulder with his vice commander.

"I've killed people. I can never explain that away."

"We kill in self-defense. The Soldati di Cristo vow to protect persecuted Christians. Period. Sometimes that includes someone's death. It haunts all of us, but it is necessary. Think of the countless people the Soldati have saved for two millennia. We have been called to serve and are willing to sacrifice our own life for others. There is no stronger love. You have nothing to be ashamed of."

As if sensing Vivienne's anguish, dark, heavy clouds blocked the sun, leaving a morning filled with secrets and lies. Even the rust-colored dome of Il Duomo di Firenze seemed diminished in the distance.

René posed a real threat to Genevieve. His life must be forfeited for her daughter's.

At any price.

During her investigation into the Spaniard's activities, Vivienne wasn't surprised by the increasing atrocities he'd ordered. Even as a boy, he could not control his compulsion to torture those around him through manipulation and lies. Age had only refined his true nature. At her brother's core lay a coward's heart. Given his penchant for notoriety and adulation, he would not hide forever.

A life for a life.

Vivienne turned to her friend. "What if Genevieve hates me? What if I lose her for a second time?"

"She's an intelligent young woman. Put yourself in her place. Genevieve has been thrust into a predicament she didn't expect, nor does she understand. We will help her put these events into perspective. Give her the only things of importance you have to give: the truth and your love. Her soul will understand. It may take a while for her mind to catch up."

CHAPTER
FIFTEEN

The Land Rover stopped in the middle of a narrow street flanked by two multi-storied buildings. The neighborhood appeared to be part of a vibrant mixed-use block of retail storefronts, apartments, and cafés. Shopkeepers were beginning to open their roll up industrial doors for the eager tourists hunting for souvenirs.

"Don't say one word," Luc warned as he pulled Blade out of the car. His hand kept a tight grip on her forearm as they approached two solid varnished wooden doors that looked as if they could withstand a siege. A modern-day keypad marred the ancient façade of the stone building.

Entering, she was disconcerted to see dozens of violins displayed for sale. Not what she expected. Behind a wooden counter, a half-dozen men and women worked on violins in various stages of development. Fumes of varnish and wood shavings filled the air, reminding her of her father's workshop. As a teenager, he'd helped her fashion a custom ax handle for her first international competition. She had thought this would bring them closer together. It hadn't.

A young boy, perhaps eleven or twelve, looked up from playing a red violin as Luc unceremoniously pressed her toward wooden stairs. An older man behind a sales counter appeared unfazed by the intrusion.

The cry of the violin carried upward as they climbed two flights to a landing. The wooden stairs and balustrade looked reasonably new, but the plaster walls, cracked and crumbling, were in serious need of repair.

The pair halted at an old, peeling door that reminded her of a voodoo shop she had visited upon moving to New Orleans. Then, as now, she was afraid of what lay behind the closed door. Curiosity about a strange milieu had driven her to turn the doorknob that day. Behind that door, she'd found an assortment of charms, gris-gris, candles, and other oddities that made her feel like exactly what she was: an outsider looking into a realm she didn't understand. She felt the same queasy sensation over the prospect of meeting Vivienne and coming to terms with a truth she didn't understand—yet.

Luc pressed the buzzer and the latch opened automatically. Blade wasn't sure what to expect behind the door, but it wasn't this. The interior elements combined patched plaster walls and arched doorways with glass walls separating work spaces. Dark walnut wood flooring covered the entire area. The juxtaposition of old-world and modern industrial worked within the cavernous space.

About a dozen people either sat at computer stations or gathered in workgroups with tablets in hand. Some glanced in their direction, but most went about their business.

Luc ushered her into an austere conference room, where he shoved her into a chair. "Stay there," he ordered as he backed out of the room.

I will get even with you before I leave Florence.

In defiance, she walked to the window to canvas the area. From this vantage point, she gazed upon a vista of terra-cotta rooftops spreading out from the Arno River. Her eyes drank in the beauty of Florence. A red-domed cathedral dominated the city sprawl—a tribute to the great Renaissance period that moved the world from the Middle Ages to modernity. Years ago, when she attended an Art History course at UC San Diego, the instructor showed slides of Michelangelo's David, Botticelli's Birth of Venus, and Donatello's Penitent Magdalene. Despite the pull of this ancient city and its treasures, she longed for home. The Spanish moss hanging from mighty oak trees, the

Mississippi lumbering through New Orleans, even the roughnecks at Gators.

"Genevieve," a woman said behind her.

Blade whipped around.

Vivienne stood, a sliver of sunlight bathing her in light. Slowly, she closed the door behind her.

Blade found it hard to swallow past the lump in her throat as she gazed upon the stranger who claimed to be her mother. Casually dressed in jeans, a white oxford shirt, and boots, Vivienne looked more like her sister. Dark brown hair, drawn into a rope braid, fell over her left shoulder.

Forming words felt like an impossibility as a riot of emotions clashed with each other. What did you say to the woman who gave you away at birth? She'd rarely thought about her adoption or biological donors, but for what felt like the first time in her life, words literally escaped her. She stood there feeling like a child, lost and alone.

"My daughter," Vivienne said in a hushed tone, as if she knelt in a confessional.

"I'm not your daughter," Blade lashed out. "My mother died ten years ago."

"*Disculpa*, I did not mean to imply a relationship. I'm only happy to meet you—after these many years."

Anger, remorse, uncertainty, betrayal, love, hate. Rampant emotions suffocated her. As a teen, after the accidental drowning of a friend, Blade's parents had taken her to a psychologist to better cope with and control events in her life. She was taught to recognize the downward spiral that could derail her personally and professionally. Blade *needed* to end this interview before she exploded.

"I wish I could say the same," she said. "You forced me here. Your brother threatened me. And your friends aren't much of an improvement. I want to forget I ever met René Martel or any of you. I want my life to go back to normal."

Normal. The word hung in the air like a half-deflated balloon. "As long as René is alive, your life is in danger. You will stay with me until he is stopped."

"Stay with you?" Blade repeated. "For how long?"

Vivienne took a tentative step in her direction, arm outstretched. Blade couldn't think beyond her breath, which came in short, clipped gasps. A jackhammer pounded in her chest. The room shrank. Her vision narrowed. She grabbed her bag and brushed past Vivienne.

She needed air.

Blade jerked the door open and ran along the bare hallway into the heart of the building. People, alarmed at the sudden intrusion in their office space, stopped their activity. Chase appeared between her and the exit leading to the stairs, his feet planted, the only formidable obstacle standing between her and freedom.

Men often discounted her ability, assuming women could not compete with them in a fight. Her Savate instructor, always a realist, encouraged women to take advantage of this weakness—seize the initiative, and never fight fair. Blade had needed little encouragement to integrate this detail into her training. She closed the distance between herself and Chase at a run and sucker-punched him in the groin, leaving him bent over and sucking in air.

Blade needed to run, leave, find someone who could help. Tourists stopped browsing and turned in her direction as she leaped over the last two steps. Near the door, the young boy played a haunting melody, setting her nerves on edge. No one followed her outside. Recalling the view from her vantage point upstairs, people congregated around the Arno, a perfect location to lose herself. Surely, among the hundreds of people on the streets, at least one person could tell her where to find the American Consulate.

"What are you looking at?" Chase growled at his fellow Soldati. They scattered, leaving the former Navy Seal alone.

With hands on knees, Chase tried to catch his breath. Bested by a nightclub performer. He'd never live this down.

He stood up and closed his eyes, willing the wave of nausea to pass. Blade was a fighter, an independent thinker. If truth be told, he didn't blame her for running. He would have done the same thing.

Luc chuckled as he slapped him on the back. "I wish someone had recorded that. You forgot one basic rule: never underestimate your opponent."

"Found that entertaining?" Chase croaked.

"She is Vivienne's daughter. I expected nothing less."

"Did anyone go after that hellion?" Chase said.

"It happened so fast. That girl doesn't just pack a punch, she can move," Luc said, grinning. "Don't blame yourself. She'll be back. That firecracker will want to hear the truth from Vivienne. Of that, I'm sure, my friend."

"She's no girl. She's a full-grown woman, and trouble. What if she goes to the Carabinieri? We're a *clandestine* organization, remember?"

Luc stared at the younger man. "You're right. If she goes to the Carabinieri, our entire organization could be blown. We have to find her. Any ideas?"

"Probably straight into a crowd, then the police."

"No," Vivienne said, sliding up behind them. "She's scared. And she doesn't know who to trust. She will go to the one place she feels safe."

The two men said in unison, "Home."

CHAPTER
SIXTEEN

November 28, 11:17 a.m.
Florence, Italy

Alec Quinn smiled at his ace in the hole.

The red dot on his cell phone moved through Ponte Vecchio, the centuries-old bridge over the Arno River. From appearances, the bridge looked more like tenant apartments than a place to buy artwork or jewelry. The oil painting he'd purchased while on holiday the previous year from one of the vendors there hung in his flat in Barcelona. He bought anything he fancied. Living on crumbs in Liverpool's slums had given him an apparently bottomless appreciation for the luxurious life Martel offered.

It didn't appear Blade held to that same philosophy. The red dot moved without pause over the bridge.

He would need to reward Dr. Pashkov, the brilliant Russian scientist bought and paid for by Daystar, LLC, for a job well done. Alec didn't particularly care about the science behind the tracking agent—only that it worked. The one drawback to this agent was the relatively short period of time it stayed in a person's system.

Earlier, the GPS had tracked her to a violin shop in the Oltrarno district. South of the Arno River could get dicey, but tourists still strolled through the Boboli Gardens or the Palazzo Pitti. He'd assumed Blade and Vivienne were there, along with the extraction team who had infiltrated the villa. A strange place to hole up. But our girl appeared to have bolted. Evidently her touching reunion with Mom had gone balls-up.

With luck, Blade was alone. Ideal conditions for his own extraction team to grab her.

Alec had his own plans for Blade.

Months earlier, Martel had dispatched him to New Orleans to gather a DNA sample from a young woman, an impalement artist performing at a local dive. *Impalement artist? A posh job title for a carny worker.* Since this was such a simple mission compared to his usual, he took time to attend her performance at the Rising Sun—and stood corrected. This Blade was every inch an artist. There was no mistaking her competence with a wide array of knives and axes. And she absolutely commanded the stage—sleek, sexy, strong, confident, with a hint of ruthlessness behind her strange eyes.

Afterward, hiding among the shadows across the street from the Rising Sun, he waited for her to emerge from the side door. Dim light poured into the alley as the door opened. Blade strode to a red Ducati motorcycle, helmet in hand. Her long chestnut hair, pulled tight into a ponytail, made her appear younger, like a typical college student and even sexier in a pair of skinny jeans and a black leather jacket.

At thirty-two, he could count the number of casual relationships he'd indulged in on his two hands. In his line of work, a love interest only left him vulnerable. Martel liked him well enough, but Alec knew he was not immune to his employer's wrath. Even family members of employees were susceptible to harsh punishments. His identity rested in being Alec Quinn—the fixer. And fixers didn't live their own lives.

Blade had been his purpose in New Orleans. She was a stunner, and he'd undeniably felt an immediate physical attraction to the impalement artist. The night at Gators had marked the first real emotion he'd experienced in years. He found her to be genuine, unlike most of the people he associated with. Sure, he'd like to shag her, but she wasn't the type for one-night stands. And his feelings for her went deeper. More than he'd thought possible. To the point that he hated himself for leading her into Martel's snare.

But he didn't kid himself. His commitment to self-preservation outweighed his feelings for her.

Hundreds of tourists scurried through the shops on the Ponte Vecchio. They moved like a herd of sheep, with their cell phones in their hands, presumably taking pictures. With head bent, he appeared to be just one more tourist looking at his phone. Alec's tracking app displayed a red dot turn left on *Lungarno degli Acciaiuoli*, parallel to the Arno.

He snapped to attention. *Bloody hell.* The office of the Consulate General of the United States was ten minutes away. Alec rushed to stop her.

"*Scusa*," a bouncy young woman said after bumping into him. She wore green camouflage cargo pants and a black tank top that revealed ample breasts. Before he could regain his balance, her bare arm fell across his hand like a sledgehammer, causing his phone to skitter away across the pavement.

"Twit," he said under his breath. But before he could retrieve it, the young woman ground her heel into his foot. He flinched in pain and tried to shove her away. She made a show of trying to help steady him, all the while apologizing loudly, calling attention to them.

Alec heard the sound of bare feet on the pavement before he saw a young boy scoop up the phone at a run. *I can't believe I fell for the oldest trick in the book.*

He made a grab for the young woman a second too late. She deftly slid into a group of Japanese tourists who were taking pictures of a storefront, then disappeared into the crowd. *Bloody gypsies. The lot of them pickpockets and thieves.*

He needed that phone.

"Stop!" Alec yelled, running after the boy. Alec could easily outrun him on a track, but the nimble lad ran in and out of tourists like the great Mario Andretti on a racecourse. Alec shoved people aside, trying to keep the boy within sight, but he turned the corner at the end of the bridge, and by the time Alec rounded it, he was gone.

It took a good thirty seconds for his rage to simmer. Only then did he think to check the inside of his jacket for his wallet. Nicked by the young woman. His tracking system, money, contacts, e-mails—all potentially exposed and, if they were to fall into the wrong hands, capable of implicating not only himself but Martel.

Bollocks. If Martel finds out.

Take a breath. The security lock on his phone would give him time to fix this problem remotely. But it did complicate his plan to recapture Blade. With no way to alert the extraction team, he would have to rely solely on himself. If she made it inside the Consulate, his life would be worthless. He sprinted down *Lungarno degli Acciaiuoli* past the *Ponte Santa Trinita* and *Ponte Alla Carraia* bridges until finally reaching *Ponte Amerigo Vespucci*. His pulse raced, his lungs burned, and his calf muscles throbbed from the seven-minute run. He rested his hands on his thighs, fighting to catch his breath.

The Consulate appeared to be about four hundred meters from where he stood at the bridge. *What a cock-up.* Three guards surrounded Blade, two with weapons aimed directly at her, center mass.

Getting closer to the Consulate, he casually pretended to admire the statue of Giuseppe Garibaldi, just east of the building. After a few minutes, a guard escorted her into the building. Time to cover his ass. First order of business—buy a burner phone and get a team in place to keep the Consulate under surveillance. Martel would expect an update on his progress in attaining Blade, but Alec needed time to calculate his next move. Now was not the time to be imprudent.

When tracking an adversary, it all amounted to patience and isolating the target. Alec kicked at a chunk of broken pavement. Blade didn't stand a chance.

CHAPTER
SEVENTEEN

November 28, 11:22 a.m.
Florence, Italy

Blade raced alongside the Arno River toward the United States Consulate. The green water of the Arno River looked unimpressive compared to the Mississippi that flowed through New Orleans. Her home. There were so many things she missed: the paddle wheeler cruising the river, Hawk Rollins playing his sax in the French Quarter, cafés au lait in the morning, and muffalettas at her favorite Italian restaurant. Once she spoke to someone at the Consulate, this hellish ordeal would be over. She could sympathize with Dorothy as she tapped her ruby slippers together—there really was no place like home.

Concrete barricades blocked the area immediately surrounding the Consulate, a sad testament of world affairs and the unpopularity of US foreign policy. The American flag waved gently in the breeze above an arched entryway into the Consulate. The squat, rectangular building looked out of place among Florence's terracotta allure. Its institutional green exterior reminded her of government properties in the States— unappealing and hopeless. *What a disgrace.* Then again, maybe this did represent what her country stood for: a square, old, shabby political system that warranted a reboot.

A lone guard stood sentry under an oversize umbrella, shouting at an elderly gentleman taking a photograph of the building. What was the big deal? There was probably an image of the Consulate on Google. She couldn't help but smile as the man flipped the guard off and snapped one more photo before turning on his heel. Talk about grand exits.

"Ciao," Blade said to the young guard, trying her best to sound friendly yet professional. "I'm an American citizen, and I'd like to speak to a Consulate staffer."

"Do you have an appointment?"

Appointment? Didn't most people probably have an emergency or at least an unexpected need when they visited a Consulate or Embassy? "I'm an American citizen. I shouldn't need an appointment."

"I'm sorry," the guard said, pasting a blatantly counterfeit smile on his youthful face. "You need an appointment."

"This is an emergency. I have something to report about a possible attack on the United Nations."

That should get his attention.

Suspicious, his hand went to a cell phone. Within seconds several guards came through the entrance, guns drawn. Not what she expected.

"Drop the backpack," the guard ordered.

Blade let the bag slip from her fingers.

After passing through a metal detector, a guard escorted her to a small interview room on the first floor.

With no clock or windows in the austere room, it was impossible to track the minutes that ticked by, but Blade had seen enough police procedural television shows to spot the intimidation tactic.

At last, a petite woman entered the room and sat on a metal chair across from her. She could have been thirty years old or fifty, her porcelain skin flawless. Black hair, cut in a severe blunt cut, and hands primly set one upon the other, reminded Blade of an exasperated parent getting ready to scold her child.

"You have caused quite a stir, Ms. Broussard," she said, pulling on her conservative black jacket. "I am Eva Rossini, a management officer at this post. I understand you have information about an attack on…the United Nations, was it?" This was delivered with a smirk that fairly ached to be slapped off her face.

"I don't have time to play games"

Sharp-penciled eyebrows lifted. "Is that what you think we're doing here? You come to the Consulate with a story about a planned attack on the UN, without proof, and you expect us to do what, exactly?"

"I expect you to warn the UN security force, or Homeland Security, or the CIA. I'm guessing here. This is your area of expertise."

The woman allowed the silence to linger. "You have told your story to one of the guards, but I would like you to tell me your story again, from the beginning."

"I overheard René Martel discussing the attack at his home two days ago. I barely escaped with my life. They mentioned TNA1—"

"René Martel, the fashion designer?" Incredulous, she went on. "*You* were a guest at René Martel's home? When the villa exploded?"

"I'm an impalement artist from the States. Martel hired me—"

"I'm sorry. An *impalement…?*"

"An impalement artist. I throw knives at people." She matched the woman's smile with one of her own. "Quite accurately."

The woman blinked at that, as though the daggers Blade's eyes were throwing had hit their marks.

"René Martel paid me to perform at his villa. Google me or call my last employer. I'm telling you, the United Nations is in danger."

Red lips turned into a frown after reading a text message on her cell. Eva stood, opened the door, and beckoned a guard with her index finger. "This office takes threats very seriously. We did a background check on you. An unemployed knife-thrower from New Orleans. René Martel is a successful businessman and philanthropist. He held a press conference this morning. The local authorities are ruling the attack an act of terrorism. The investigation is ongoing, of course. What we don't do is take part in smear campaigns or assist publicity hounds. I could have you detained, but I think that would be a waste of everyone's time. Don't you?"

Blade silently berated herself. Of course, the media would devour the story as Martel shaped it. The paparazzi followed René Martel like shadows. An explosion at his villa, with a hint of mystery, would be front-page headlines. Fodder for the masses. Going to the Consulate had been a mistake. Eva Rossini didn't believe her, and could have detained her.

Without consciously thinking, she turned right on Via Palestro, away from the Arno River and Vivienne.

A motorcycle tore past her as she hurried past an apartment building and underground parking. The Italians must be more trusting than Americans, she thought as she passed a bicycle secured to a street sign. In New Orleans, teenagers with time to kill would have stolen the bike by now. Fiats, Citroëns, and other small cars lined both sides of the street.

No one followed her. She passed few pedestrians, although rows of bikes and scooters were parked at the intersection. Florence felt profoundly unfamiliar, even alien to her, steeped in culture, architecture, religion. Each building with a host of stories to tell. She wondered whether she'd make it out of this alive and whether her ghost would haunt the narrow streets of this city.

Her stomach rumbled as she passed a trattoria. People were seated in an outdoor patio area, with pizzas and glasses of wine covering the tables. Damn, it smelled delicious. On impulse, she headed to the hostess station and within minutes was seated in the corner of the patio. After ordering a Peroni and pepperoni pizza, she leaned back in her chair and guzzled the cool water placed in front of her.

Already half the day was gone and she had accomplished nothing. A headache pulsed behind her eyes, but the steaming pizza and cold beer should remedy it. While devouring the pizza, all she could think about was Martel. He could not afford to leave her alive, even on the outside chance she could get anyone to listen to her. With unlimited funds and employees like Alec to do his bidding, she wondered how long it would take before he captured her.

By her calculations, she had four hundred dollars cash and a credit card, which she could use to book a flight home. If only she could borrow a phone. She caught the eye of a young man, but he quickly looked away. Pale and thin, he wore skinny black jeans, a black T-shirt, and a black fedora. What caught her attention were the colorful tattoos that ran the length of his arms and neck.

She had read that in Italy, it was considered rude for a server to bring the bill, and she didn't want to offend. But she needed to get to the airport. The young woman at the cash register happily took her credit card but became suspicious when Blade asked to borrow a phone.

"*Necesita usar un teléfono?*" the pale young man asked, standing directly behind her and holding up his phone.

Assuming he'd understood her conversation with the hostess, she accepted the phone he held out to her. Maybe the guy only looked sketchy.

"*Afuera?*" The young man gestured to the door with a hand.

She walked outside, waiting for the young man to pay his bill. He'd forgotten to enter his password on the phone. Men. Past the lunch hour, there were few people on the street. She looked through the window and saw the young woman leading him to the back of the *trattoria*. What could they be doing?

A white van swept into the empty parking stall adjacent to the restaurant's front door. Probably a delivery. The driver's door opened, and an attractive blonde woman stepped onto the pavement. She wore jeans, a short puffer coat, and a baseball cap. The side door opened, and two men piled out to stand behind her.

"Hello," the woman said.

"You're American," Blade blurted, surprise and familiarity overriding suspicion. If she couldn't directly lend Blade a hand, she could at least offer the use of her phone. Perhaps she could still book a flight home.

The tattooed man belatedly exited the *trattoria* and stood behind her. The hair on the nape of her neck prickled. Too many fronts to track at once. She tensed, preparing to flee. But before she could bolt, the tattooed man grabbed her from behind while the two other men seized her legs. She fought back, sinking her teeth into an arm and drawing blood. One of the men cursed while she kicked and screamed. With one leg free, she unleashed a vicious piston-action kick that landed squarely on a knee. One of the men released her other leg.

"Keep her *still*, you idiots," the blonde screamed.

With her legs under her, Blade twisted out of the tattooed man's hold.

He fired a jab into the side of her head, momentarily stunning her. Good thing she'd drawn back just before impact.

She blinked her eyes, feeling oddly weightless. Only just managing to stay on her feet, she heard departing footsteps, an engine revving, and wheels screeching as the van sped away.

"Are you all right?" the young woman from the restaurant said in halting English as Blade's knees buckled. By this time, bystanders hovered all around her, speaking rapidly in Italian. Something wet dripped from her chin. She wiped at it—blood. But not hers.

What the hell just happened?

She'd narrowly escaped them, but Martel and his people were relentless—the threats becoming more intense and dangerous. Would she ever be safe again?

But the more pressing question—how had they tracked her?

CHAPTER
EIGHTEEN

November 28, 12:02 p.m.
Gstaad, Switzerland

Martel threw the French doors open leading to the upstairs terrace and breathed in the fresh mountain air. The resonate clanging of a cowbell rode the wind, the chill air invigorating his body and spirit. This was the only place on the planet where he felt at home. An entire year had passed since he last visited. He'd missed its rustic beauty, the solitude, the landscape. Pine trees covered the hillside. The Jungfrau Peak, part of the Bernese Alps, touched the ice-blue sky with its snow-covered summit. Most CEOs withdrew to acclaimed retreat centers to disconnect from the everyday grind, but no other setting he'd encountered better enabled him to clear his mind—to focus—than the green pastures and picturesque view before him.

In less than two days, an upheaval of the world's governments would initiate his rise to power. Within three years, with the United States in his back pocket, predetermined individuals would be established in positions of power in other countries. And with the threat of nuclear missiles, he would begin the final phase of his ambitious stratagem—global domination. He could taste the sweet satisfaction of country after country falling like dominoes. Under his rule, the populace would be governed by distinct regions with his overlords implementing his agenda. A strong authoritarian government would take time, but eventually all armed resistance from dissidents would be suppressed. He was born for greatness. People would hail him as their Supreme Leader.

But first he had to smoke out the serpent within his ranks.

Graciela's silence on the flight to Gstaad had sparked distrust. Usually, her lively conversation about the newest fashion trends or tabloid gossip kept him occupied. Today she seemed aloof and brooding. After the limousine driver had deposited the luggage in the great room, she'd thrown her jacket on a nearby table and went upstairs without a word. He could hear the shower running and knew from experience he wouldn't see her for the next hour.

"Alexa, play *Obsessão*," he commanded. The passionate voice of Amália Rodrigues filled the chalet with suffering and abandonment as he laid his head back on the cinnamon leather sofa and closed his eyes. The Portuguese guitar and viola wept with all of life's struggles—love, betrayal, and death—an entire life span in one song.

Vivienne was his obsession. Since her disappearance nearly twenty-seven years ago, he would catch glimpses of women through the years who reminded him of his twin, then ultimately be disappointed when they came into full view. Until a few months ago, when he caught the profile of a woman at an art gallery in Paris. He searched the entire building for the illusive woman. His pursuit proved fruitless. But his gut never failed him, and a few weeks later the surety of seeing his sister was cemented when he saw the *Maxim* photo of Blade.

Finding himself on edge, he reminded himself that his long road of unfulfilled need was about to end. He would soon have Vivienne and the entire population subjugated and bent to his will. But only after he identified the traitor within his inner circle. Once he'd confirmed that, punishment would be meted out, the delicious possibilities endless.

Once again, he ticked through the list of people closest to him.

Over the past sixteen years, Alec Quinn had earned his trust by working his way up in the organization, from thief to bodyguard to lieutenant. Martel considered the small fortune spent on Quinn's education smart money. The man always followed through and never made mistakes. When it came to enticing Genevieve to Mallorca, Quinn had been the obvious choice. Martel not only respected Quinn, but honestly liked him. It wouldn't be an exaggeration to say that he considered him the son he may never have.

Ellis, expatriated from America, reveled in her work as an assassin. She studied the art of killing as she tackled any assignment—with tireless energy and laser-like precision. She reminded him of a thoroughbred racehorse, at times too spirited to control. Loyal, intelligent, and beautiful. Although her judgment could be clouded by her thirst for killing, that talent undeniably came in handy.

Although Quinn handled the extensive background checks and hiring of the security team, Ellis directly supervised them. All the men and women were ex-military with combat experience. The only exception being Cruz Vega, the *loco* SOB whose fealty lay with Ellis and her alone. Troubling.

That left the alluring Graciela.

For generations, the Belmonte family had worked on the Martel *dehesa* in Seville. The legendary fighting bulls were large, fierce, and cunning, much like Martel's grandfather Francisco. As the Martel fortunes flourished, so did the Belmontes'. The two families were tied together by sweat and blood. Diego, Graciela's brother, had been Martel's lieutenant until a car accident took his life five years ago.

Martel had often visited the estate and marked Graciela's transformation from a gangly girl who begged for treats to a stunning young woman. With an unerring eye for talent, he'd hired the fifteen-year-old to model his summer clothing line in an ambitious ad campaign. With her lithe body, mane of dark luxurious hair, and exotic beauty, she became an overnight sensation.

After Diego's death, Martel comforted the sultry beauty by bedding her and taking her virginity. Since then, he had regarded her as his castellan, with absolute power to handle all administrative duties pertaining to his household and grounds staff. She knew every nuance of his daily routine.

Their fiery temperaments ignited into instant combustion in and out of bed. This was great in the sack—not so much in the day-to-day living. Eventually, Graciela had learned to accept his libertine nature, to co-exist in relative harmony. Impossible to think of Graciela as the traitor. Except...

Graciela's appearance still excited him as she came into view wearing a fluffy white robe, wet hair piled on top of her head in a messy bun.

"Come, sit next to me," Martel said, patting the seat beside him.

Ignoring him, she padded to the wine rack, finally settling upon her favorite merlot. Carefully, she uncorked the bottle and poured herself a glass. Taking a seat on the fireplace hearth, she kept the massive coffee table made from a teak tree root between them.

"I had time to examine the security footage from Genevieve's bedroom on the flight over," he said. "And guess what I discovered?"

Shrugging her shoulders as though beyond caring, she nonetheless looked wary, like a bird about to be stuffed in a cage.

"You searched her luggage, Graciela? Confiscated her knives, made the room escape-proof. *Si?*"

Defiantly, she grabbed the fireplace poker and battered it against the hearth. Again and again until she sagged against the wall. "You want to know what's bothering *me*, René?" she asked, meeting his gaze. Did you order Diego's death?"

Martel never shifted his gaze from her. "Your brother died in a car accident—five years ago."

"*Si*, you said a car accident killed him." Her voice rose in agitation. "That is what you told *mi familia*. But I read the police report two weeks ago. It says someone rammed his car off the road deliberately. A hit-and-run, with no witnesses. Convenient, no? Did you order it?"

"I trusted Diego with my life. I considered him a friend. Why would I want him killed? I read the report when he died," he said, then added more gently, "I asked Ellis to look into the hit-and-run. I vowed Diego's death would not go unpunished. But the trail grew cold."

"He worshipped you. He trusted you," Graciela said, pushing herself from the wall and pointing a finger at him. "Ellis murdered him. That bitch! I will kill her myself. She was always jealous of your relationship with *mi hermano*."

"Enough," he roared, flying at her. Squeezing her upper arms with both hands, he threw her onto her back on the sofa and lunged atop her, keeping her immobile with his body.

She struggled, trying to kick her way out from underneath him. But he easily pinned her with his leverage and weight.

"*Idiota!*" he shouted. "You betrayed me because you think Ellis murdered Diego?"

"I have never betrayed you," she hissed.

"I saw the footage. You missed a set of lock picks in the room. And you are the only person with access to my personal computer." He moved his hands from her arms to around her neck. "I could kill you," he said, squeezing until she almost lost consciousness. "But I have a better idea."

He dragged her to the soundproof safe room he'd built in case of attack. "Think about what you would like to say next during your brief stay," he said to her prone body, locking the door behind him.

CHAPTER
NINETEEN

November 28, 2:53 p.m.
Florence, Italy

Sirens screamed through the streets, coming closer to the *trattoria*.

Blade was in over her head. She should have heeded Vivienne's warning. Barely escaping with no apparent injuries, she may not be this lucky again.

Get up and run!

Blade grabbed her backpack and stood, swaying to find her equilibrium.

The young girl spoke to her in Italian, motioning to a chair, but Blade knew that if she stayed, the *polizia* would ask questions that she couldn't answer, not after the disastrous encounter with the Consulate. They would almost certainly detain her, and she had no time to spare.

Her options were shrinking. She considered returning to Vivienne and the Soldati, but that felt like admitting defeat. What she needed was time —and, most immediately, the freedom to move once she decided on a course of action.

Blade took off at a dead run, turning on a narrow cobblestoned street. There she slowed, not taking the chance of falling on the uneven surface. She came to a T at a busy street. Few tourists could be seen in this depressed and derelict area. An elderly woman trudged into a building smeared with graffiti, its exposed wiring an obvious fire hazard, the windows marred with shutters that were filthy, the peeling paint a barely discernible green.

An underground parking garage lay ahead. Blade hurried into the dark structure. Her arms felt tender to the touch where the man with tattoos had held her. Those hands and every other inch of exposed skin were a sea of color. And the hard-eyed American woman, the blonde, probably from Georgia or the Carolinas, appeared to be the leader.

Blade couldn't remember when she'd been so sore or tired. Every muscle in her body ached. She sat on the concrete, not caring about the dirt or smell of urine. Little light came in through the garage's narrow windows, and the dim overhead lighting flickered. It seemed like a place the homeless would wander into overnight. If not offering warmth, it had to be better than sleeping in the elements.

It had only been a few days since her last training session in New Orleans, but she felt wiped out. She yawned and couldn't seem to keep her eyes open. *This isn't normal.* Nothing about her trip was normal. Leaning over, she made a pillow of her crossed arms and closed her eyes. Just a few moments of rest.

An awful, scraping sound—metal against concrete?—snapped her awake. It took a few panicked moments to orient herself. The parking garage. *Damn.* She'd fallen asleep. That sound, though. It was getting louder.

A ragged man, trailing a shovel behind him, shuffled in her direction. Probably just a panhandler—but why would he be carrying a shovel? And why was he advancing on her? It was obvious he saw her.

"*Sei al mio posto!*" the panhandler said, raising the shovel above his head. *What the hell?* It was only then that she noticed a gathered blanket and a battered suitcase tucked away in the corner just behind her. Unintentionally, she had intruded upon his safe place.

"Hey hey hey!" she said, scrabbling away from him, her palms held up as if in surrender.

Time to leave. Working her way around him, she backpedaled out into the street, leaving him grumbling in his cave.

The bright afternoon had turned a cold gray. She'd maybe slept a little more than an hour. Enough to clear the fog from her head. She headed east.

After twenty minutes, she came to a large plaza lined with cafés and high-end shops. Children squealed as they rode a carousel tucked away in the corner. A couple in a horse-drawn carriage ambled by while pigeons scattered out of the way. That's all it took to summon a lump in her throat, triggered by a vivid memory of her first carriage ride through the French Quarter—a vacation with her father, another attempt to rebuild their relationship, which had only served to draw them further apart. Especially after he'd told her he planned to remarry a woman she'd never met. That had sealed their estrangement.

Blade started across the plaza when she saw a group of men in navy blue uniforms huddled near a van and police car. The *Carabinieri*. They seemed to be laughing over a joke, relying on their mere presence to serve as a deterrent to thefts or petty crimes.

Seeing no need to take any chances, she turned on her heel and high-tailed it in the opposite direction.

Ahead, a woman holding a Hard Rock Cafe shopping bag stood in line before an upscale restaurant. There must be a store nearby. Changing her appearance might buy some time. After turning the corner, she saw the red awning with the iconic logo. She went in wearing borrowed clothing, she came out wearing new black jogging pants and matching hoodie.

Noting an organized group of tourists being led by an Italian woman, Blade drafted behind, close enough for someone to believe she was part of the group, yet hopefully far enough away to escape the tour guide's notice.

Ten minutes later she stood before a church in awe—Il Duomo.

Hundreds of people filled the square before it, some taking pictures, others on tours, and about a dozen artists at their easels drawing or painting the Gothic structure. Controlled chaos. She'd never seen a church so magnificent. It dwarfed everything in sight. Various shades of green and pink marble tiles, bordered by white marble, adorned its exterior.

The adrenaline that had fueled her since that morning's kidnapping attempt burned itself out. Exhausted, she longed to lay her head on a pillow and forget the past few days without worrying about something blowing up or being assaulted or meeting her biological mother. Maybe a pillow would be too much to ask for. But just a private space, to think about her limited options. By the look of the line that curved around the church, though, it would be impossible to get inside. There wasn't even an empty seat at any of the nearby cafés. She dropped her backpack on the ground, dejected.

"Impressive, isn't it?" an attractive man in his mid-forties said, bending to retrieve a dirty brochure from the pavement.

Wary, Blade scrutinized him. He appeared harmless, but she wouldn't be taken by surprise again. "It's unique," she agreed.

"Ah, American. Happy to meet a fellow countrywoman. Catholic?"

Blade shook her head.

"Well, no one's perfect," the man said with a smile. "I'm Father Sean McCann, originally from Minnesota but now a resident at the Vatican. I'm on holiday, but I can't resist the pull of Italian cathedrals."

He wore no clerical collar. Dressed in a conservative navy suit with athletic shoes, his wire-rimmed glasses and the leather satchel over one shoulder gave him a scholarly look. "Genevieve Broussard," she said. "On holiday, too."

"Here for the tour?"

"It appears I may be too late, if the line is any indicator."

"Would you like to see the *Cattedrale di Santa Maria del Fiore*? There isn't an entrance fee to the cathedral itself, and the inside is spectacular." He winked. "I've been here for a few days, and I do have connections."

"Do you often give tours to perfect strangers?"

"Pope Francis says we're to be among Christ's people. To me, that means talking with strangers and being authentic. Perhaps more personal."

"I'm not a believer. I don't want to waste your time trying to convert me."

His contagious laughter brought a smile to her face. "Are you kidding? How often does a guy like me have an opportunity to hang out with an attractive woman like you? I'll answer that question for you: next to never. Come," he said, reaching down for her backpack.

"I can carry that," Blade blurted.

Father McCann, not offended by the brusque response, merely handed it to her.

After entering the cathedral, Blade stopped abruptly, taken aback by its vast expanse and beauty. The high-domed ceilings, the mosaic flooring, the stained glass windows, the marble arches—all worked together to create a place of almost surreal tranquility.

"Not what you expected? I felt the same way the first time I visited. Somehow all the elements blend together to make one feel at peace."

Father McCann continued to lead her through the church, side-stepping other tourists, but stopped mid-way. "Look behind us. The clock above the main door is liturgical and still works. It's a one-handed clock that shows the twenty-four hours of the *hora Italica,* or Italian time, a period of time ending with sunset at twenty-four hours. Used until the eighteenth century."

"I think you're more a historical enthusiast than a priest," Blade remarked as he led her on the tour. Not that she had ever associated with priests or any other religious institutions. Father McCann was an unexpected surprise. She liked him.

He blushed. "Perhaps. I do get consumed when history and architecture collide. I suppose it's my own form of worship. C'mon, I want to show you the dome."

Although Blade and Father McCann were about the same height, she found herself hustling to keep up with the exuberant priest. "Look," he said, pointing to the ceiling. "This is a representation of *The Last Judgment* and in my humble opinion just as beautiful as Michelangelo's at the Sistine Chapel. Giorgio Vasari and Federico Zuccari painted this from 1572 through 1579."

"I could use a pair of binoculars."

The priest laughed. "I agree. There is one more thing I want to show you before your eyes glaze over."

Dusk was darkening the interior of the church. "I'm sorry, Father," she said, "but I really need to get going."

"Of course," he said, leaning closer to Blade. "I could help, or try to help, with your situation."

Blade wondered if priests could read minds or souls. "I don't have a situation."

His eyes rested on her forearm. Embarrassed, she pulled her sleeves over the purple bruises already forming.

"You say that you don't believe, yet God led you here. Fate doesn't exist. God orchestrates divine interventions. He uses ordinary people like me to do his work on the ground. I'm not here to judge. If you're in trouble, I can help. Trust me."

Those two words carried a weight few people understood, much less demonstrated. How she wanted to tell the priest her story, to unburden herself. But she couldn't draw him into the mess she'd stumbled into through her own greed and bad judgment. She should have stayed home and never set foot on that private jet or accepted the outrageous payout. This was her burden, and she wouldn't put Father McCann in harm's way.

"Thank you for the offer, but I can take care of myself."

She practically ran out of the cathedral, as if the very demons of hell were nipping at her heels.

CHAPTER
TWENTY

November 28, 3:14 p.m.
Florence, Italy

"Did you think Dr. Pashkov would keep your little secret?" Ellis asked, her sugary drawl setting Alec's teeth on edge. "I've been tracking your tart ever since she escaped."

Earlier, when he'd told Martel about Blade entering the Consulate, he'd realized the bugger was even more paranoid than usual. This business about Vivienne and Blade continued to push the Spaniard to his limit. While Alec had studied his employer and mentor over the years, learning all he could from a master of finance and manipulation, he'd also observed Martel's slow decline from fashion magnate to psychotic genius bent on controlling the world through nuclear threats and advanced surveillance techniques. As a consequence, his own life had come to remind him of living in prison—always watching his back, never living his own life. Although Alec could talk his way out of most situations with the man, he felt sure his boss would make him pay for this particular setback. Alec needed both women alive—at least for the time being.

"I'm ordering all of you to leave off," Alec growled, addressing Ellis' security team, especially Cruz Vega, the barmy bastard. "I'm handling this situation—my way."

"I'm head of security," Ellis said calmly, screwing her silencer into her Sig Sauer P320. "I answer to Martel, not to you."

Alec had chosen this hotel, west of the Pitti Palace near the Piazza di Santo Spirito church, to meet with Ellis and her team. But after hearing about the botched abduction at the bistro, he needed to sort out exactly what Ellis knew and what Martel might suspect. Tourists stayed away from this area, and the guests kept to themselves. The room, large for an Italian hotel room, featured a living area separate from the bedroom.

Ellis handed the gun to Vega and nodded at the two men riveted to a soccer match on the television.

Before Alec could stop him, Vega shot each man in the back of the head. Brain matter and blood sprayed over the coffee table and rug. Some of the debris splattered on Vega. He didn't seem to notice, just turned and smiled at Ellis. Their relationship, forged by blood and terror, was dangerous. Not only to Alec, but to the organization. The two could be brash and undisciplined. They were the reason Blade was in the wind.

"You bloody nutters! Martel wants Blade taken *alive*. You might as well have given her a neon sign saying we can bloody well track her," Alec shouted. "You've brought undue attention to Martel's business affairs. You will be lucky to make it out of this alive. People have died for much less."

Ellis looked up sharply. "Martel is becoming distrustful of you, darlin'. Why do you think we're here?"

"A nightclub entertainer bested the lot of you," Alec chided. "I reckon Martel will get a kick, hearing about this cock-up."

He was pleased to see a pall of terror pass over Ellis's usually smug demeanor. "She's more like Martel than I had anticipated, I'll admit. Perhaps he should consider bringing her into the fold. She could be an asset."

Not a bad idea, Alec thought. Lucky for Vega and his gang of merry men that Blade hadn't had a knife with her. Would she have the juice to kill someone, though?

Blade was essential to his evolving plan. Unlike his increasingly psychotic boss, he didn't need to rule the world, only a small portion of it. With Blade in his pocket, Vivienne and her team would take out Martel for him. He presided over the Spaniard's empire, leaving Martel to run the legitimate side of his business. With Martel gone, he would proceed, business as usual.

Alec grabbed his jacket and headed for the door.

"Where are you goin'?" Ellis asked.

"Out to finish the job."

"I come with you," Vega said in his halting English.

"You're not going anywhere with me."

Vega advanced, his gun still in hand.

"Give me the gun and go take a shower. You're covered in blood," Ellis told him. "And Quinn, be careful. You just never know who will sneak up behind you."

"Oh, I've already updated Martel. My advice? Head back to the States. And clean up this damn room."

He closed the door behind him and leaned against it.

There was no other choice but to surveil the violin workshop and hope Blade would return.

———

Alec moved the curtain a fraction of an inch to check the street below. No sign of Blade. She could be cunning, resilient, and willing to take risks. Traits he admired. No one had ever escaped from Martel's stronghold. He grinned. The cheeky bird was full of surprises.

Streetlights would make it possible to distinguish Blade from the dozens of tourists that raced from one store to another hunting for the perfect souvenir. The stores would be closing soon. That could work to his advantage. Once the plonkers scurried back to their hotels, he would move to the street and work within the shadows to surprise her.

He'd chosen this flat carefully, picking the locks of several contenders before deciding on it. It afforded a perfect view across the street from the violin workshop. After looking through the closets, he surmised that the occupants were an elderly couple that favored floral dresses and white dress shirts. A gallery of family pictures hung on the walls of the living room. Crucifixes and pictures of the Virgin Mary were everywhere else. The devout pair were most likely on holiday, judging by the empty refrigerator and bathroom counter.

Catholics…their Jesus, Mary, the saints, communion. Rubbish, all of it. His mum—or Jackie, as she insisted he call her—had entered a recovery program through the Catholic church when he'd been about twelve. With no family close by, social workers had forced him into foster care. The church extolled the sanctity of life and the family unit. Hypocrites. There was more honor and character among the disenfranchised on the streets than in the foster care system or the church.

Bloody hell. Could Mum still be alive? Such a possibility hadn't occurred to him in a long while.

Impulsively, he threw a statue of the Virgin Mary across the room. The painted porcelain shattered into bits of fragmented color. The splintering sound echoed in the small confines of the living area. What a stupid blunder. The other tenants of this block of flats probably knew where the occupants were and that no one should be here. He stood, motionless, listening for any doors in the hallway to open. Nosy neighbors could unravel his entire plan. After thirty seconds, he let out a breath. No interruptions.

Earlier, he had dragged an end table to the window when there was still minimal light coming through the lace curtains. He unzipped his rifle case, removed the Remington 700, unfolded the stock, and attached the bipod. He slowed his breathing, holding the butt to his shoulder. Even just preparing to shoot calmed him.

He placed the rifle on the table and commenced to zero the rifle. He adjusted the scope until a young girl came into focus. She extended a hand to touch one of the violins. One pull on the trigger would obliterate the delicate features.

Once again, he scanned the street.

Before long, he let out a repressed sigh. *Finally.*

Blade drifted up the street, hips gently swaying, eyes observing the area . He smiled as he viewed an old woman slap her husband on the shoulder as he craned his neck to see her backside. Not a bad view, Alec had to agree.

He lost sight of her after she entered the shop. A good operative always knew their surroundings. He felt sure Blade would make a formidable partner, or opponent, depending on how this game played out. He sensed a ruthlessness in her. Life with Blade in it made it more interesting. Desire flooded through him. Her lips on his, her long legs wrapped around him...

His cell phone vibrated in his right jeans pocket. Not the replacement phone Ellis gave him; that was in his left pocket. Martel hired top surveillance talent, operatives who looked more like teenagers than someone who could find anyone at any time. Privacy was extinct, like the bloody dinosaurs. Fortunately, workarounds for Alec's personal business affairs still existed.

"Is everything going as planned?" a woman's voice purred on the phone.

Teresa Escobar could be insufferable, but she was pliant and an essential piece to the puzzle. The last time the two had rendezvoused in Paris, she had used her considerable skills to seduce him. He had laughed in her face. As if a bit of tail could turn him into a trained monkey.

"Are you calling me on a secure line?"

"What do you think?" Teresa said. "I've been at this game quite a bit longer than you."

He held back a biting response. "Have you kept your part of the bargain?"

"I don't want to raise alarms, but that has proven...problematic."

A headache started to throb in his left temple. Alec put the phone on speaker and began to gently massage both temples, hoping to head off the migraine that too often plagued him under extreme stress.

"Do you need additional funds?" he said, clenching his teeth against a wave of nausea.

"That would help."

"I'll transfer them. Keep me informed."

He disconnected and sat heavily in one of the brocade chairs in the sitting room. He needed to *relax*. With any luck at all, Martel would kill Vivienne. The Soldati would eliminate Martel. And the attack on the UN would eradicate the loose ends. In Alec's experience, survival of the fittest prevailed, and there was no one fitter than he.

And what of Blade? He wasn't ready to address that question.

CHAPTER
TWENTY-ONE

November 28, 7:05 p.m.
Florence, Italy

Even though Blade's feet ached after hours of rambling through the streets of Florence, she couldn't help but appreciate the city's beauty as darkness descended upon it like a shroud. None of that could distract her from the unsettling fact that every turn led her back to the Arno River and the Soldati headquarters. Scenario after scenario drew her back to Vivienne and Chase. The only two people who would believe her about the impending attack on the UN, aware of what René Martel was capable of.

Alert for any threat as she walked over the Ponte Vecchio, her eyes scoured over crazed shoppers anxious for their last big buy before shops closed for the evening. How could she hope to tell the good guys from the bad guys? As she approached the Soldati headquarters, she could only hope the knife she carried in her waistband would help compensate should she make the wrong call.

With a surge of relief, she could see the overhead lights shining brightly through the workshop window. The old man stood stoically behind the counter, making eye contact with her. After a slight nod of his head, Blade headed for the narrow stairs to the second floor. She stopped at the same peeling door, except this time, she noticed its sturdy hardwood. Not easy to breach. She knocked on the door and waited.

Confiding in Vivienne rubbed against the grain of her subconscious, yet her mind kept replaying the few minutes with her biological mother. Maybe she'd been rash to flee from her like that. If nothing else, she'd hardly exhibited mastery of her emotions.

The door was opened by a middle-aged man with salt-and-pepper hair. He wore an unbuttoned red polo shirt that exposed a deep one-inch ragged scar that seemed to encircle his neck. His eyes, the color of smokey quartz, assessed her from head to toe. She balked at the scrutiny, but stood firm.

"You made it back," he said with a pronounced British accent.

"Who are you?" Blade blurted. "Part of Vivienne's muscle?"

"I am *the* muscle," he said with a grin. "Thomas Kazir. I lead this band of misfits." He opened the door wider. "Come in. I've sent everyone home, including Vivienne. You caused quite a stir today. I thought everyone could use a little time to…decompress. You look like you could use a drink."

She followed him in and locked the door. *A drink and an airline ticket home.*

Thomas followed Blade's gaze to the inscription above an arched doorway. *Lux in tenebris lucet.* "The light shines in the darkness," he translated, leading her into a glass-enclosed conference room. "Words we take seriously."

Blade released her breath, patience spent. "Okay, Mr. Boss Man. No more games. No more secrets. I think I deserve the truth."

Thomas poured brandy into two snifters. "Young lady, you don't *deserve* any consideration. But, in your case, I can understand how overwhelming this must be for you."

"Who do you think—".

"Before you bolt again, I suggest you take a seat and hear me out." Smiling warmly, he sat across from her and slid a snifter to her. "We are formally known as the *Soldati di Cristo*, Soldiers of Christ. It's a mouthful, so we just go by Soldati."

The enemy of my enemy is my friend. Clever words in a movie she'd seen some time ago. Only now, those words carried weight, and there was no denying the price Shen had paid. She didn't trust anyone, but the Soldati could very well be her ticket to safety—away from Martel and his hit squad.

"Is the Soldati a religious cult?"

"Not a cult, a calling. After the crucifixion, Christians became the target of both the Jewish traditionalists and Roman politicians. In 64 A.D., a fire destroyed much of Rome. Some of the populace believed Emperor Nero started the blaze in order to rebuild the city in the Greek style he preferred, but, being a politician, he shifted the blame to Christians. Believers were fed to dogs, women were tied to bulls and dragged through the streets, and Nero impaled Christians to use as human torches to light his garden parties. From this depravity, the Soldati rose along with its mission: securing the rescue of defenseless and vulnerable Christians."

"Thanks for the history lesson," Blade said, hoping her sarcasm masked the sudden lump in her throat. "From my standpoint, you're no better than Martel. Your Soldati killed people at the villa."

Anger flickered behind the dark eyes. "Christians are still being killed or persecuted in North Korea, Nigeria, Pakistan, Somalia, just to name a few countries. Boko Haram extremists kidnap children and use them as suicide bombers to target Christian communities. In the past year, nearly six thousand Christians were killed for their faith."

"The end justifies the means?"

"Not by a long shot. A few of our entrusted brethren don't agree with our methods or mission. During the course of our work, we never intend to harm anyone. In most cases, we don't use lethal force. But we do defend ourselves. As commander of the Soldati, all I can do is seek God's will and soldier on."

She heard his deep commitment and sorrow. But what he said only reinforced her own feelings about a non-existent God. If there was a God, why would he condone the use of children as suicide bombers, or murder, or the death of her own mother? Belief and trust in God were for fools.

"I didn't come back here to debate," she said.

Thomas took a moment before responding. "Why did you come back?"

A psychologist, hired by her parents when she was a teenager, once said people choose what to do with pain. They either retreated, gave in to fear, or fought back. She stood and poured another drink. "I prided myself on being a good judge of character until the past few days. I couldn't have been more wrong. But my gut tells me to trust you. I need your help. The world needs your help."

"I'm listening."

Blade recounted the little she had overheard about the planned attack on the United Nations.

"When is this to take place?" Thomas demanded, rising from his chair.

"They didn't say. But they mentioned TNA1, and two of his people are already in Geneva."

"Dear God," Thomas breathed as he hurried to the door. "Are you coming?" he said, looking over his shoulder at her.

Blade sprang up. "Where are we going?"

"To the war room. I'll assemble the team, and I need you to tell us every bit of information you can remember. According to news reports in the last few days, the President of the United States will be addressing the UN in seventy-two hours. I don't know what TNA1 is, but it's most likely some sort of killing agent like Novichok. Martel could be planning to assassinate your President and every other head of state who attends the meeting."

Two factions warred within her. One wanted nothing more than to unload her burden and fly home. The other needed to stay and pay Martel back—in full.

"I want to help," she said, following him out the door. "I want to kick Martel's ass."

"We all want a piece of that man," Thomas said.

Concealed within the headquarter's second story, soundproof walls protected a state-of-the-art conference room. A massive oval table domi-nated the space, with a semi-recessed area at each end to accommodate a laptop. Six large LCD screens were affixed to the side and back walls, allowing anyone sitting around the table to view information being shared.

The Soldati might be a centuries-old organization, Blade thought, but they clearly embraced technology.

Thomas had told her to find a seat at the table, then disappeared. Bone weary and feeling out of her element, she felt compelled to choose an inconspicuous seat, but due to the room's design, no such refuge presented itself. She opted for a chair facing the door, so she'd at least have some warning when someone entered. Just when she was beginning to feel she'd been purposefully marooned or forgotten, Thomas showed, followed by a young Asian woman whose venomous eyes locked on Blade as she sat at the laptop closest to the door. Hatred sparked from the woman like a touch of a finger connecting to a live electrical switch plate. It momentarily baffled Blade, but she steeled herself for the even more difficult interaction to come.

Thomas cleared his throat, and as if on cue, Chase, Vivienne, Luc, and Finn trooped into the room. Vivienne and Luc sat opposite her. With no way to escape Vivienne's probing stare, Blade turned her chair to face Thomas, who stood directly at the head of the table. The two other men sat behind her, but she didn't want to chance a glance to see who sat next to her.

"Before we start," Thomas said, "shall we take a moment to pray for our fallen brother and friend?"

All heads bowed. The air in the room seemed to freeze as if time itself stood still in memoriam of Shen. Blade offered no prayer, but she joined in the silence. He had sacrificed himself to give her a few extra seconds to escape. She would forever be in his debt.

"We're all grieving Shen's death," Thomas said, taking a moment to collect himself. "As Christians, we are assured he's with our Savior. But that doesn't make his passing any easier. The Psalmist says God heals the brokenhearted. But we must postpone our grief until this crisis is over. Xiu, perhaps you should take some time off. You don't need to be here."

"You're wrong, Thomas. You won't catch Martel without my help," she said, dry-eyed.

And there was the answer to Blade's question. Xiu was Shen's sister. She understood and sympathized with the young woman's hatred of her.

Someone had to pay the cost for death. Blade's own mother was killed by a drunk driver; if only she'd been older at the time, the man responsible would have suffered more than a jail sentence and pitiful fine.

"Blade, tell the team what you told me," Thomas said.

Careful not to make eye contact with Vivienne, Blade once again replayed the conversation she'd overheard.

"I told you my brother is dangerous," Vivienne said after she'd finished, turning an accusing look on Thomas. "We should have killed him weeks ago. If you had listened, Shen would be alive, and my daughter would be safe."

The outburst unleashed a cacophony of words and accusations that ignited the room like a wildfire, hot and destructive.

"Enough!" Thomas bellowed. "We cannot waste time second-guessing. If Martel plans to use a biological or chemical weapon, how do we find him? His villa is destroyed. Where else would he go?"

"He isn't on his yacht," Xiu said, with a hint of a Chinese accent, "and I have not been able to track him through usual methods. No credit card usage, no flight plans. He's off the grid."

"We could call the Secret Service or the UN security force," Finn offered.

"Use me as bait," Vivienne said, rising to her feet. "He won't be able to resist coming for me."

Thomas lifted a palm to the room. "If Martel hasn't changed his plans, we have three days to find and stop him. I agree with Finn. We must inform the Secret Service and the UN security force. But that means we expose the Soldati. Are we willing to do that?"

"You've all made it clear that I'm not part of this team, but there may be another way," Blade said.

CHAPTER
TWENTY-TWO

November 28, 7:48 p.m.
Florence, Italy

"The man covered in ink and the blonde American. Who the hell are they?" Blade demanded. She was playing a game of chicken and the one piece of information she still held might be nothing at all. But, it could also be the key to finding Martel before his attack plunged the world into chaos.

Vivienne nodded to Xiu, granting her permission to bring up two pictures on the monitors.

"The two are Cruz Vega and Ellis Stephens," Vivienne reported, matter-of-factly. "Both work for René. Assassins, killers, the pair are intelligent and have successfully kept under the radar from law enforcement agencies."

"How have they been tracking me?"

Vivienne shrugged.

Blade started rummaging through her backpack. *A deal is a deal.* Within the side pocket lay a business card, the only remaining shred of evidence from what she'd taken from Martel's desk on Mallorca.

"I think this may be useful in finding Martel," Blade said, holding the business card between her fingers.

"What?" Finn said, barely able to keep his contempt under control. "Unless that piece of paper has coordinates to Martel's location on it, don't waste our time or our manpower."

"Not so fast," Xiu said, rising from her chair and practically leaping on the card. "Aebischer-Graf Properties in Gstaad, Switzerland. This may be the bread crumb I need." Without looking at Blade or waiting for more discussion, she marched out the door, already concentrating on the task at hand.

"You can't be serious," Finn said to her retreating back. "Crack on, then. As for you," he said, pointing to Blade, "never think you're part of our team." He threw himself back from the table and rose to his feet.

"Get your head out of your ass," Chase said to him. "We're working lean, with one man short and no room for error...or theatrics from you."

Finn's countenance darkened, then his gaze flicked to Thomas as though in appeal.

"Remember North Korea last year?" Thomas asked him. "No food, no water, leading a ragtag group of Christians with the Korean People's Army on our tail." He waited for Finn to nod that yes, he remembered. "We didn't doubt each other then, and we will not doubt each other now. Let's get to work."

He gestured toward the door, ushering the men from the room.

This left only Vivienne and Blade in the uncomfortable hush that followed their exit. From the street below, high-pitched laughter drifted on the night's air—people living their lives, oblivious to danger right next door to them. But that was the thing about danger, it looked innocent enough until it struck like lightning, indiscriminate and deadly.

As the silence stretched between them, anger, resentment, and a profound sense of loss passed through Blade. She removed the knife from her waistband, clutching it in her hand like a lifeline, thankful for the cold, hard metal that helped keep her grounded. It occurred to her that perhaps Vivienne wanted to keep her secret of Blade's adoption buried. Sometimes secrets should stay hidden, in the dark. Maybe they both wanted their lives to go back to normal.

"Do you plan to stab me with that?" Vivienne asked.

"Not today," Blade said, leveling a cold stare at the stranger sitting across from her. Marie would always be her mother, but given her current situation, she could accept nothing less than the truth.

Blade leaned back in her chair, evaluating the woman who sat across from her. Their uncanny resemblance surprised her, and she understood how René Martel had made the connection when he saw her picture on the cover of *Maxim*. The same full lips and high cheekbones. Vivienne's hands, folded on the table, were replicas of her own—strong and capable.

Vivienne exuded strength and purpose. A woman to be wary of, feared. A woman who gave orders, a leader who wasn't afraid to get her hands dirty.

"Genevieve," Vivienne said gently, "you were named after my grandmother."

Blade's head whipped up, causing her to mishandle the knife. She could feel the sharp sting of a knife cut—biting in the palm of her hand.

"You're wrong. My mother named me after Saint Genevieve, the patron saint of Paris."

Vivienne shook her head. "Thomas brought Marie and I together. We became close friends while I was pregnant with you."

"I don't believe you. And since my mother is dead, I can't verify your story."

"But Dom is still alive and well in Florida. With a wife and stepchildren."

Stunned by the revelation that Vivienne knew her parents, Blade questioned what she'd been told her entire life. It felt like her very being was collapsing around her. Dom had chosen to remarry, although he knew this decision would forever thrust a wedge between them. She didn't begrudge him love. But he never tried to include her into his new family. Their last communication, via text message, was six months ago.

"You have no right to talk about my father," Blade said haltingly. "Not after giving me away as if I were a piece of garbage."

"It wasn't like that. I never wanted to give you up for adoption. Marie and Dom promised to keep you safe. None of us meant for René to find you."

"And yet, here we are. Martel still found me," Blade said, her voice rising an octave.

Silence cut the room.

"Marie was my guardian angel," Vivienne said, wiping away tears. "An answered prayer."

"You all talk about God as if He were alive, breathing, and gave a crap." Blade stood and walked to the window, lobbing the knife from one hand to the other, grappling with feelings that made her chest ache. Her parents had deceived her. Not with outright lies, but by omission. The taste of betrayal bitter in her mouth, she pivoted, anger taking control because she feared everything else.

"Who's my biological father, or do you even know?"

Vivienne winced.

"John. John Andrews. We met at university in England. His father, an Ambassador for the United States, sent him to study foreign relations. I went to party and escape from René." She eased off the chair and walked around the table. "He proposed in a beautiful garden, the scent of jasmine and gardenias in the air. I'll never forget that moment of complete happiness. You were already growing within me."

Blade's windpipe had contracted, making it impossible to utter a syllable.

"And then," Vivienne said, "René killed him."

Moments stretched like a rubber band, ready to snap.

Blade struggled to absorb the words. *René killed him.*

"You ran away," she said at last. "You allowed Martel to get away with murder."

All these years, she'd been complacent, never willing to hurt her parents by asking questions about her adoption. Without realizing it, her parents and Vivienne had placed her at a disadvantage by shielding her from the truth. If only she'd been warned about Martel.

Vivienne shook her head. "You don't understand. René was obsessed with me, by our bond. He never would have allowed me a life of my own. I couldn't take the chance that he would somehow take you from me."

"You took the easy way out. Admit it, you never wanted a child."

Vivienne rounded the room, now only five feet away from Blade.

"I've bought you a plane ticket home and made arrangements to hide you until this is over."

"You have no right to make decisions for me. I can take care of myself."

"I have every right to protect my daughter."

The two women faced each other, their energy repelling them like two poles of magnets, forever alike but forever separate. The crushing ache in Blade's chest exploded into a blind rage. "You may be my biological mother, but we have no relationship, no connection. The past few minutes don't make up for twenty-six years. Got it?"

Eyes glittering with unshed tears, she considered the knife between her fingers before hurling it at the far wall with such force the knife quivered. A solid hit. "*That's* what I plan to do when I see Martel. Not because of you. No one tries to kill me and gets away with it. I don't run away from my problems."

Blade shoulder-checked Vivienne as she tore past her, pulling the door open and marching to Thomas's office. She saw Chase and Luc in her peripheral vision, sure they'd been posted there to guarantee she didn't run again. She guessed not many people disagreed with Vivienne. Somehow, her own refusal of her made her smile.

CHAPTER
TWENTY-THREE

November 29, 11:28 a.m.
Gstaad, Switzerland

René Martel leaned back in the driver's seat as he gunned the black metallic Mercedes AMG GT Roadster up the hill to the Müller Hütte, about five thousand feet above Gstaad in the Swiss Alps. He drove his car like he drove his company: precisely, brutally, savagely. There were no gray areas in Martel's life.

With the black soft-top down, the sun did little to warm the icy air. Martel's heart pumped in anticipation of the upcoming meeting, where his strategy to control the United States would be consummated. *What a rush.*

Martel parked behind an Audi Q3 and surveilled the area. Patches of white snow pockmarked the glistening green hills. Clear skies belied the approach of another storm due to hit by this evening. The man pacing on the weathered sunporch was United States Senator Daniel Williamson, Speaker of the House and part of the advance team in preparation of the president's address to the United Nations in Geneva.

Seven years before, Martel's avid interest in horse racing had led him to the Kentucky Derby—and an introduction to the one man whose ambition could be used to turn the United States into one huge nuclear weapon against the world. The charismatic senator, all smiles and handshakes, had practically salivated at Martel's interest. Sensing an opportunity, Martel had given millions to Williamson's campaign and sponsored lavish vacations for the senator and his family. Williamson was his prime acquisition in the West. Through the senator's connections, Martel's defense companies had made billions.

He set the parking brake and got out, inhaling deeply as he admired the picturesque view of the Gstaad and Saanenland region. His own chalet, nestled about two kilometers from here, overlooked the same area. Still, the less Williamson knew about his personal life, the better.

"Damn, this is a helluva place to meet," Senator Williamson said. "I about froze my *cojones* off."

"Americans." Martel stuffed his hands in his pockets and marched up the worn wooden steps of the hut. The senator followed, rubbing his hands together to keep them warm.

Heat welcomed the pair as they entered. Knotted-wood paneling gave the place a rustic feel. Two overstuffed chairs, with an animal skin draped over one, sat before a blazing fire. A cold lunch was laid out on the dining room table.

"Why all the covert crap?" Williamson said, standing with his back to the fire.

"We need to talk, without interruption, *hombre a hombre*," Martel said, pouring them both a drink from the Pappy Van Winkle's Family Reserve fifteen-year bourbon he had ordered especially for the occasion.

"You remembered," the senator said as he drank his whiskey in one gulp and helped himself to another generous pour.

"It pays to remember the small details. I trust your accommodations have met your expectations?" Martel didn't care if the senator did indeed freeze his *cojones* off or what he thought about his time in Switzerland. Williamson was on the payroll, whether he wanted to admit that to himself or not.

"No complaints. Miranda loves the place. She hired a nanny to corral the kids so she could fully appreciate the spa. It's a beautiful country."

"Take a load off, as you Americans say," Martel said, smiling as he sat in the dark brown leather chair.

Senator Williamson sat in that chair's mate and stretched his legs out in front of him. The Speaker of the House had recently gained weight; his complexion was waxen in the sunlight. Excessive drinking and whoring could age a man. Quinn had dredged up enough intel to ruin the senator, although, after today, he would never again have the opportunity to compromise his allegiance to Martel.

"Tell me, Daniel, are you ready for the upcoming week?"

Williamson nodded. "I'm ready. The president will be flying into Geneva tonight. His daughter will accompany him. Pretty damn sick, if you ask me. But the girl is media savvy. She'd be a damn good presidential candidate herself. It's too bad she won't get the chance. The two will attend a dinner hosted by the Federal Council that evening, and the president will address the United Nations precisely at eleven o'clock the next day."

"Once the president is killed by a terrorist attack, you'll be able to ascertain the location of the vice president?"

"I can assure you, I'll know."

Martel swiveled his head, his amber eyes boring into Williamson.

"I'm the Speaker of the House, René. Once the president is dead, I'll be second in line to the presidency. There are protocols in place. Don't worry. The media will be like a pack of wolves, tearing into each other to get a scoop. A nice distraction from our agenda. And I'll be the grieving senator, teary-eyed and thankful I wasn't killed, too."

Martel nodded. "*Bueno.*"

"We have a deal." Williamson's voice had a steely edge to it. "You promised I'd become president if I delivered one of our nuclear warheads to you. I believe you took possession of it last week."

Martel stood and walked to a cupboard, withdrawing a wooden box. He came back to the senator, opened the lid, and offered him a cigar.

"Try one of these. I created my own unique blend, which I always smoke after I've cemented a deal." Martel took one of the cigars, brought it to his nose, and inhaled. "Smell that, Daniel. It's the heady aroma of success."

Williamson smiled. "I knew you wouldn't disappoint."

"One cuts the cigar just so," Martel said, using the guillotine-style straight cutter to snip the end of the cigar off above the cap line.

"This isn't my first rodeo," Senator Williamson said, reaching for the cutter.

"The trick to lighting a cigar is to gently rotate the end over the flame —never directly into it."

The senator scooted to the edge of the chair. "Dammit, René, I'm not some hick that needs a tutorial on smoking a damn cigar."

"I thought this might be a good analogy to explain a few truths to you," Martel said, drawing the smoke in, absorbing its flavor. "You are the cigar. I am the aficionado. But in your case, I believe I will need to hold you over the flame. You are a dispensable part of *my* plan, under *my* control."

A flush rose up the senator's neck and face. "Listen, you Spanish degenerate. Just to be clear: I could destroy you with a snap of my fingers. Do you really think your money can *buy* me? Do you think that's what we've been doing? That I'm, what...under your thumb? That's laughable."

Martel smiled coolly. "A Russian friend tells me you have been negotiating an oil deal with President Novikov. I say that is putting the cart well before the horse, Daniel. Forgetting your place."

"And what if I did? I don't need your permission for any damn thing I might do. I certainly don't need you anymore, if I ever did. We don't need each other."

Martel flew from his chair. Before the senator could react, Martel locked his arm around the man's fat neck and began to squeeze.

"You have overestimated your importance, *mi amigo*," he practically whispered into his hairy ear, "and that could be a fatal mistake. With only two days before the UN meeting, I don't have time to replace you. But the wife," he said, taking a look at his watch. "She's had a horrible allergic reaction to shellfish."

"What?" Williamson croaked, clawing at the arm around his neck.

Martel gradually released his hold. "The poor, grieving senator. No one will suspect you had anything to do with this terrorist attack."

Senator Williamson slid off the chair to his knees. "What are you...? My *wife*?"

"You will be President of the United States within a few days, Daniel. This required a price, one significant enough to warrant the honor of the position. I think you'll agree in time. Miranda would not make a fitting first lady. Now you can be who I need you to be."

A wooden cuckoo clock, with an intricately carved stag's head, marked the half-hour.

"You son of a bitch," Williamson growled. "You prick!" he screamed.

Unfazed, Martel strolled to the table laden with food. "You must try the fresh shrimp. It's to die for."

CHAPTER
TWENTY-FOUR

November 29, 1:45 a.m.
Florence, Italy

Blade pummeled the punching bag, reliving her failure yesterday with each jab. She should have taken out all four attackers at the restaurant. Her savate instructor always said, "There are no excuses in fighting. You are either in the fight or already defeated." Exhaustion had caused her to be unfocused, distracted. How many times would Lady Luck save her butt?

The training facility took up the entire third floor of the building that housed the violin workshop and Soldati headquarters. It smelled like lemon disinfectant rather than sweat and old leather like her gym in New Orleans. The area, divided into four quadrants, held free weights, cardio equipment, rowing machines, and a mat area for martial arts or wrestling practice.

She had never envisioned a scenario in which she'd be in fear for her life so far away from home. The gig in Mallorca should have been the catalyst for a new start. Instead, she was dependent upon people, essentially strangers, that she didn't fully trust.

She stood in a fighting stance, raised her arms in the en garde position, pivoted her support foot, and turned her hips to deliver a high whipped kick to the bag, followed by a fouetté. Thinking about the blonde American, she countered with a savage uppercut. For the next thirty minutes, she delivered kicks and punches to the bag until sweat covered her body. She scanned the room for a towel, but not seeing any, used her shirt to wipe her face. A state-of-the-art gym, but no towels. Go figure.

"You're good," a male voice said.

Blade whirled around to find Chase leaning against a support beam with a grin as wide as Texas. Fine lines crinkled the corners of his cobalt blue eyes, making him look less imposing than he had on previous encounters. Chiseled features and casual attire that accentuated his muscles screamed G.I. Joe action hero. Women probably threw themselves at him; there was something irresistible about the strong, silent types. Personally, she'd had her fill of men.

"Not good enough yesterday."

"You escaped from professional killers, Blade. Your skills and muscle memory served you well. Looks like you could use this," he said, throwing a white towel to her.

Should she be insulted or grateful? She caught the towel one-handed and began putting it to use.

"Do I have you to thank for my new wardrobe?" she asked. Earlier, when she'd arrived back in the guest room, she'd found new clothes hanging in the closet, including a black leather jacket. Neatly arranged on the bed were lingerie, nightclothes, and fitness attire. And in the center, propped up against pillows, had rested a designer backpack.

"Hell no," he said. "I couldn't be trusted. Vivienne sent someone with a little more fashion sense than I have."

"I appreciate the surprise. I feel almost human again."

"We aim to please."

"Your headquarters is impressive," she said. "Hiding in plain sight?"

"Exactly. We move every few years, and we have several places like this one in other countries. It isn't easy to stay off the radar for centuries."

"No, I suppose it isn't," she said, taking a seat on an exercise bench. "Aren't you afraid I'll blow your cover when I leave here?"

"Your little jaunt to the American Consulate actually worked in our favor. You've been labeled a nutcase."

She nodded. "You'd allow me to walk out of here today?"

Chase stiffened. "You aren't our prisoner. But René Martel is a real threat. Not only to you, but to all of us. His plan to use you proves that he will go to any lengths to capture Vivienne. Besides, I want to show you something. If you're going to stay awhile, I thought you should be prepared." He started away from her, then paused before rounding a corner near the far wall. "Are you coming?"

Blade grabbed her water bottle and jogged to catch up. "Where are we going?"

He shrugged and rounded the corner.

"Surprises haven't worked out for me lately," she said to his back as she followed him.

"I'd agree with that assessment."

"What branch of the military were you in?" she asked.

He glanced back at her. "Is it that obvious?"

"Civilians rarely say the word 'assessment'," she said. "You carry yourself like a man who's seen some crap. And then there's the hair." His black hair, cut in a military-style crew cut, did not detract from his appealing good looks.

"You should do that more often," he said, stopping at a mirrored wall.

"Do what?"

"Smile. It suits you."

Blade saw her reflection and realized she was indeed smiling, like a schoolgirl flirting with the high school quarterback. Heat flooded her face. She slipped behind him, out of his line of vision.

What is wrong with me?

He placed his hand on a small, square security device.

This reminded Blade of a recent spy movie she'd seen. Like magic, the mirror slid open, exposing an armory that looked like a candy store for boys playing soldier. Racks of automatic rifles and handguns, crossbows, and sniper rifles lined the walls to her left and right. A workbench with multiple drawers hugged the far wall.

"Impressive, but maybe a little over the top?" Blade said. The last time she had seen so much firepower in one room was at a San Diego gun store. She remembered her father listing all the benefits of gun ownership before she moved to New Orleans. After a tug-of-war of words, she'd allowed him to buy her the 9mm Glock for his peace of mind—not hers. She'd never touched it after hiding it under a stack of blankets in her closet.

"We have our main cache of weapons at a warehouse near here. But there are times when we're deployed at a moment's notice. To make it easier, we've categorized our ordnance. We have our handguns, rifles, both sniper and 50-caliber, automatic and semi-automatic guns, the Ruger MP9, M16s, flash-bangs, grenades, and missile launchers. The ammo is kept in the locked cabinet in the corner, although we normally use rubber bullets to minimize the number of wounded or killed."

"And here I thought you were a humanitarian organization."

Chase ignored this. "Ever shoot a gun before?"

Blade shook her head. "Got any knives?"

"Affirmative." Chase opened the top drawer of a metal workbench to reveal a variety of knives. He brought out two.

"I recommend the Ka-Bar or the Glauca B1. Both are exceptional weapons. Good for close-quarters situations, as well as cutting plastic restraints or wire-cutting."

She took the Ka-Bar in her hand, testing the weight and balance. "This will do. How many do you have?"

Chase pulled out another five. "Six altogether. But Martel's forces aren't our usual adversaries. You can't rely on being close enough to throw a knife without being blown apart. Since you've never handled a gun, I'll start with the basics."

Blade held one knife in each hand and threw them in quick succession at an empty space on the wall. The knives stuck one inch apart, each vibrating from the force of the throw.

"Sweet," he said. "I searched you on YouTube. Liked the act. But throwing a knife into something is different than throwing a knife into a human being, or engaging in hand-to-hand combat. You should be familiar with a firearm."

"I can handle myself."

"When you're under attack, everything changes. Just like yesterday. Hard training pays off." Chase's cobalt eyes drilled into her. "You're not prepared for Martel's army. They're mercenaries, ex-military. I've been in combat situations that kill civilians. If anything happens to you, Vivienne will never forgive herself."

"You weren't kidnapped and threatened. According to Vivienne, I won't be safe unless I go into hiding."

"She's right. You should fly home and lay low until this is over."

Blade removed the knives from the wall, balancing the tip of one on the index finger of her left hand. "In the last three days, I've been imprisoned, shot at, and almost kidnapped at the restaurant by Martel's goons. I plan to see this through. Are you going to help me?"

"You're stubborn, just like Vivienne. Don't tell me"—holding up both arms in surrender—"you don't want to be compared with her. Just making an observation. Let's get to work."

For the next hour, Chase demonstrated the fundamentals of using a 9mm Glock and Ruger MP9, how to load and reload, the correct stance when firing the weapons, and the proper way to aim.

After a hundred or so firing repetitions under his tutelage, Blade said, "Am I going to get any firing practice?"

"You're going to be a natural. You already have excellent hand-eye coordination. We have a firing range built into our warehouse. If we leave within the next few minutes, we'll be back before dinner."

"Leave it to a man to think with his stomach."

As they made their way downstairs, Chase said, "Dinner is on me if you make fifty percent of your shots. If you don't, dinner is on you. Deal?"

But before she could answer, a fire alarm screeched.

What could be happening now?

CHAPTER
TWENTY-FIVE

November 29, 1:25 p.m.
Florence, Italy

High stakes mean high risks.

Alec sat at the dining room table and stacked antique teacups into a pyramid. Marking time during operations drove him crazy. Stuck in this flat with the smell of mothballs and old people didn't help. Why *did* old people smell? This reminded him of the few months spent with his malodorous grandparents as a lad; their incessant chatter and shuffling gait drove him mad. In a temper, he swiped the teacups to the floor, the sound of shattering glass on linoleum centering him.

He dragged one of the wooden dining room chairs to the window and sat with his rifle leaning against the windowsill.

"You, my friend, are bloody brilliant," he said to his reflection in the glass, remembering the conversation between himself and Martel. It had been child's play, wrestling control of this operation from Ellis. Martel had screamed his displeasure at the ineptitude Ellis demonstrated at the restaurant. He currently controlled Martel's mercenary force—and his own.

One move closer.

His six-member team was hand-picked for its ability to operate quickly and aggressively in hostile situations. Four were positioned on the street, ready to capture Vivienne alive. The other two mercenaries were placed on the roof with an RPG-7 and long-range rifles to take out the Soldati headquarters. Vivienne just needed a reason to run into the street.

A pity the woman would serve as the sacrificial lamb for his ambitions. She was a class act. Beautiful, intelligent, passionate about her cause, and committed to protecting her daughter. Five months before, Vivienne had sat, utterly at her ease, across from him at an outdoor café in London. Such a striking, intriguing older woman. He'd listened, rapt, as she recounted for him the details of Martel's illegal activities and his own involvement with Daystar, LLC. She should have been an international spy, rather than a Christian crusader. He still couldn't suss out how she'd unearthed his identity or who he worked for.

At first, he'd thought she worked for a government agency and blew her off. But when she approached him a week later in Spain, he guessed her interest in Martel was personal. It wasn't until much later that he learned of her relationship with his employer. She'd even tried to recruit him into the Soldati di Cristo, as if he could ever believe in God after witnessing his mother's transformation into a skag head. Ironic that he traded in the very pursuits that had ruined his own boyhood.

Eventually, he began to deduce the benefits of helping Vivienne destroy Martel. Martel would be dead, and the Spaniard's entire network his. When he began to siphon off bits of intel to test her capabilities, she and the Soldati surpassed his expectations.

Blade's cover shoot on *Maxim* accelerated his plan. Once Martel saw her picture and read the article about the up-and-coming "impalement artist" with strange eyes, his employer had become obsessed with her. After Martel had sent him to New Orleans to collect a DNA sample, Alec found himself no less in her thrall. He couldn't forget the lithe woman with the hairline scar along her jawline. Or the killer body.

Once Martel verified Blade's identity, his obsession with capturing Vivienne intensified into an insatiable need. Alec knew Martel's Achilles heel was the need to oversee every detail of every situation. His employer would not rest until he had answers to the questions Blade's existence elicited. Alec doubted Vivienne would make it out of this alive. But he'd be one rich Scouser. Maybe he'd buy a soccer team. Or a casino in Monte Carlo or Las Vegas. Blade could be the headliner for his new venture.

He took out his cell phone and made the call.

"*Hola,*" Vivienne said.

"Get out of there. Martel is going to blow the place."

"Throw the fire alarm!" Vivienne yelled from the cafeteria. "Get out! Everyone, get out!"

Soldati staff jumped to action. Running to her nearby office, Vivienne grabbed a Sig Sauer P226 and stuck it at the small of her back. No time to gather more weapons.

"Genevieve!" she yelled over the din of the fire alarm.

Vivienne saw Thomas and a small contingent of the Soldati heading for the fire escape and caught his eye. He shook his head—no, he had not seen Genevieve. The others ran through the door and down the stairs. She knew Blade could take care of herself, but burning doubt plagued her. She could not lose her—not like this.

Where the hell is she?

Alec disconnected the call before Vivienne could ask questions.

Within seconds, a fire alarm began to blare. People from the building ran into the street. Other pedestrians on the block stood motionless, gawking, hoping to catch the first licks of fire consuming the building. Bloody plonkers, fascinated by violence yet crying when they got a paper cut. He wouldn't mind getting rid of the lot. But first, Vivienne needed to make it out.

"On my mark," Alec said through his headset.

He adjusted the scope for clarity. Shooting people at this distance would be better odds than shooting ducks at a carnival game. He imagined a carney barking, "Step right up and test your target shooting skills! Just land your eyes on a lucky duck, aim, and shoot!"

And . . . there she is. My lucky duck.

131

Vivienne had run out into the street, holding a young boy's hand. It was the prodigy violin player who played Niccolò Paganini's *Violin Concerto No. 1* as if he'd been performing for decades. Vivienne's brow furrowed in frustration as the boy wriggled out of her grasp and ran back in. He came back tugging on an old man's hand while clutching a violin case to his chest.

"Team 1—don't harm the boy," Alec said. Music had always been his ticket to escape life on the streets rather than drugs. Living with his mother taught him that lesson. He was no expert in classical music, but this lad had the juice. Talent like his shouldn't be splattered on a dirty street.

Vivienne and the old bloke were having a row. The boy joined her side and began pulling on the old man's sleeve. He resisted, planting both feet firmly on the pavement.

Bugger me. Alec tightened his grip on the rifle, considering shooting the old man.

Losing her cool, Vivienne grabbed the violin case in one hand and the boy's wrist in the other and ran full out away from the building and the old man. Sirens could be heard over the blaring fire alarm.

He couldn't wait any longer.

"Fire away," he ordered.

A fireball engulfed the third story. The concussive force of the explosion shook nearby buildings. Car alarms went off, adding to the pandemonium. Black smoke quickly filled the street. Fragments of plaster, metal, and concrete rained on parked cars and people as they ran. Residents spilled from flats to join screaming tourists fleeing from nearby shops.

A second explosion shook the building's foundation. People took cover while others huddled in doorways. The third floor imploded and collapsed upon the second. Even from Alec's distance from across the street, he threw himself on the floor, protecting his head as the glass window shattered. Pictures fell from the wall as the concussion shook the building.

Alec slowly rose to hands and knees, waiting for his ears to clear.

"Target acquired," a mild voice said into his headset.

"Affirmative," Alec said. "And the boy?"

"Alive."

As the dust settled, Alec saw the entire building was now a shell, the exterior walls barely intact, a mound of rubble covering the ground floor. Adjacent buildings sustained some damage with blown-out windows and collapsing stone walls. He doubted anyone could make it out alive.

Alec brought the rifle sight to his eye, hoping for a glimpse of Blade. People stumbled away, except for one man who was covered with tattoos.

CHAPTER
TWENTY-SIX

November 29, 1:55 p.m.
Florence, Italy

Bollocks. What the hell is Vega doing here?

Alec blinked, not believing what his eyes registered. There was no mistaking Vega, though. The man was a walking advertisement, a neon sign demanding attention. The nutter wore no hat, and even from this distance, he noted scrambling onlookers taking a second glance at him.

Sweat trickled from his brow, dropping on the linoleum floor. Ellis had effectively declared war by sending Vega to the workshop. Martel might excuse the debacle at the bistro with Blade, but usually mediocrity at this level in Martel's organization was dealt with permanently. Ellis, desperate to prove herself, exposed her need to come through in a big way—which could only mean capturing Vivienne alive—and killing him.

Not only was Ellis able to track Blade, but she'd probably planted a tracking bug on him. *Damn her.* The bitch probably knew exactly where he was standing at this moment.

Only one thing to do—eliminate the threat for good.

Vega's head swiveled, much like a barn owl triangulating its next meal. If he were here, that meant Alec's team had already made it away with Vivienne undetected and were on their way to the hangar. He brought the scope to his eye, searching for Ellis. No sign of the ice queen.

The desire to kill Vega on the spot almost overpowered his sapience. *Patience*, Alec reminded himself. If Ellis were in the vicinity and reported back to Martel, his own life would be forfeit. Best to wait this out.

He scanned the debris for any sign of Blade. Regrettably for Vivienne, he had no choice but to hand her over to Martel. But perhaps he could still save Blade. Deep pain in the pit of his stomach ached. With surprise, he admitted the attraction he felt for Blade was real. He needed for her to be alive. The curves of her body and those soft amber eyes pulled powerfully at him, but they were nothing compared to her tenacity or the left hook she'd landed at the villa. His jaw still felt tender to the touch.

He spotted a dark-haired man crawling through the rubble of splintered wood and shards of glass. Desperate, the man tore at the glass and wood fragments, heedless of the cuts he sustained, until he lifted a small slab of concrete and uncovered a long curl of chestnut hair. Her arm shot out, valiantly trying to grab onto something.

Blade lived.

A slow smile emerged on his face as Alec viewed the action below. Even pressed under a pile of debris, the woman was a warrior.

With deliberation, Alec weighed the pros and cons of killing the dark-haired man who'd freed her. Could he be useful in the long game? Alec settled the scope's crosshairs on the back of the man's head. He made his decision: he would take the kill shot. Slowly, he expelled his breath, then began to gently squeeze the trigger. It wasn't possible, but the dark-haired man seemed to preternaturally sense his presence. For whatever reason, he looked straight into the crosshairs. Alec eased back the trigger —then stopped, reconsidering. This man could be the weapon that destroyed the Spaniard.

Meanwhile, Vega had crept closer, only fifty feet away from them.

Blade coughed, the stench of smoke and centuries-old dust filling her lungs. Particles of debris floated in the air like gray snowflakes. Someone leaned over her, trying to hold her still. She lashed out with little strength, her ears ringing.

"Easy. You may have a concussion or broken bones," Chase said as his hands brushed over her arms and legs. "Anything hurt?"

She relaxed, recognizing Chase's voice. They were alive. Others could be alive, too. The persistent clamor of a klaxon made her head throb. She turned her head from side to side, wiggled her toes, and clenched and unclenched her hands. No pain yet.

A low gray haze hovered above the entire block like a bad omen. Fire alarms, car alarms, police sirens, people's screams, and children's cries all melded into a cacophony that scared her.

Where is Vivienne?

Blade struggled to sit up, pushing Chase's hands away as he tried to stop her. The block looked like a war zone, with crumbled walls and debris in the street. A young woman huddled in a doorway with a toddler safely in her arms. She rocked back and forth, unable to tear her eyes away from the crushed building that had once held the Soldati head-quarters.

"The old man," Blade rasped, searching the crowd for the familiar face. She closed her eyes tight and remembered. The fire alarm, running to the first floor, then the explosion. Before her world blew apart, the old man was trying to tell her something in Italian.

Struggling to her feet, she saw a tattered trench coat draped over a body merely fifteen feet away. The once shiny brown loafers were covered in gray dust, his brown dress pants shredded by flying debris. Why wouldn't the old man come with her? He kept repeating the same word, *rapito, rapito*. What did that mean?

"We need to get out of here," Blade said, recognizing the man with tattoos coming at them. "Now."

***

The Carabinieri turned the corner, tires squealing, sirens blazing. All-or-nothing. Alec's finger tightened on the trigger. Vega's brain matter and blood sprayed over the area. Alec congratulated himself on the head shot. "Sometimes it's necessary to get your hands dirty," his retired British SAS firearms instructor had liked to say, "but if you use a gun, it isn't so dreadfully messy."

Panic gripped the crowd afresh, the gunshot sending them off in all directions like a herd of maddened wild horses. Many of them rushed the recently arrived Carabinieri, pleading for assistance.

"*Scendere*, get down!" an officer yelled above the mayhem. "Take cover!"

Another of the policemen pointed in the general vicinity of Alec, although they could not possibly have pinpointed the shot's origin. He quickly disassembled his rifle and placed the parts neatly into the compact gun case. One last look out the window. The dark-haired man seemed to be checking Blade for broken bones. Emergency personnel swarmed over the site, looking for survivors, while a half dozen *polizia* ran toward his building. Check-out time.

He opened the door to a stampede of older residents tottering to the stairwell. These geezers could still move when prodded. He'd lay odds ninety percent of them had been glued to their windows, their attention riveted on the aftermath of the explosion across the street. Alec turned in the opposite direction, making for the fire escape, when he collided with an elderly woman who reminded him of an overweight Maggie Smith. Her filthy apron looked like she'd been butchering a pig, which may not have been far from the truth.

The old woman grabbed his arm with claw-like fingers, her finger-nails yellowed by age and smoking. "*Cosa stai facendo in quell'apparta-mento?*" She gestured with her head, indicating the door he had recently closed.

"*Fatti gli affari tuoi.*" The crone should mind her own business.

Alec tried to shake her off, but the old woman's fingers curled around his forearm.

Everyone and everything inside this building reminded him of his Gran—a clawing, mewing woman who'd turned his stomach every time his mum delivered him to her doorstep. He wanted to smash this woman's nose into her skull. He settled for merely shoving the woman, hard. She staggered back, hitting the wall with a thunk.

Someone shouted from below.

The old woman's knees buckled as she melted to the floor. A trace of blood spotted the cracked plaster wall.

He regarded the old woman's prone body with contempt before looking out the window leading to the fire escape. The Carabinieri were already canvassing the area below. There was no way to go but up.

He climbed the metal stairs until he gained access to the roof. The architects of the historical center of Florence wasted not one square inch of real estate. The roofs were close enough to traverse to the Arno River, although the pitches were different. Once there, he could blend into the panicked crowds.

The vantage point from the rooftops reminded him of the old times in Liverpool when he'd been a fit and agile teen. For fun, he and his mates would scale buildings, jumping from one roof to another to evade detection after stealing whatever they could resell later.

Smoke began to move in a northerly direction, the wind casting and pitching ash through the area. His eyes watered from the acrid smell of fire, slowing his progress across the rooftops. He pressed on, knowing he must cross the Ponte Vecchio before the Carabinieri closed that access point.

At last, he made it to the river. Smoke and filth from the rooftops clung to his clothes and skin. No fire escape, no door leading to a stairwell, and six floors between him and the street below.

No other way but down a bloody pipe.

Removing his jacket, he stashed the rifle case inside an old vent. He'd come back for it later. He positioned himself over the pipe and muscled his way down, hand over hand, just like old times. The crowd, intent on getting over the bridge, barely noticed him. He became part of the throng. Surveillance cameras covered the entire length of the bridge due to the amount of gold and gemstones sold at the jewelry stores. He would appear to be just another tourist caught in the chaos.

As he looked up into the smoke-filled sky, Alec's own future seemed uncertain. With so many variables at play, it was imperative to reach the hangar before Ellis. He must kill her or pay the ultimate price for betraying the Spaniard.

CHAPTER
TWENTY-SEVEN

November 29, 2:01 p.m.
Florence, Italy

Blade swayed on her feet, bile rising after seeing blood and gore spray into the air behind the tattooed man's head. Even as the man was still toppling backwards, Blade flashed to what she recalled of Shen's death: the blur of his blood through the night air. While that carnage, that death, had only been suggested, as though rendered with a quick, deft stroke of charcoal on gray paper, the hot white light of day had illuminated the violence of the tattooed man's death in such a cruelly high-definition, Technicolor display that she doubted she would ever stop seeing it.

Chase grabbed her wrist and dragged her behind him through the uneven rubble beneath them. "We need to make it across the street under one of the awnings," he said. "Get out of the shooter's line of sight."

Blade could not seem to tear her eyes away from the woman and toddler still huddled together in the recessed doorway of the building across the street. The terrified woman leaned out to get a better look. Blade wanted to warn her to stay where she was, but her feet, now on automatic, kept moving after Chase. Whether emboldened by their own retreat or some sixth sense, the woman gathered the child in her arms and made a dash toward the sirens, away from the sniper.

Once they made it safely under an awning, Blade took a knee, trembling.

"We've got to get out of here before the police take control of the area," Chase said gruffly. "Are you up to it?"

Of course she wasn't up to it. Her ears were still ringing from the explosion and she couldn't stop shaking. She glanced up to see a battle-hardened soldier, confident and strong. *Pull yourself together.* The sound of a bullet pinging off a metal address plaque about six inches from her head startled her. Heart pumping wildly, she stood unsteadily.

"Martel's force is trying to corner us or drive us into a trap. We need to keep moving." He squeezed her shoulder before leading the way around the corner to a side street. They ran in a zig-zag pattern as bullets pelted the pavement until Chase veered into a recessed doorway, Blade on his heels.

"Close," Chase said.

"Too close."

"Were you hit?"

Before she could answer, they both heard someone running—hard. Presumably tracking them. Chase tried to open the door next to them, but it was locked from the inside. Without weapons, they were easy targets. As he positioned his body before her as a shield, she rooted under her workout bra to find a push dagger she had stashed there earlier. It reminded her of a talon, a discreet palm-sized weapon designed to inflict damage through muscle and tendons. No one would get the drop on her again.

Blade tried to muscle her way to the front, but Chase wouldn't budge. Precious seconds were ticking away. Finally, she conceded and tapped Chase's hand with her forefinger, placing the weapon in his palm.

He gave an imperceptible nod of thanks and switched it to his right hand.

The attacker slowed. Blade could feel Chase tense, even as her own muscles reacted to the threat. Fury flooded through her. She wasn't going to stand here and allow this assassin to murder them—not without a fight. Martel's people had inflicted enough damage for one day.

Before she could move, Chase exploded from the doorway. Flying after him, she saw that he'd plunged the dagger into the attacker's abdomen and was trying to drive it upward. But something—a kevlar vest—stopped its ascent. The attacker shifted his gaze to Blade and brought his right arm up to fire his gun, but Chase, sensing the threat, knocked the man off-balance. The shot missed wide. The two men grappled for the weapon, making it impossible for Blade to unleash a kick or jab.

She watched in horror as the attacker brought the gun to within inches of Chase's forehead. In such close quarters, and with a gun pointed at her ally's head, she couldn't risk his life by misjudging a strike. The dagger still dangled from the man's abdomen. If only she could pry it from his body, she might be able to disable the man.

As though perceiving Blade's intention, the man lashed out with his leg, kicking her mid-thigh, never losing his grip on the gun. She lost her balance, finding herself on all fours.

The distraction bought Chase some time. He reared back and drove his forehead into the attacker's face, although this only seemed to rouse the man. He drove his knee into Chase's rib cage, all the while maneuvering the muzzle of the gun at Chase.

Blade launched herself at him. In that mid-flight instant, she saw his finger find the trigger. Simultaneously, she sighted the barrel, guiding it upward with her outstretched hand as her body drove the man back against the wall. The gun fired, missing Chase's head by inches.

Chase seized the opportunity. With one final boost of energy, he pulled the dagger from the man's abdomen and thrust it through his larynx. The man collapsed to his knees, his eyes full of fear. Then he slowly dropped sideways, his cheek hitting the sidewalk hard.

Blade covered her mouth with her hand, unsure if it was to stifle a scream or to keep from being sick. Rationally, she knew it was either the assassin's death or theirs, but the reality of seeing a dead body at her feet caused her senses to flatline—except for a pinpoint of vision, focused on the man's empty eyes. She didn't believe in God, but if she did, his death would surely leave a stain on her soul that could never be washed away.

Chase gently shook her shoulder, his breathing still labored. "I need you alert. Our protocol is to meet at our safe house in Rome. If anyone else has made it out alive, that's where they'll be. Are you up to traveling?"

She got to her feet, stiffened her spine, and nodded.

"Search his pockets for anything useful," Chase ordered as he wrenched the gun from the dead man's hand and set about checking the magazine.

The street was still empty of people. Blade reluctantly slid her hand into his pant pockets. Nothing terribly useful except spare change, five hundred Euros, and a hotel room key-card. No identification or cell phone.

After reporting this to Chase, he nodded and pulled her to her feet. "Stand still," he said, and set about slapping the dust from her clothes. He did the same to his own.

Looking upon the man she'd helped kill, she felt like a murderous robber who'd just rifled through their victim's pockets. Dirty and wrong. She knew it had to be different for Chase, who'd trained to kill the enemy. She was just a civilian with blood on her hands. A low, shuddering moan escaped her lips.

"Hold it together," he ordered, glancing at her. "First, we can both clean up and buy new clothes at the train station. Now move."

It was easy to rely on his expertise to get through the day. She matched him stride for stride. After a few minutes, her mind began to clear. She could do this. "Why take the train? Isn't that dangerous? Why not steal a car? Or a motorcycle?"

"I'm not sure how they're tracking us, but they are. It's better to draw the enemy out in a controlled environment rather than being on the road and used as target practice."

Blade prided herself on being self-reliant and in control of her life, but she found herself under siege in a foreign country with no passport and only the clothes on her back, at the mercy of a man she'd met only days before.

"Shouldn't we look for Vivienne? Or your friends?" she asked, hoping for some sort of reprieve from running—again. Maybe a chance to catch her breath and cope with what just happened.

Chase whirled on her. He grabbed her shoulders and leaned into her, leaving inches between their gazes. "These people are my family. You're the outsider. People are dying all around us. This isn't a game or some reality show. This is what I *do*. You either follow my orders or you leave. But if you stay with me, you will do exactly what I say."

He didn't wait for a reply before heading off again. Blade stared icily at his back, fuming at the insult. After what they'd just been through, his dismissal of her stung like a slap to the face. For a few brief hours, she thought the two had forged the beginning of a friendship.

To think I'd started to like the ass.

With the five hundred Euros in her pocket, she could hole up in a hotel room, get some rest, and think.

To hell with Chase and his damn Soldati.

She could be in New Orleans within a day. Surely the Consulate would make the arrangements to rid themselves of a nutcase if she made a pest of herself. But what of Vivienne? Her biological mother.

That word. Having it just pop up like that rocked her to her core. Blade's love for Marie was undeniable, but could there be room in her heart for Vivienne? There was no denying the ties that bound them. The pull to know her was more potent than she ever thought possible.

As Chase's broad shoulders slipped through the crowd of tourists like a knife through butter, Blade followed in his wake, resolve coursing through her.

First, she would find her mother. Together, perhaps they could save the UN *and* destroy René Martel.

CHAPTER
TWENTY-EIGHT

November 29, 2:10 p.m.
Florence, Italy

With his rash decision to kill Vega, the chain reaction Alec started was irrevocable. And all because of a damn woman. Somehow, Blade had gotten under his skin. At the moment he tensed his finger to pull the trigger, he realized he *needed* her alive. He wasn't naive enough to think they would ever have a normal life together. But allowing the likes of Vega to kill her? No bloody way.

Alec saw the flashing lights of a police car at the end of Ponte Vecchio. Two *polizia* were trying to direct the terrified crowd, but the mob's fear outweighed their reason. One overweight woman tripped and fell headlong onto the bridge, her red dress flying over her head. She screamed as people trampled over her. Alec felt the crunch of bone under his foot and assumed it was either the woman's fingers or hand, as the mob spilled onto *Via Por Santa Maria*. He remained with them until he saw a sign pointing to *Piazza Della Signoria*.

He splintered off from the crowd, intent on one thing—to get back to the hangar as soon as possible. Pigeons covered the plaza, scavenging for any food dropped by tourists. Alec kicked at one that didn't move as he strode across the plaza. Tourists roosted on the steps of the Loggia dei

Lanzi, an open-air sculpture gallery, flocking together after the recent explosion—just like the bloody pigeons.

Guarding the gallery like sentries rested The Medici lions, a pair of huge marble sculptures. One rested its massive paw on a sphere—triggering the recognition in him that Martel still controlled him. He was gambling his life on this roll of the dice. Ellis, desperate to appease Martel, would do anything to save her own neck. He assumed she had dispatched Vega in one direction while she took another. To her credit, she came close to capturing both Blade and Vivienne. If not for his ingenuity and forethought, this could be his death sentence.

Two years ago, he and Francesca, a brilliant woman earning her doctorate in Renaissance Studies, visited every museum in Florence. As a reward for dragging him through the city, she arranged for a private tour of Tuscany by scooter. An excursion of a winery amid the Tuscany countryside had netted results in the bedroom that still brought a smile to his face. If he remembered correctly, the tour company veered off this very plaza onto one of the side streets.

"*Mi scusi, Mi scusi,*" a middle-aged woman apologized as she tried to navigate her red scooter through a line of customers in front of a sandwich shop. She seemed incapable of turning the scooter around. Alec couldn't ignore providence. In a matter of seconds, the woman was floundering on the ground while he hopped on the scooter with cries from onlookers carrying on the wind.

It would take at least twenty minutes to drive to the Aeroporto di Firenze-Peretola. The Gulfstream, fueled and ready for takeoff, awaited him there at a private hangar. There would be no way Ellis could know about Vega's death—unless she followed him. Either way, Ellis would eventually make her way back to the airport hangar.

Usurping a psychotic billionaire was a delicate business. Martel's death must not be traced back to him. Not if he wanted to live. Even the most brutal drug cartels lived by a code of conduct—no one betrayed the boss, or *El Jefe*, and lived to tell the tale. He had to be honest with Vivienne—to a point—and somehow convince her to keep his role as informant to herself. If she was unable to kill Martel while at the chalet, well, accidents happened. One way or another, she would be his sacrificial lamb. Ellis would just be roadkill.

CHAPTER
TWENTY-NINE

November 29, 2:24 p.m.
Florence, Italy

After Blade's first few disastrous performances at the Rising Sun, the Great Mancini took her aside to give her two pieces of advice: Planning is imperative to the art of illusion and sleight of hand. And, more importantly, having a back door was worth more than a 401K plan.

Taking the train to Rome felt more like an invitation to Martel's killing squad than an escape route. Chase had accused her of being an outsider and a rank novice. But that didn't mean she couldn't be effective, or that she didn't have skills to add to their already impressive arsenal or that she was a complete idiot.

They couldn't rent a car without a driver's license, which was Chase's rationale for the two-hour train ride to Rome. The Soldati probably frowned upon boosting a car, but surely saving the world and finding Vivienne were worth the transgression. Maybe she should accept his decision, but damn, she *knew* this was a mistake. It left them vulnerable, and she already felt like a hunted animal and didn't like the odds.

She followed Chase for fifteen minutes, allowing her anger to simmer. When he slowed at the Basilica di Santa Maria Novella, Blade stopped next to him to appreciate the façade, a palette of white and green marble used to create squares, rectangles, circles, and other design elements. Together they created a masterpiece of symmetry. It reminded her of Il Duomo. The entire city truly did possess a treasure trove of architectural delights.

Perhaps one day I'll come back.

She studied Chase—his set, square jaw, the way his eyes misted over as he took in the church. This sliver of emotion surprised her.

"My wife loved architecture," he said. "Especially stained glass windows. I've been here a few times. You'll find most churches in Europe have their own unique workmanship. Something we don't see much of in the States."

"You were married?"

Chase exhaled loudly as if he'd been holding his breath for an eternity. "Yes," he said, back in motion, striding across the street. "So. Are you in or out?"

Messy divorce. Infidelity? Not the type. She'd lay odds he had no children.

"In," she said. "But I don't blindly obey orders."

"The Soldati follows a strict chain of command, just like the military. Our survival depends on it."

"Well, I'm an outsider, like you said. And outsiders, pretty much by definition, don't conform to rules. I'm in this to find Vivienne and stop Martel. Period."

Clearly irritated, Chase squinted ahead in the afternoon sun. "We're almost there."

The nondescript Santa Maria Novella train station was an eyesore among the elegance of city center. It reminded Blade of the Union Passenger Terminal in New Orleans—drab, lifeless, ordinary. The Renaissance architects, like Brunelleschi, would have cringed at this abomination.

Chase paused to survey the area. When she joined him, Blade saw a camouflaged military vehicle parked just outside the terminal. The entire city was probably on high alert due to the explosion. Four soldiers wearing camo and red berets stood at the ready, each carrying an automatic rifle, index finger on the frame, just as Chase had instructed her earlier.

"I'll need the Euros for our tickets and clothing," he said. "It shouldn't take me long. I'll meet you downstairs."

"I still think the train is a bad idea," she said, taking the money out of her zippered pocket.

"The train is the simplest way to get from point A to point B. I'll be back in ten minutes."

An escalator was just to her left. Hundreds of people moved in and out of the terminal. A young girl, perhaps five or six, skipped alongside her mother without a care, oblivious to the overburdened woman, who looked more like a pack mule than a tourist. An elderly couple struggled with an ATM machine, targets for any vagrant in need of easy cash. And the never-ending stream of millennials armed with their backpacks and Bluetooth earbuds. No one and nothing seemed out of place.

She rode the escalator to the level below. Sure the ten minutes would stretch to twenty, she followed the signs to the restroom. A half dozen women waited to use the facilities. Blade caught a glimpse of herself in the mirror. A layer of dust covered her. She longed for a shower, but a sink with running water was better than nothing. She put her hand under the soap dispenser and rubbed a generous amount over her face and hands. It felt delicious on her skin. Women gave her sidelong glances, but Blade continued rinsing off the suds. There wasn't enough room to stick her head under the faucet, so she bent over and did her best to shake the dust out of her hair.

When it was her turn, she stepped into a stall, unsure whether she'd have access to a women's bathroom again or the time to sit and breathe normally. Minutes passed, and with it, the knot of women who'd entered with her and filled the space with their chatter. She closed her eyes and listened to…silence. The ebb and flow of people probably revolved around the train schedules. Still, Chase might be pacing near their rendezvous point, fuming at her delay. Unlatching the door, she again examined herself in the mirror. She'd missed a smudge of dirt under her chin.

As she tugged a paper towel from its dispenser, the door opened. A tall blonde woman waltzed in. Ellis. Before Blade could react, the blonde attacked with a high kick to the head, followed by a punch to the abdomen. Blade doubled over.

"Sugar, I don't appreciate being one-upped," Ellis said, grabbing a handful of Blade's hair and dragging her back into the stall she'd just vacated. "And you're goin' to *pay*."

The kick to Blade's head had almost knocked her out, but she fought through the fuzziness.

The snap of a switchblade triggered a memory of another attack where she had succumbed to fear. She wasn't going to die in a bathroom stall thousands of miles from home.

Tears welled in her eyes as Ellis pulled on her hair, forcing her head back to reveal the soft part of her neck. *She's going to slit my throat. Time to fight or die.*

"A blade for a Blade," Ellis whispered near her ear.

Using the stall door frame as leverage, Blade pushed hard with her legs, driving Ellis back, wedging her between the toilet and wall. There was no time to think—only react. Blade delivered a headbutt into Ellis's face.

The switchblade clattered on the floor.

Blade rotated, using her body weight to gain the advantage, but the blonde thrust the heel of her hand into Blade's throat. Ellis scrambled over her body and lunged for the knife. As her fingers touched the handle, Blade rammed her fist into the side of Ellis's head, flipped her on her back, straddled her, and threw a few more punches to her face.

"How are you tracking us?" Blade hissed.

"I have no idea what you're talkin' about."

"Tell me, or I'll break every bone in your face."

"You don't have the stomach for that."

Before she could begin to show her otherwise, the door handle rattled.

In a flash, Blade balled her hand into a fist and drove it into Ellis's temple. Out cold. Quickly, Blade bent over the prone body, pretending to give Ellis CPR while a young mother holding a toddler with one arm and a diaper bag in the other came in. One startled look at the floor and the young mother practically ran back the way she came in.

Blade stood, grabbed Ellis's ankles, and strained to pull her into the farthest stall. She couldn't just leave her here, unconscious in a bathroom. Smiling, she removed the shoelaces from her athletic shoes, and used them as rope to tie Ellis's hands behind her back. Next, she removed her bra, wrapped it around Ellis's ankles twice, and tied it securely. One last bit of insurance—she pulled a wad of paper towels from the dispenser.

This should keep her quiet.

Blade stuffed the wad into Ellis's slack mouth, then crammed her between the commode and wall. Before locking the stall door from the inside, Blade retrieved the switchblade, crawled underneath, and headed out the exit door.

She ran to the escalator but opted for the stairs. Hundreds of people filled the terminal. A head taller than most of the travelers, Chase was easy to spot. Ruggedly handsome, every woman who passed him did a double take.

Shoving through the crowd, she reached him and grabbed for his free hand. "We need to get the hell out of this train station."

"Whose blood is on your shirt?" Chase said, assessing her.

"Ellis. She nearly killed me. I left her tied up in the restroom."

"Damn," he said as he checked around them. "Looks like the new clothes will come in handy."

"Clothes are the least of our problems," Blade said, realizing she spoke too loud as a couple holding hands glanced their way. She lowered her voice, "I'm not getting on a train. Didn't they teach you how to hot-wire cars in the military?"

Chase stiffened.

Blade smiled. "Finally, my talents will come in handy."

CHAPTER
THIRTY

November 29, 3:12 p.m.
Florence, Italy

The extraction team gathered their equipment and rolled out of the hangar in a black Mercedes SUV. Alec had paid for the best in the business, and Vivienne's inert body lay in the aft cabin as proof. The doctor on the team guaranteed she'd be out for two hours. He would need some time to broker a deal with the woman before handing her off to Martel.

He boarded the jet, leaving the airstairs down in order to hear anyone approach, and helped himself to a Guinness as he waited for Ellis. The dust and physical exertion had left him parched. He tilted his head back and enjoyed the ice-cold brew. The jet, the Ferrari, the clothes, the women—he would not give up this lifestyle without a fight. If not for Martel, he would probably be in prison or dead. For years, he'd thought of Martel as his mentor, saw himself forever indebted to the man for recognizing his potential and pouring thousands into his education. Unfortunately, bad things happened to bad people. Martel would be another casualty of war, and he would reap the spoils.

His body tensed at the sound of a car door slamming outside the jet. Ellis hummed an old nursery tune as she ascended the air stairs. Her killing song. Usually, it set his nerves on fire, but today it gave him fair warning. He set his beer on a side table. This was when he felt most alive.

Bring it on, bitch.

Ellis's damaged face made him feel almost sorry for her. Almost. Her left eye was nearly swollen shut, her nose definitely broken.

She surveyed the main cabin. "Why Sugar, you look like the cat that swallowed the canary. Where's Vega?"

Alec laughed. "What the hell happened to you?" He slapped his thigh. "Blade got the best of you, didn't she? You just had your arse handed to you by a bloody impalement artist. Brilliant."

"You didn't answer my question," she said, ignoring the bait. "Where is Vega?"

"Haven't seen him. You two were supposed to wait here."

"I don't like waiting."

She made a show of sitting in one of the tan leather chairs, one long leg crossing over the other. "I could use a drink," she said, gesturing to the beer in his hand.

"Help yourself."

She glared at him but stood and made her way to the bar. "I prefer whiskey to beer. Beer is so…ordinary."

Alec scooped up his beer and took a swig. "Your loss."

Her eyes roved about the cabin, evaluating its layout and analyzing her options for a successful attack on him. She could be so transparent.

Shite. I can't wait to kick her arse.

"Did you find Vivienne? Or Blade?" she asked sweetly.

"What do you think?"

"I think you're a bastard with too much power. You don't fool me. Once I arrive at Gstaad, I will expose how you allowed Blade to escape, although you won't be around to reap what you deserve," she said, drawing within striking distance.

Alec stood. "Vega's dead."

"I know."

He threw the beer bottle at her. She ducked, as expected, but the beating she'd taken earlier had slowed her reaction time by a fraction— just enough to allow Alec to seize her by the lapels and throw her across the cabin. She slammed into a table and still landed on her toes, like a damn cat.

But when she looked up at him, she wore a lop-sided grin. "You know what's gonna happen now, Sugar? Because I love making people happy?" She licked her bloodied lips clean. "I'm gonna leave you alive long enough for René to finish you off."

Then she was lunging for his throat—and nearly getting to it, too. She was quite an athlete. Astonishingly fast, really. Using that very speed against her, Alec rolled and threw her onto her belly on the floor, then fell upon her with all his weight.

Some people, like Ellis, considered the act of killing a hobby. For him, it meant only survival. He wrapped one arm around her neck and set about the business of choking off her air. Kicking and thrashing and twisting, frantically using the seats for leverage, she attempted to use the strength in her legs to dislodge his hold, but he stayed in position and squeezed harder, her neck firmly ensconced in the crook of his arm. It was hard, dirty work. His muscles bulged and his head hammered from the exertion. He took no pleasure in any of it, least of all the increasingly pitiable sounds she made as she struggled. But in this game, there could only be one winner.

At long last, the cabin fell silent except for his own labored breathing.

He had taken out the Queen; the next move would be checkmate. The King would fall.

CHAPTER
THIRTY-ONE

November 29, 3:30 p.m.
Enroute to Rome, Italy

Thunder cracked overhead as the November sky grew sullen with rain clouds. The red Lamborghini Aventador SVJ loosed a monstrous growl as Blade turned the corner. Chase's instructions had been simple—choose a car that was inconspicuous. And yet…come *on*. She'd had her pick of countless Fiats, Renaults, and Citroëns. But the Lamborghini! It was a no-brainer.

Chase had his back to her in front of the Tourist Information Center near the Basilica di Santa Maria Novella, their pre-arranged meeting place, so she revved the engine. Chase turned, surprise registering on his usually stoic face. Blade smiled to herself. If she were going into battle, she would need a worthy steed to carry her to Rome—not some nag. The Lamborghini would do.

"I thought I told you we needed to blend in," Chase said as he folded his tall frame into the tight confines of the passenger seat.

"This may be my only opportunity to drive a Lambo. Besides, I thought you would want to make it to Rome in record time."

Earlier, they had stopped to buy new clothes—a necessary, but pretty mild countermeasure. Certainly no guarantee they weren't being followed. Every shadow, around every corner, a possible ambush. If not for her Savate training, she might already be lying dead in a bathroom stall. Ellis had underestimated her. That lapse would not happen again.

She stole a glance in his direction. The blue plaid flannel shirt Chase had selected and the light stubble on his cheeks made him even more ruggedly handsome. His bearing exuded a solid, self-controlled, sober-minded individual determined to avenge the attack on the Soldati—but she suddenly became aware of the menace just below the surface. It unnerved her.

"We should be in Rome by 1900 hours if we take the A1/E35. Follow the signs."

"I already programmed the navigation to the Vatican. You can update the directions at our next rest stop. I promise not to peek—since I'm on a need-to-know basis."

Chase didn't take the bait. People often accused her of being difficult to work with. It was a coping mechanism—a sure way to protect herself from being hurt or relying on others. Being dependent on Chase grated, like fingernails on a chalkboard.

"Do you think we'll find anyone at the safe house?" she said, weaving fluidly through traffic. How she loved speed.

He nodded, studying every car they passed.

He laid the confiscated revolver from the assassin on his lap.

"Expecting company?" she said.

"No. But I've learned not to take chances."

Minutes ticked by, each quiet with their own thoughts. Once on the A1/E35, Blade set the cruise control at 130 kilometers per hour and turned the radio on, selecting the first English speaking channel—classic rock. The music was familiar, yet her mind drifted to Vivienne, whether she wanted it to or not. She replayed Vivienne's admission about Martel murdering her biological father and her own decision to give Blade up for adoption. It seemed inconceivable that the actions of one man could redirect the lives of so many others. Martel was guilty of murder. Perhaps it was unfair to accuse Vivienne of cowardice. Blade knew she couldn't leave matters as they stood between them. They both deserved better.

Suddenly finding the silence oppressive, she blurted, "How did you meet Vivienne?"

"That's a long story."

"We have time."

He rubbed his forehead with his right hand as if the motion would conjure up memories best left contained. "Six years ago, I hit rock bottom. I didn't re-enlist in the Navy and started drinking, not caring whether I lived or died. Worse, I stopped believing in God."

"Is that when your wife left you?"

"She didn't leave me. She died."

This hung in the air, like a dark cloud blotting out the sun. Blade wanted to crawl inside herself and disappear. When would she learn that assumptions were dangerous? She tightened her grip on the wheel, searching for the right words to say. Why was it hard for her to have a normal conversation with someone?

"Sometimes," she said, "I speak without thinking."

"My past isn't a secret. The Boko Haram murdered my wife. Cheyenne wanted to save the world, one person at a time. She insisted on joining a mission team through our local church to share the gospel with villagers in Northern Nigeria. While on leave, I joined her. The scum besieged the small village. All the villagers had for protection was me and one Glock. Six Christians arrived at the village, only one left."

"Did Vivienne find you there?"

He reclined his seat and closed his eyes. "After I finished my tour, I traveled back to the village. The Boko Haram had taken the children and left a few old people alive. The elder told me Cheyenne hit me on the head with a frying pan before being shot herself. Knocked me out cold. The Boko Haram left me for dead."

"I'm so sorry," she whispered.

"I enlisted to protect our country, but I failed my wife and those kids. That's hard to live with," he explained. "I roamed around the Middle East for a while until I found security work in Dubai. I stayed drunk during my off-hours. One night I picked a fight with the wrong people. Four men against me—until Vivienne showed up."

"And what did she do, talk them to death?" Blade asked, remembering their recent encounter.

"She did try to reason with them at first, but the men were intent on teaching the American a lesson in manners. It took about fifteen seconds for Vivienne to lay all four flat on their asses. I wish I could recall the rest, but I blacked out. The next thing I remember is waking up on a private jet to Italy."

"Vivienne recruited you?"

"More like rescued me. I owe her my life. Through my work with the Soldati, I found my faith again."

"Faith. Believing in a God you can't see. For me, it's a stretch to believe in an omniscient God."

"Once you experience God at work, you can't help but believe." Chase rested his gaze on her. "What do you believe in?"

"I create my own destiny. I don't believe in a God who would take life indiscriminately. Or in a God who condones war, murder, and rape."

"You being here, at this moment, is no accident. God has plans for you, Genevieve Broussard."

She rolled her eyes. "I've read John 3:16. Do you really believe your wife lives on in eternity?"

"Absolutely. I've never been so sure of anything in my life."

"I don't get it. Blind faith can rob you. When I bartended, I heard my share of hard-luck stories. People would give their life savings to an evangelist or church only to be disappointed because their prayers weren't answered. If a God existed, wouldn't he take better care of his people?"

The rolling hills of Tuscany unfurled as the Lamborghini sped by. The countryside was postcard-perfect, with the occasional stone villa peeking from behind oak trees. The Tiber River bobbed adjacent to the highway, evoking memories of the Merced River, its turbulent waters above the Nevada Falls carrying her friend Lucas to his death. All she could do was gape at him, clawing at the water, struggling to stay afloat. She vowed to never be that helpless again.

"Bad shit happens," Chase said, "but God is still in control. Cheyenne's death caused me to lose myself. Do I wonder why that happened? Of course I do. If she were still alive, we'd be living in Tennessee, raising a family together. Instead, I'm with the Soldati trying to save your butt."

"Save my butt?" she said, pressing her foot on the accelerator. "I'm the one who carried a dagger in the alley, who kicked Ellis's ass, and who boosted this car."

"Whoa," Chase said, "didn't mean to get you riled up. Slow your speed unless you want to get pulled over."

The speedometer read 168 kph. She lifted her foot off the accelerator, letting cruise control take over again. Chase was right. They couldn't risk being stopped by the *polizia*.

"I'm not much of a team player," she admitted. "But I think you forget it's only been three days since I arrived on Mallorca. You, Vivienne, the Soldati, the God connection—it's a bit much to absorb."

"You're right. Once we reach Rome, our operation to halt the attack on the UN will go into overdrive. Go big or go home. Words to live by. Are you ready for the fireworks?"

Rain pelted the windshield as if on cue. Blade turned on the wipers without answering.

Am I ready?

CHAPTER
THIRTY-TWO

November 29, 3:43 p.m.
Somewhere above the Apennine Mountains

"Wait in the main cabin," Alec ordered.

The physician checked the patient's vitals once more before leaving the room.

Vivienne lay unconscious on a bed in the aft cabin, but not for long. The doctor had administered ketamine after her capture, which, according to his estimation, should be wearing off soon.

Alec would take no pleasure in the upcoming conversation or in handing her over to Martel, but it was either his death or hers. He chose hers.

He perched on a tan leather side chair and waited. Her hands and feet were bound in flex cuffs. Dark hair spilled over the white pillow, and for the first time he noticed strands of silver through the thick tangles. The doctor had replaced her filthy clothes with a modest nightgown. For the moment, she looked small and vulnerable.

Damn, with a woman like Vivienne as his mum, would the trajectory of his life be different?

After their first meeting, new possibilities had materialized. It was like scoring all the bank account numbers in Switzerland. Untold riches and power. He fed Vivienne intel to draw her in, earn her trust. Simple but not easy. She was cautious, well-trained, and suspicious. There was also Martel to consider. The bastard had a nose for informants…and traitors.

The two met in person only twice during their brief association. She captivated those around her, a quality that Blade had clearly inherited. Martel had no idea what he had unleashed when he brought Blade to Mallorca. Alec had once seen a film on the telly about female bears protecting their cubs. If he was any judge of character, Vivienne would go to any lengths to protect her daughter. He was betting his life on it.

He checked the time on his cell phone. The plane would land in less than an hour. Plenty of time, if Vivienne would just wake. Deals must be brokered, sacrifices made.

He stood to fetch the doctor when he noticed movement.

Her amber eyes finally met his. "Alec?"

"Drink some water." He helped support her to a sitting position and held a glass of cold water to her lips. She tried to bring her bound hands to the glass, but they fell useless to her lap. "We haven't much time."

"Time for what? Is Genevieve alive?"

"Yes. And I'd like to keep her that way."

Vivienne tilted her head back to rest against the headboard. "These binds are unnecessary."

He grinned. "Let's just say I respect your skills and resourcefulness. In fact, I'm counting on them."

Flashes of what happened to the Soldati headquarters buffeted her consciousness—pulling the fire alarm after Alec's warning, running downstairs to look for Genevieve, members of the Soldati force moving frantically, gathering what they could before escaping. No sign of her daughter. Spotting Paolo trying to convince his grandfather to leave the violin workshop. Without thinking, only reacting, grabbing the boy's hand and running, hoping Signor Bertinelli would follow. Then the blast. Then the men. Then nothing.

She paused before responding. "You betrayed me."

He replaced the glass on the table. "You should have known better than to trust someone willing to betray Martel."

She coughed, trying to clear her lungs. "I never fully trusted you. But I never thought you would stoop to this," she said, indicating the cuffs.

Alec leaned over and opened the window shade. Lightning flashed through the thicket of gray clouds. A snowstorm loomed over Gstaad, ripe conditions to restrict Martel's movements for the next twenty-four hours.

"What do you want?" she said.

"To strike a bargain."

Her eyes narrowed. "Bargain with you? I'd rather deal with the devil."

"I need Martel gone and I need your help."

"That is what I wanted from you, *recuerda*? Why do this when we both want the same thing?"

"Circumstances have changed. I chose Blade's life over two of Martel's trusted inner-circle. I've been compromised. I'm a dead man if he finds out I'm the traitor."

"You expect my assistance?"

"I expect you to believe I will keep Blade alive if you cooperate."

"Trust is something one earns. I should have seen you for who you are," she said, her voice growing stronger. "But I was consumed with discrediting my brother and holding him accountable. It affected my judgment."

Alec stepped to the coffee table and poured himself a brandy. "We are on our way to Gstaad, where I will deliver you to Martel—and you will kill him. There is no other way."

"And how am I supposed to get to him, trussed up like a turkey?"

"Martel plans to use a serum to kill world leaders at the United Nations in Geneva, including the President of the United States. Crazy, huh? He will want you close, to witness his victory. You will have one chance—probably only a slight chance—to strike."

Alec verified what she already knew about her brother, he performed better with an audience. As a boy, he would strut about their *Abuelo's* ranch wearing the traditional *Traje de Luces* that every bullfighter wore in the ring. He looked ridiculous in the oversized suit, but no one dared laugh at Francisco Martel's grandson.

"What if I fail?

"If you fail, I'll have no other choice but to kill him myself."

"Why drag Genevieve and me into this if you were willing to kill him anyway?"

"You dragged me into your shit-storm," he chided. "You found me. I only recognized an opportunity and seized it."

Temper flaring, she said, "You're planning a coup and you need me."

He chuckled. "Damn straight. But I promise Blade will make it out of this alive. Will you cooperate?"

She could still feel the weight of Genevieve, still smell her hair. Could still feel the avalanche of despair as she handed her baby into Marie's waiting arms. Twenty-six years later she found herself at the same crossroads. Except this time she would entrust her daughter to a snake rather than an angel. She recalled her *abuela's* admonition—*el diablo siempre deja su huella.* The devil always leaves his mark.

The Martels, ambitious and glory-seeking, had forsaken God long ago. Her grandmother, a healer among the people, swore she saw the devil's hand on René. Her *abuela* was never wrong.

While she still drew breath, there was a chance to make amends with her daughter. Sweeping aside all her regrets, she vowed to see Genevieve once again, even if that meant killing her brother. In the meantime, if she was willing to kill, an empty promise meant little. "I will keep your treachery from René and kill him in exchange for Genevieve's safety."

Alec lifted his glass in a toast. "Cheers. To our new alliance."

CHAPTER
THIRTY-THREE

November 29, 6:30 p.m.
Gstaad, Switzerland

"Headache, *hermana*?" a familiar voice cooed. "I'm afraid my acolyte gave you a strong sedative for the flight—for your own safety, of course."

René.

Vivienne breathed through the hatred and rage brought on by being in her brother's presence, using it to fight through the fog. She recalled Alec and the bargain they'd struck to keep Genevieve alive.

Still bound by flex cuffs, she noted the surroundings, avoiding making eye contact with her brother, seated in her periphery. A burly man stood at the door of the room. The lamps on the nightstands cast a faint romantic glow in an elegant bedroom decorated in various shades of taupe and brown. She tried to focus on the recessed dome ceiling with exposed wooden beams, but the polygonal shape made her head spin. She closed her eyes as a wave of nausea hit her.

"I'm thirsty."

René snapped his fingers and the big man left the room.

She squashed the stirring rage in order to play the helpless victim. Her brother sat in a modernized version of a Queen Anne chair near the bed, facing her. Photographs did not do him justice. He was still hand-some. Age had softened his features, the disheveled salt and pepper hair giving him an aristocratic air, like an aging rock star who could still seduce young women half his age. This evening, he resembled a country gentleman in jeans and a turtleneck sweater.

"Pardon the restraints," he said, "but I thought it prudent until we have a chance to get reacquainted."

"Genevieve?" Vivienne croaked. *I must be believable.* All of her skills at disguise and manipulation must be on point to save her daughter.

"Most likely dead."

Alec must have decided to share as much truth as possible.

"I will kill you," Vivienne promised, eyes glistening in hatred. "You will regret leaving me alive."

"Who said you were going to be left alive?" René said, a savage smile twisting his face. "But first, I need information from you, and you will tell me—one way or another."

Alec had accurately predicted her brother's reaction. He would keep her alive long enough to witness his crowning achievement, just as he'd always needed her approval.

An outdoor floodlight turned on, illuminating the evening. Delicate snowflakes swirled in the wind, weightless and ethereal near the window.

She must get free of these cuffs.

Taking a few deep breaths, she asked, "Where are we, *hermano?*"

He followed her gaze to the winter display. "I don't want to spoil the surprise. First, we dine. There is much I want to share."

After all these years, he still relished a theatrical performance. How exhausting it must be to live an entire life masquerading as a normal person rather than what had surely been revealed by him, over and over, as his true nature—a pathological liar and psychotic killer.

Years of hatred and fear coursed over and through her. She tested the restraints, the plastic cutting into her flesh.

The words she'd kept buried for years spilled out. "You killed John. Did you not think I knew?"

He pushed the sleeves of his sweater up to his elbows, exposing muscled forearms. Wealth had not enervated her brother, and it would be a mistake to underestimate him or the lengths he would go to. He reminded her of a cantil viper, luring unsuspecting quarry with its tail and killing it with poisonous venom. How many people lay scattered across the globe, seduced by her brother's good looks and magnetism, only to be murdered for sport or financial gain?

"John Andrews," he said, smiling. "That is a name I haven't thought of in over twenty-five years." He leaned forward in his chair, elbows resting on his knees as if about to recount a favorite childhood story. "I merely eliminated a roadblock. You could never have been happy with an American politician. I did you a favor by killing him."

"You were friends."

He leaned over the bed, bringing his lips close to her ear. "I have no friends. You were the only person I trusted. No one was going to take you away from me. Not John, not our parents."

"Our parents?"

Salvador and Pilar Martel had died in a car accident after attending a charity dinner in Barcelona. Not unusual for the couple to participate in events on most weekends. On this particular Saturday evening, Salvador had lost control of the vehicle and driven over a cliff on their way home. According to the toxicology report, her father had been drunk, twice the legal limit. A tragic accident that had left the twelve-year-old twins orphaned. Thank God for Aunt Leticia and Uncle Tomas. The couple, childless, had raised them as their own. They'd never accepted payment from the trust fund to support them—only showered them with love.

"You never suspected?" he asked, shaking his head. "I drove a scooter to the event after you went to bed. I knew the old man would stay until the very end, drinking and patting the asses of anyone who would let him. I cut the brake line. It is easy if you follow simple instructions."

Vivienne strained her neck, trying desperately to escape his words.

"*Monstruo*," Vivienne spat out.

"Admit it. Our father and mother were the monsters," he said with some heat, pinning her shoulders to the bed. "I *saved* you. Father would have bedded you. His eyes never strayed from you. And our mother knew the truth. She cared more for her social standing than for her own children. Why do you think he and mother were going to send me away to boarding school? To protect each other, their precious way of life. They couldn't afford a scandal."

Chills rolled through her body as she recalled, against her will, how her father would put her on his lap while his hands lingered too long on her body. His dark eyes drinking in her movements. She closed her eyes, remembering all the nights she would sneak into her brother's bedroom, where she felt safest. And their nearly nonexistent mother, always too busy to even give a hug.

"You know what I'm capable of. You've always known, in here," he said, pointing to her heart.

"We were only twelve years old," she whispered. Her naked eyes bored into his.

"Who are you to judge me? You gave away your own child." His brow furrowed, just as it always had when he was displeased with her. "Get some rest. You will need it for tonight's festivities."

He brushed her cheek with the back of his hand before striding to the door. It closed with a soft click.

Alec claimed Genevieve still lived. She prayed he told the truth, at least about that. Hope welled like a spring inside her. She peered out the window. The snow fell like a white waterfall, cleansing the earth of its filth. God, in his grace, had given her a second chance with her daughter. She refused to squander this prospect at redemption.

Vivienne prayed for the safety of Genevieve, Luc, and her Soldati family, for the strength and wisdom to destroy the one man who threatened the world—who threatened her daughter—even if it meant sacrificing her own life to do it.

'Vengeance is mine, I will repay, says the Lord.' Why did that come to mind?

A shadow passed by the window. Vivienne squinted to see a white dove hover through the glass for an instant, and then it disappeared. God, indeed, did listen.

CHAPTER
THIRTY-FOUR

November 29, 7:10 p.m.
Rome, Italy

"You've driven cars like this before?" Blade said as Chase navigated the Lamborghini through traffic, nearing the outskirts of Rome.

"Hell yes. I'd forgotten how much fun driving a car like this can be," he said, grinning like a kid who had just hit his first home run. My dad was a crew chief for a NASCAR team. I kinda grew up traveling throughout the country, following the major races."

"You could have hot wired this car," Blade accused. "You let me do the dirty work."

"I wanted you to feel useful," Chase countered, his grin widening into a full-blown smile.

Blade couldn't help but roll her eyes at the playful exchange.

The Lamborghini rounded a corner near Castel Sant'Angelo. "Saint Peter's Basilica is just over there," Chase said, nodding in the direction of an illuminated night sky.

A beacon of hope. Like every other normal person on the planet, Blade wasn't immune to the stab of hope of finding Vivienne alive as they raced to the safe house.

At this hour, the city still bustled with mini cars and scooters. The streets looked like polished obsidian from the recent rain storm. Blade rolled down the window to take in the aroma of Rome. She expected the fragrant scent of baked bread and pasta. Instead, the reek of the Tiber River greeted her, much like the giant Mississippi that rolled through New Orleans. She missed home—po'boy sandwiches overflowing with fried shrimp, strolling along the Garden District, listening to live music at the Bent Note. Sadly, there was no such thing as going home by merely clicking a pair of ruby slippers together.

"We should be at the safe house within minutes," Chase said.

They turned onto a narrow street flanked by five-story buildings. The façade looked centuries old, with shuttered windows and balconies. Chase pulled into a driveway barricaded by a six-foot black wrought iron fence.

"Wait here," he said, jumping out of the car. He jogged to a discreet keypad near the corner of the terracotta building. Each shuttered window displayed ornate floral pediments. Through the windshield, the building reminded Blade of the Spanish colonial architecture on Jackson Square where, according to her friend Madam Avril, tortured souls roamed the historic structures. With over two millennia of history, it wouldn't surprise her to hear tales of the ghosts of gladiators or Roman soldiers haunting the Colosseum or streets of the Eternal City.

The fence slowly opened to a small parking lot on the side of the building as Chase hurried back. Four parking stalls were empty.

"There's a light on inside the building," Blade said. "That's a good sign, right?"

He shrugged his shoulders, noncommittal, as he pulled the car into the small lot and claimed one of the stalls.

A shiver ran through her body as they covered the short distance from the parking lot to the building. After the rain, the night air felt wet and cold. There were no pedestrians, only a single scooter traveling along the desolate street.

"Now what?" Blade said.

"We go in." He placed his hand on a touchscreen pad near the front door. A menacing bronze lion's head adorned the lintel, and not for the first time did she begin to second-guess herself. Still, she followed him through the threshold, hoping to see Vivienne. The living room, devoid of personality, stood empty.

Chase's shoulders slumped as he trudged through the house to another door. Lagging behind, she felt ashamed at failing to notice how heavily the fate of his friends weighed on him. She wanted to touch his shoulder, to commiserate with him. But the moment vanished, just like every other time she'd been tempted to show any authentic emotion with a man.

He placed his thumb on a fingerprint scanner and the door popped open, allowing a sliver of light to shine through. His hand, skinned and raw, grabbed the door and flung it open to reveal stairs leading to a converted basement. They bounded to the bottom of the stairs and stood in an open area filled with computer stations and monitors. She heard rather than saw someone launch at Chase. Blade's muscles tightened, but before she could move, Chase had caught a woman around the waist and twirled her around the room. A loud *whoop* erupted from his throat.

Xiu—not Vivienne.

There was no one else in the room.

"Have you heard from anyone?" Chase asked with a hint of optimism.

Xiu lowered her eyes. "Not yet. I've been reviewing all the surveillance footage I could find." She glanced at Blade before addressing her friend. "A team snatched Vivienne off the street but left Paolo alive. The van headed south, but I lost them," she ended in a whisper.

He rubbed his face, then looked heavenward. "I'm going to get rid of the car. When I get back, we'll sift through every piece of intel we have."

Observing the other woman's lingering gaze as Chase left the basement, Blade thought, *She's in love with him.* Sadly, Xiu couldn't hope to compete with a ghost who not only held his heart but had saved him with a sacrificial act so profound that his sense of honor and chivalry would never betray her.

Not sure how to articulate her own feelings about Shen's sacrifice, Blade said softly, "Shen—I'm so…"

Xiu held up a hand to stop her. For the first time, she saw Xiu's features soften. "Shen vowed to give his life for others. There is no

169

greater love than that. If he could speak, it would be to assure you he is in a better place."

A better place. Words failed her. Everyone grieved in their own way. Blade closed her eyes, and for the first time since her mother's death, pondered the notion of an afterlife. Her mother had hated confined spaces, but her father had refused to consider cremation. As groundskeepers lowered the casket into the ground, Blade wondered what her mother would think about the ceremony. For months afterward, nightmares of her mom in complete darkness, underground, with no way to escape, plagued her. Perhaps Christianity, with its promise of eternal life, was better than facing death with no hope.

"Any ideas on where to start?" Blade asked.

The IT genius hesitated for a moment before moving to a computer station. "The business card you gave me from Aebischer-Graf Properties led to this." Her fingers flew over the keyboard, eventually opening a folder that contained dozens of documents. "One of René Martel's holding companies purchased a chalet in Gstaad five years ago."

"How is this relevant?"

"Gstaad is a two-hour drive from Geneva. I've downloaded a copy of the deed, a map, and a list of surveillance equipment purchased for the property. The equipment includes fiber-optic cable, heat-detection and night-vision cameras, and even a few drones. Overkill for a chalet unless that chalet is owned by a very paranoid and wealthy individual."

Behind them, Chase cleared his throat. The two women jumped in unison. "Good thing I'm not one of Martel's mercenaries, or you'd be toast."

"I take it you've been eavesdropping," Xiu said, her brows knitting together. "There is more. I hacked into the Bern Cantonal Police network. An American woman died at a high-end resort in Gstaad earlier today, but the authorities are keeping a lid on the news."

"Who is the American?" Chase said.

"Miranda Williamson. Senator Daniel Williamson's wife."

"What does this have to do with Martel?" Blade said.

"I realize this all seems circumstantial, but I've looked into Senator Williamson's financials. He is living the lifestyle of someone who spends millions rather than the two hundred thousand he earns annually. Neither the Senator nor his wife have wealthy relatives. One has to wonder where the cash inflow is coming from."

"There must be a connection between Martel and Williamson. It's like a vortex forming in and around Geneva." Chase began to pace around the room. "Vivienne was captured alive. They could have killed her on the spot."

Blade leaned against a wall, exhausted and discouraged. It felt like they were spinning their wheels. "How are we going to get Vivienne back and stop the attack on the UN?"

"Divide and conquer," Chase said.

"There's only three of us," Blade said.

"More than enough to take care of business. Trust me." Chase stopped in front of her, his two hands pressing into each of her shoulders. "The next few hours are going to be hell. I need to know I can count on you."

Blade had never been part of a team, not in high school or her brief stint at college or her chosen career. Her whole life had been self-centered and competitive, always striving to be better than someone else. Chase and Xiu needed her. Surprisingly, she did trust Chase, without any doubt or hesitation.

"I won't let you down."

He nodded. "Xiu, let's take another look at the map. We're also going to need the jet."

CHAPTER
THIRTY-FIVE

November 29, 7:30 p.m.
Gstaad, Switzerland

Vivienne ran her hands over the black silk, feeling half-naked in the backless dress that René had insisted she wear for dinner. At first, she had refused to even touch the dress, much less wear it. But when the same burly security guard from earlier threatened to dress her himself, she relented.

The dress was exquisite. She couldn't help but admire her reflection in front of a floor mirror, imagining Luc's reaction to the side-slit that exposed her leg from ankle to thigh. At this moment, she felt like a woman rather than a soldier—sexy and desirable. She walked to the window, drinking in the beauty of freshly fallen snow. She could not deny her love for Luc any longer. So many wasted years of pretending they were merely friends, comrades-in-arms. Shame and guilt, responsibility and duty, always seemed to form an indestructible wedge between them.

If I get out of this alive, I'm asking him to marry me. To hell with convention.

She closed her eyes against the reality of what awaited her. René would not let her go. No matter what happened, she could not falter. Genevieve's life was at stake.

A fist pounded on the door before the security guard barged in. "Mr. Martel wants to have a word." He grabbed her upper arm and jerked her in front of him. His massive arms and chest strained against the knit turtleneck he wore. The man was like an army tank, all power and bluster.

She carefully descended the stairs, her three-inch heels clicking against the hardwood.

"The tattoo on your back is making me horny," Tank said. "Maybe you can show me the whole blade when I take you back to your room."

Vivienne often forgot about the body art that decorated the length of her spine. For twenty years, this spear had reminded her of the first Roman soldier who had dared risk his own life to save Christians during the great fire in Rome, and her own commitment to the oath she'd sworn.

"It isn't a blade, moron. It's a spear."

"Bitch," the guard said, seizing her forearm and squeezing until his fingers hit bone.

"I think you forget I'm René's sister. Touch me again, and he will probably kill you. If he doesn't, I will."

With two remaining stairs left, he shoved her—hard. Uncuffed, she caught herself on the handrail.

She stood at the bottom of the stairs, taking in the immense living area. A stone fireplace dominated the room, a roaring fire warming its occupants. Over the mantel hung a bull's head with two swords above it crossed at their tips. René had always fancied himself a man with the heart of a fearless matador.

Impatient, the guard grabbed her wrist and pulled her behind him, throwing her onto a leather sofa. "Threaten me again and I'll cut you," Tank said, holding a switchblade against her cheek.

Before she could respond, Tank stood ramrod straight with a look of disbelief, then emptiness before his knees gave way. Standing behind him were René and two other guards, one of which held a bloodied knife in his right hand.

"I detest bullies," René said. "Get this man out of here before he ruins the carpet."

Each guard grabbed the man under his arms and dragged him out, blood soaking the dead man's shirt.

"Brawn doesn't always equate to brains," René said, breaking the silence. "Don't think me weak because of our familial connection. No one lays a hand on you unless I order it."

René sat on the sofa across from her, casually crossing his legs as the fire crackled in the grate. He wore a black and silver baroque jacquard tuxedo. Both were overdressed for the casual ambiance of the room.

The overhead antler chandelier reminded her of the rustic inn she'd visited in Wyoming after one of her more difficult rescue operations. No one within the Soldati guessed her trip encompassed more than recuperation. It coincided with one of Genevieve's knife-throwing competitions. Just before Marie died. Vivienne could still remember the mountain breeze filled with the faint scent of pine trees as her daughter, poised and unshakable, outperformed most of the competition. It was a bittersweet moment filled with love, pride, regret, and sorrow.

"You look stunning, Vivienne. After all these years, I never doubted that you and I would find each other again."

"We haven't exactly found each other."

"True. But you are here, back in my life. I hope we can amuse ourselves during your last few days on earth." René slapped his hands on his knees and stood. "I have a surprise for you, *hermana*."

He snapped his fingers and a guard brought in a woman strapped to a wheelchair. Wide gray duct tape covered her mouth, each ankle securely tied to a chair leg. A red silk scarf bound her hands, which rested on her lap. The once-expensive clothes, rumpled and torn, looked as though she'd been wearing them for days. Vivienne didn't recognize the woman.

"I assume the two of you are acquainted," René said.

Vivienne looked into the eyes of the younger woman and saw stark, naked hatred. Her eyes flashed hot, like twin lumps of coal that had burned for hours. Proximity to René had that effect on people.

"I've never met this woman in my life," Vivienne said.

Alarm settled into her bones. *Why should I know her?*

"Don't lie to me!" He held up his index finger, giving himself a moment to collect himself. "We are quite isolated here. I'm confident we won't be disturbed," René said as he moved the furniture to clear a space. "But as a precaution, I also have guards stationed around the perimeter of the property." He laid out a thick plastic sheet, covering the area rug.

"I need information from the two of you, and I'm afraid it may take some coaxing. But I'm sure in the end, I will get what I want."

Vivienne's heart rate began to accelerate. *Lord, I shall not fear, for you are with me.*

René hefted a side table to the middle of the plastic sheet and squared the wheelchair to it.

"Ready to tell the truth, *hermana*?" he said.

She kept her eyes fixed on the plastic, praying for strength and agility. The plastic made a crunching sound as he moved closer.

"No?" He held her chin in his hand and forced her head up. "I think you are stalling." He slapped her hard across the face. "Perhaps that will clear your head."

Visibly shaken, she cowered in the corner of the sofa, drawing her legs off the floor.

"Such an actress," he said, towering over her. "A Martel never cowers."

This could be her only chance. She broke free from his grasp and drove the heel of her hand into his nose. Blood gushed as he sagged to the floor. Grabbing a handful of hair, Vivienne pulled his head back then slammed his face into her knee. He fell on his side, stunned. Quickly, she wrapped her hands around his neck, willing all her strength to cut off vital oxygen.

"Die," Vivienne whispered. "Die."

Something cool rubbed against her temple—a gun muzzle.

In her bloodlust, she had failed to see or hear a security guard enter the room.

Damn, damn, damn!

Vivienne couldn't bring herself to look at the other woman. With the failed attack on René, neither one would make it out alive.

A second security guard hurried into the room and helped René rise to his feet. He rested his hands on the sofa, gulping air through his mouth. The slight bruising under his eyes gave Vivienne a sense of victory.

"*Hermano*," she said, gloating over his distress. "Every time you look in the mirror, you will think of me. The sister who almost killed you."

"You will pay for this. But not before I interrogate Graciela." René spewed out a glob of blood and mucus on the pristine plastic.

Vivienne knew her twin's strengths and weaknesses, even after all the years of separation.

"You think you are so superior. You've been duped for months, and you never realized it until last week. The great René Martel, bested by his sister and a group of Christians. I feel sorry for you."

"Tie her up," he ordered. "And make it hurt."

CHAPTER
THIRTY-SIX

November 29, 8:30 p.m.
Gstaad, Switzerland

Blood splatter covered the table, plastic sheet, and René's once-crisp white shirt. Graciela sat slumped in the chair, passed out from the pain. Her bloody hands lay limp in her lap.

Vivienne viciously rubbed at a fleck of blood on her wrist, wishing she could obliterate the past hour. Not one word or scream, not even a whimper escaped Graciela as René tortured her. Over and over, he'd asked Vivienne how she'd made contact with the woman. But Vivienne repeatedly denied an association with Graciela or anyone else in his organization. God, she wanted to weep for this innocent woman. Graciela had paid an enormous price for Vivienne's vow of silence.

Guilt and shame clung to her like old friends. It took all her willpower and resolve to keep Alec's secret. Intimately aware of René's character, she and Graciela were already dead—but Genevieve could still be saved.

René sighed as he poured himself a glass of red wine. "I don't believe you, *hermana.* You are a strong woman. Why didn't I realize this earlier about you?" He sat on the sofa next to her, keeping a respectful distance. He sipped his wine, taking Vivienne's bound hands in his. "Who knew you possessed the heart of a lion? You are just as ruthless as I am. We could rule together. Just tell me who has betrayed me."

Vivienne shook her head. "How many times do I need to say it? I didn't need an informant. You are so predictable. Once we observed your attempt to blow the armament plant in India, we surveilled you and your pathetic force," she sneered. "Especially the man with tattoos. He stands out in a crowd."

Graciela began to groan like a wounded animal in a cage. Her body shifted in the chair. When she tried to use her hands for leverage, the moan became an agonized cry.

René slipped behind her, gently rubbing his knuckles along her collarbone. Graciela sat up straighter, consciousness returning, her eyes locking onto Vivienne's.

"Please take the tape off her mouth," Vivienne pleaded.

"Why, so she can tell more lies?" His hands splayed open, caressing Graciela's shoulders. Vivienne saw her wince, but no other sound came from behind the tape. This woman would not give René the satisfaction of knowing his touch caused her pain.

He brought his fingers around Graciela's neck and began to exert pressure.

"*Alto,* René," Vivienne cried, reliving the moment her brother had choked the life out of her John in the middle of a park on a beautiful September evening. Even after twenty-seven years, she still felt the anguish of that moment in the pit of her stomach.

"Do you honestly think you can win this game?" he said, releasing his hold on Graciela. He made a show of admiring his hands. "I hold the power of life and death, *hermana.*"

"Remember when father locked us in the closet for fighting over a toy? We were about seven years old. With no light, I was afraid. You took my hand and swore nothing would happen to either of us. That you and I would live and die together."

His eyes narrowed. "Is there a point to this story?"

Vivienne sneered. "For years, you have lived in my dreams. Ones where I killed you. Sometimes I stabbed you to death, other times I shot you, and tonight I almost strangled you—a dream come true! We have lived together. And we will die together."

René laughed, a rich, deep rumble that made Vivienne's hair stand on end.

"What *mierda*."

His red-rimmed eyes grew intense. He bent to wrap his arms around Graciela from behind, caressing her cheek with his right hand. He looked at Vivienne and beamed. It was the same expression she'd seen when René wrapped his hands around John's throat. Except this time, rather than hide behind bushes, she launched herself at her brother. But with her ankles bound together, she landed on her hands and knees instead. With a grunt of satisfaction, he cupped Gabriella's chin in one hand, and lovingly placed the other hand on her head. In one swift motion, he jerked her head up at an angle and twisted, effectively breaking her neck.

Shock turned to rage.

He bowed as if performing to an audience. "Do not insult my intelligence again. I could easily do the same to you."

"I swear I will kill you, René," she said, hitting the floor with her fists.

"No, *hermana*, when you have seen my *pièce de résistance*, I will kill you."

God, forgive my silence.

After the two security guards wheeled Graciela's body out of the room, René ordered one of them to keep Vivienne under constant supervision. Cutting the bindings around her ankles, the guard shepherded her back to the bedroom.

"I've been ordered to secure you," the guard said curtly. "Bed or chair?"

Vivienne made a show of heading to the chair, inching closer to the guard. Without warning, she pivoted, and with a cracking kick to the knee, the guard reflexively bent to protect himself. With her hands bound, she managed to swing into his temple like a baseball player hitting a home run.

"This…is…for…Graciela." Again and again she kicked his torso until she was spent.

She thought about killing the guard, but she couldn't bring herself to *actually* kill someone defenseless—no matter the circumstances. She did find a Swiss Army knife in his pocket and went about cutting the bindings around her wrists.

Free at last.

Vivienne yanked off the evening gown and ripped it to shreds. If only she could rip apart her memories of René so easily. After rummaging through the closet, she dressed in a new pair of jeans and pullover sweater. Much better. Someone had left her combat boots on the floor. Once laced and tied, she strode over to the guard and kicked him hard in the kidney, adding to his pain.

"And that's for me."

Returning to the chair, she pulled a throw over her legs. If only she'd gone to the *policia* after John's murder. Regret weighed heavy on her. Perhaps she could have kept Genevieve and been part of her life. René would have been sent to prison or executed. Many lives would have been saved if she'd believed in God and leaned on His strength.

René wasn't specific, but she could feel the time in her hourglass running out. She leaned into the night. Storm clouds still obscured the moon and stars, but she'd much rather see the snow. The world renewing itself.

She continued to look into the darkness, scanning the area for a rescue team. Not that she expected one. The threat to the UN took precedence over one life. The Soldati could not be compromised, even if that meant sacrificing a soldier of Christ.

A shard of moonlight shone on the mountain peaks, reminding her of Psalm 23: *...though I walk through the valley of the shadow of death, I will fear no evil; for You are with me.*

"Lord, if it be your will, let me die bravely."

CHAPTER
THIRTY-SEVEN

November 29, 9:35 p.m.
Over Italy

Blade noted the dome of St. Peter's Basilica disappear from view as the jet banked northward.

At the safe house, Chase had decided that Xiu would remain in Rome to monitor and direct activity while he and Blade would fly to Switzerland. Before leaving, she took a shower and changed clothes, thanks to Xiu's scavenging. She'd felt refreshed, albeit exhausted. There would be time enough to sleep once they'd recovered Vivienne and stopped Martel.

Across the jet's narrow aisle, Chase pulled out a laptop and map from a bag and laid them on the table where Blade sat. He settled in opposite her.

"We could be wrong about finding Martel and Vivienne in Gstaad," Blade said, examining the location of the chalet on the map.

"We follow the trail. That's all we can do."

"I shouldn't have lost my temper the last time I spoke to her."

"Don't beat yourself up. Everyone needs to let off a little steam. Vivienne understands that more than most."

"How do *you* let off a little steam?"

Chase grinned, and Blade's defenses melted into that smile. In the last few days, she had observed his combat mode: menacing, fierce, explosive. He'd also exhibited a tender side whenever he'd spoken of his late wife. She found herself drawn to him, willing to follow his lead. He wasn't patient like Joe Mancini, but the two men shared a no-nonsense attitude. She respected that.

"Not by throwing knives," he said, easing back in his chair.

"The power of a knife depends upon the person wielding the blade." To make her point, she padded to the galley and withdrew a knife from one of the drawers. "In the right hands, it can be a prop," she said, balancing the knife on her index finger while stepping closer to him. "Or a razor," she said, drawing the knife close to his cheek. "Even piercing a heart," she said, bending forward and whispering in his ear.

"I'll keep that in mind," he said, his cheeks reddening. "I think I could use a glass of water."

A fire extinguisher, more like it.

Blade was tempted to laugh at his awkward attempts to appear cool and unruffled. He took his time at the small icebox, reaching for a water bottle and chugging half of it down before retaking a seat.

"We have a little over an hour to finalize our plan," he explained. "We fly into Geneva, where I disembark to deal with the UN attack. You'll stay onboard and fly to Gstaad. They have a private airfield there."

"We're splitting up?" she said, her voice rising an octave. "I thought we were in this together."

Chase responded, flat and professional. "I can't be in two places at once, and my primary responsibility is to the UN. Vivienne would understand." He took her hand in his. "I don't expect you to make contact. This is a reconnaissance mission only. Xiu has rented a chalet a half-mile from Martel's. You'll be in direct communication with her the entire time and she can guide you through the paces."

She pulled her hand from his. "What sort of information do you need?"

"Report anything and everything. The number and types of vehicles parked there, the number of guards you see, whether you get a visual of Vivienne or Martel inside the chalet."

"How in the hell is that helpful? You expect me to sit on my hands if I see Vivienne? What if she's hurt? Do I call the police?"

"I should be back in Gstaad with an extraction team in the morning. I can't promise anything more."

I thought you were one of the good guys," she said. "A man of honor, no soldier left behind and all that drivel." She shook her head, releasing a bitter laugh. "You said Vivienne saved your life. Some repayment."

"We risk our lives every day and make hard choices," Chase said curtly. "Shen sacrificed his life for ours. I don't expect an entertainer to understand a soldier's moral code."

"You claim the Soldati are family. It's better to be an orphan than part of *this*." She stood, gathering the map and papers in a fury. "I'll be sure to call Xiu for further instructions. From this point on, don't bother trying to contact me. But if Vivienne's already dead, I'll be coming for you," Blade said, jabbing a finger into his chest.

Blade stayed locked in the aft cabin while Chase disembarked at Geneva as planned. She wouldn't give him the satisfaction of betraying to him how inadequate she felt. The two of them—together—had made it out of Florence alive. And at this critical juncture, he thought it a good idea to separate. No one at the UN would believe Chase without proof. If only the two had stayed together. She felt sure they could have subdued Martel and forced him to make a confession.

Chase, just like her father, had proven to be stubborn and obstinate to the core. Although she'd hoped he would change his mind, he'd left without saying a word.

An ass to the end.

Cold air greeted her as she exited the plane. The airstrip lay in a valley flanked by snow-covered peaks. According to Google, Gstaad was filled with ski slopes, bike trails, upscale shopping, and luxury hotels that catered to the wealthy. A winter wonderland for the likes of Martel.

Marie would tell her this was a fool's errand. In this case, she would agree. But Blade could do this, it was a simple enough task. Drive to a chalet, call Xiu, follow instructions, and wait for Chase to show up with reinforcements. Common sense told her Martel would be on high alert after Mallorca. Would a half-mile distance between the chalets be enough? Martel would expect a rescue attempt by anyone surviving the blast in Florence. She couldn't afford to underestimate him—not if she wanted to live.

Ever since she'd arrived on Mallorca, her life had spiraled out of control, as if she were on a Tilt-A-Whirl at the carnival. Her freedom hijacked. Her identity gutted. Martel wasn't invincible and she might be the woman to prove it. She slung her backpack over her shoulder and headed for the only lit building along the runway.

A dark blue Audi Q3 sat parked about one hundred feet away. Unusual to see an SUV this far on the tarmac...granted, she knew little about private airstrips. The glow from a cell phone cast a garish light onto a woman, reminding Blade of the B-movie horror films she loved.

The SUV door opened and the woman stepped out. It was obvious she was here for Blade.

"Genevieve Broussard?" the woman said in a Scandinavian accent.

Blade released a shaky breath. Thoughts of being murdered in this deserted place flitted through her. She evaluated the threat standing near her. The Scandinavian was every inch the millennial executive, dressed in a black pantsuit, looking severe with her blonde hair pulled tight into a chignon. She seemed harmless enough, but Blade slipped the backpack off her shoulder and set it on the ground six feet away from the woman, allowing her space to drive a *chassé bas* to the knee or deliver a back leg sweep that would knock the woman off-balance.

"This is for you," the millennial said, extending a white envelope. "I've also left the car keys and a phone in the center console."

"I don't understand," Blade said, accepting the envelope.

"Read the card inside the envelope. It explains everything." The young woman turned on her heels and headed to the terminal.

Perplexed, Blade retrieved her backpack and took a seat behind the wheel of the Audi. With the interior light on, she examined the contents of the envelope. She found money, a passport, and a handwritten card written in a woman's hand.

. . .

Blade, I called in a few favors. The car is yours. Check out the cargo area. It's the best I could do. C

"C"—Chase, a man of few words.

Curious, she pressed the button on the key fob to open the cargo door. Nestled among steel cases, presumably the surveillance equipment, lay a wooden box. Blade pulled it to her, drawing it closer to the light. An antique, possibly walnut or other dark wood. She lifted the lid to reveal ten knives, identical to the ones she used during performances. Shivering and unsure whether to laugh or cry, she cradled one of the knives in her hand. Chase knew her better than she thought. The gift gave her a slice of the familiar, a means to protect herself if need be. She pressed the button to close the door, taking the knives with her.

This car didn't rival the Lamborghini in speed or design, but the Audi was considered by some as a status symbol. An over-dressed, over-paid clod had taken her out to dinner about a year ago, driving an Audi GT. He thought the price tag for getting laid would be a mere high-priced meal and bottle of wine. His ego surpassed the car. She could still remember the look of surprise when, after he tried to force his way into her apartment, she delivered a chassé frontal kick that knocked him out cold. She never dismissed the element of surprise. Perhaps this would work.

The address to the rented chalet was already entered into the navigational system. With a few changes, she would soon find out if their hunch was right. Blade pressed her foot on the gas, revving the engine, listening to the power under the hood. She gripped the tan leather steering wheel and floored the accelerator. Delicate snowflakes twinkled in the glow of the headlights, disappearing instantly upon hitting the windshield. Thirty minutes to the chalet, perhaps a bit longer if the weather continued to escalate. She turned on the stereo system, not daring to think about the shitstorm she was hurtling toward.

CHAPTER
THIRTY-EIGHT

November 30, 12:33 a.m.
Gstaad, Switzerland

The blanket of snow made it nearly impossible to see the road, although pinpoints of light from a scattering of chalets filtered through the trees. Her last vacation with her mother had been at Snowmass in Colorado. It had been snowing on that particular day, too, when Marie, always a competitor, had challenged her to a downhill ski race. Blade recalled the surge of power she'd felt on that mountain, the feeling of invincibility as she mastered the slope, her legs easily moving in rhythm as she passed her mother to the imaginary finish line.

What she needed was that same power, that feeling of invincibility to go up against Martel and his band of mercenaries. With a mile left to go, Blade pulled into a driveway, leaving the engine running and lights on. Time was running out for Vivienne, she was sure of it.

Removing two knives from the antique box, she opened the car door and popped the cargo door. Laughter and the smell of burning wood carried on the cold wind. Nothing like a party to keep warm on a winter's night. She could use a brandy just about now to steady her nerves.

Will I ever warm my hands over an open fire with friends or family? Or am I destined to be alone?

Blade placed the knives on a steel case and surveyed the cargo area once again. There had to be something more useful than surveillance equipment. She stacked the cases to one side until revealing something dark in the corner. Grabbing the coarse material, she held it out before her—a tactical vest. It probably weighed around five pounds, but would it really stop a bullet? Once she strapped the vest in place, she immediately felt ungainly. It wasn't the weight, but the restriction. Afraid it would inhibit her fluidity, she thought *Always test the equipment before a performance.*

She snatched up the two knives, and taking a stance in the low beam of the headlights, aimed at a large burl on one of the pine trees. Her usual throw felt awkward and unnatural. She missed by about three inches. Unacceptable—this wasn't going to work.

"Screw it," Blade said, taking off the vest and throwing it back amid the containers. She'd meet Martel on her own terms. The Great Mancini always said nothing thrilled an audience more than the unexpected. Martel would be far from thrilled, but perhaps doing the unexpected would give her an edge.

The three-story chalet stood like a lighthouse, a stalwart against the onslaught of swirling snow. Although it was after midnight, floor-to-ceiling windows cast a warm, candlelit glow in the darkness. A refuge in the storm. A ridge of pine trees bordered the structure on three sides, allowing an unobstructed access to the circular drive and front door.

Blade slowed the Audi into the driveway. Shadowy figures emerged from the blackness, encircling the car. *What the hell am I doing here? I should have kept driving to the rental rather than play Mission Impossible.* Sheer will moved her to stop the car and open the driver's door.

After taking a few cautious steps, one of the men threw her against the hood, sweeping her legs apart as a woman snickered in front of her, gun drawn. As he patted her down, his hands lingered over her breasts then traveled further below her hips. His touch made her skin crawl.

"She's clean." The man turned her around roughly and shoved her hard to the ground.

No one touched her without permission.

She vaulted up, attacking with a *fouetté* roundhouse kick followed with a *crochet* blow to his temple. A knockout in the first round.

Damn, that hurt. Her hand tingled from the cold and contact with the man's bone.

The woman aimed her gun directly at Blade's torso.

"Martel!" Blade yelled. "Call off your dog!"

A wash of light flooded the front porch as the door opened, revealing Vivienne with her hands tied in front of her and gray duct tape across her mouth. Martel stood behind her with a gun pointed to her right temple.

"*Déjala pasar,*" Martel called to the guard. Let her pass.

The guard lowered her weapon and motioned for Blade to move ahead with a slight nod of her head.

No one showed much concern over the lifeless man on the snow-packed ground. Blade squared her shoulders, drew back her foot, and kicked him in the stomach before continuing on.

"*Bienvenido,*" Martel said, keeping his hand on Vivienne's neck as he drew her back into the chalet after him. "You have inherited the Martel *fuego.* I wonder what else you've inherited from our bloodline."

She found herself in an immense, open room that welcomed with a huge stone fireplace alight with a roaring fire. A black bull's head mounted above the fireplace mantel stared at her with empty glass eyes.

Blade held her hands to the fire, giving herself time to stop shaking. *This is insane. What was my plan again? Walk in and rescue Vivienne? Me against all these professional killers?*

As if summoned by her thoughts, armed men appeared, guns at their side. There could be a dozen of Martel's force here. All with weapons, all trained to kill. She had been impulsive, charging into a situation without any reconnaissance. She and Vivienne would need nothing less than a miracle to escape.

Sparks flew from the crackling fire. A newspaper sat on top of the firewood, probably to be used as kindling. A picture of President Argyle dominated the front page above the fold. He would be dead within hours unless Chase convinced the authorities about Martel's threat.

Her gaze swept past the beautifully decorated great room to observe the red stains marring one of the upholstered chairs, a broken piece of glass resting against a floorboard, and the marks left by a coffee table on the multi-colored rug. The room had been cleaned, but not thoroughly.

Eventually, Blade allowed her gaze to fall on Vivienne. Her birth mother. The woman who'd desperately wanted to protect her from Martel, and did the only thing she could—given her to a loving couple to raise an entire continent away. She couldn't fathom the emotional pain Vivienne suffered these many years. And it might be too late to thank her. Assure her the decision had been the right one.

"Leave us," Martel ordered. The guards, conditioned to obey commands, double-timed out of the room.

If there is a God, please let us live through this.

"Only a coward would hold a gun against a defenseless woman," Blade finally said.

"My sister is hardly defenseless."

Blade almost smiled, examining Martel's face. It looked like he'd been through a few rounds in the ring. Maybe she had inherited the Martel fire. If she could free Vivienne, the two of them, together, might just stand a chance.

Alec lay prone against soft snowpack, cursing the storm as the cold seeped through his alpine camo snowsuit. He'd elected to cover the last two miles to the chalet by cross-country skiing. Every muscle ached from the exertion. The wind-driven snow reduced visibility. At this distance, he couldn't see into the chalet, much less shoot anything with any accuracy.

Luck and a pair of brass balls had landed him here—his one shot to unseat the Spaniard and take control of Martel's illegal operation. Only a few people knew the Spaniard's identity—and most were dead. Martel and Vivienne would be killed in an unfortunate accident, leaving no loose ends. And the investors in Martel's scheme would be eradicated, like any gutter rat. He didn't need to dominate the world, he only wanted his small slice to control. Since he ran the daily operations of the business, the transition would be seamless. And he would not make the same mistake Martel had made.

Alec would trust no one.

Headlights emerged through the storm. Who the hell could be arriving at this hour? He reached for his rifle and looked through the night-vision scope.

"Bollocks," he said slowly, as he observed a blue Audi stop in front of the chalet. He pounded the ground with a gloved fist when he spied Blade.

The only person, the one loose end he couldn't bring himself to destroy. The last time he'd seen her she'd stood covered in debris, with that dark-haired nob left alive. Fighting side-by-side with her at that dumpy bar in New Orleans had affected him. Without hesitation, she'd thrown herself into the fray to protect him, pegging him an underdog worth saving. The only woman in his entire life who had come to his defense. Bloody hell, the woman continually amazed him.

Damn. He shook his head.

He brought the night vision scope to his eye again. A two-man security detail approached Blade. There was some sort of kerfuffle that was tough to track, and only one guard remained in view. Then the porch light illuminated Martel as he opened the door with Vivienne shielding him. Blade slogged through the falling snow to the door, her posture defiant and utterly confident.

When the door closed, the upright security guard helped the one who'd disappeared to his unsteady feet. *What a woman.* In another moment, she'd no doubt have dispatched the second guard.

Alec donned a pair of snowshoes, gathered his pack, and headed to the tree line. He would need a better position to lock on a target through this storm.

Time was running out.

CHAPTER
THIRTY-NINE

November 30, 12:49 a.m.
Gstaad, Switzerland

Sweat trickled down Blade's spine. The cavalry wasn't coming. Chase wasn't coming. How stupid she'd been to believe he cared about her or Vivienne. The Navy Seal valued honor above all else, yet he had abandoned them to save the world.

Screw the world.

"Sit," Martel ordered.

"Not before you remove the tape from my mother's mouth."

He raised the gun and fired.

Blade staggered back, first from the shock, then from the intense pain. The bullet had passed through her right arm and struck the stone fireplace, showering her with chunks of rock and dust. The wound felt like a red hot poker being thrust through her arm. She tried to staunch the flow of blood with her left hand, to no avail. Her mind flipped a switch, returning her to the Merced River, the genesis of all disaster in her life. Standing at the water's edge, tracking Lucas's struggle to stay afloat, trying desperately to swim against the current. Then watching him disappear over the falls. Incomprehensible for a thirteen-year-old. She'd compounded the tragedy by telling the worst lie of her life that day.

This would not be that. She would use her pain and guilt against the one man who threatened to tear away her future, her very existence.

Rising to her feet, Vivienne strained at the cuffs, the tape over her mouth making it impossible to hear her muffled screams.

"You don't take orders well," Martel said coolly. "Sit next to your mother, now."

"Bastard," Blade said, standing on wobbly legs, then stumbling to the sofa. She leaned against the soft leather, leaving a smear of blood before complying.

"You found my private sanctuary. Well done, *sobrina*." His gaze fell upon Vivienne. "And you had no right to take her from me—from our *familia*."

Blade glared. "Be thankful you weren't involved in my life. I would have taken you out long ago. My friends are surrounding this place as we speak. The only way you'll be leaving here is in custody or in a body bag."

He laughed. "American crime movies." He shook his head. "Family should never lie to one another. Some members of my security team are positioned a mile away. There are no friends, no rescue party. It is just us."

"And you're delusional. What you should be considering is, how did I find you? What else aren't you aware of?"

Martel's eyes brightened. "Perhaps you can help me solve a dilemma. Which one of you should I kill first? This is *delicioso*. If I kill you first," he said, pointing the gun at Blade, "slowly and painfully, your mother will suffer more than I could ever inflict upon her. Finding her daughter, only to have me kill her." He closed his eyes.

"You should have been in the theater." Blade laughed through her pain. "You look as if you've just lost your virginity."

Vivienne warned her off with a slight shake of her head, but Blade persisted in taunting him.

"Ahhh, I get it," she said. "You were in love with your mommy and jealous of Daddy. Freud would have had a field day with you."

"I am in *control* here," Martel growled, the veins in his forehead pulsating. His hand shook visibly as he pointed the gun at her.

"Control? You've never been in control. Not when you killed my

192

father, not when you sent Alec Quinn to find me, not when you sent your mercenaries to kidnap me, and not when you attacked the Soldati headquarters. You've overreacted continually. I don't know how you've managed to amass a multi-billion dollar company with your temperament."

He tore the tape viciously from Vivienne's mouth, stripping the delicate skin underneath.

"Vivienne, tell your daughter to shut up, or I will kill her."

"You won't kill me before you attack the United Nations. Killing your audience would be too anticlimactic for you." Blade saw his look of surprise. "You didn't think I knew about that? Your grand plans to control the world are doomed."

He glowered at her for a moment with eyes narrowed to slits, then mastered himself. "You have no proof. All the plans are here," he said, tapping his head. "Believe me when I tell you everyone will be dead five minutes after my weapon is released. And you are right, Genevieve, we"—throwing his arms wide—"will have a front-row seat! The President of the United States and other government leaders will convene at ten o'clock this morning. Which means you have about nine hours to live."

"René," Vivienne begged, "there is still time to stop this madness." She spoke slowly, working her mouth awkwardly. "Ask God for forgiveness and turn your life around. I can help you."

"You think I care about forgiveness from God?"

Blade sat motionless, observing a security guard on the other side of the vast picture window light a cigarette through the snowfall. He took a long drag, the tip of the cigarette glowing through the haze until the ashes floated among the snowflakes. The man fell to his knees before toppling over. She waited for an alarm or shouts, but only the steady drone of Martel's diatribe against God filled the room. A weight lifted off her chest. They could be out of this hellhole in minutes.

Blade needed a distraction to give the Soldati time to storm the chalet. "You look like you've been hit by a sledgehammer, Uncle. My mom kicked your ass, right? I'll bet money she always bested you when you were kids."

"*Cállate!*" Martel bellowed, spittle flying from his lips. Kicking the coffee table aside, he towered over Vivienne. "For the finale, I want to see you beg for your daughter's life. On your knees, sister."

Vivienne used Blade's knee as leverage to shift from her seat to her knees, but Blade stopped her.

"My mother doesn't beg, and nor do I."

"You will get on your knees!" Martel roared.

The gun exploded.

Vivienne screamed in agony as the bullet tore through her knee. Blood splattered the sofa in bold strokes as she collapsed sideways on the sofa, holding her knee, writhing in pain.

Flecks of blood fell from Blade's clothing like red snowflakes on a cold winter's day. A dam exploded inside her, setting free a vast, white rage in which she reacted by instinct alone, pure animal survival.

Something erupted outside.

"What the hell?" Martel shrieked.

His car burned orange-bright through the stark white blanket.

Milliseconds ticked.

Now or never.

Blade bolted up despite the pain that ran the length of her arm and ran away from Martel. In a race against Martel's reaction, she lunged for the fireplace and leaped for one of the swords. She landed surefooted like a prima ballerina. Still surprised by the blast outside, Martel aimed and fired his gun wide.

She charged, screaming incoherently like a banshee, and drew the sword back with her left hand and swung. Martel's reflexes were good, but not optimal. The sword tip sliced the carotid artery, a spray of blood escaping a perfect cut.

He sank to his knees. Blood spurted through his fingers in rhythm to his heartbeat. He fell over, his breath coming in gasps.

Blade bent over the prone body. "Tell me about the attack," Blade shouted, trying desperately to shake an answer from him.

Vivienne pulled herself to her brother. "René, there is still time to pray for forgiveness."

He tried to speak, but too much blood was bubbling from his mouth. Eyes wild, terrified, he focused on Vivienne for a long moment, then stopped breathing.

"I killed him," Blade said, just above a whisper.

"No choice," Vivienne croaked. "He would have killed us."

Blade kneeled next to her uncle. With head bent, she felt light-headed, her fingers numb from the gunshot wound in her arm. Blood seemed to be everywhere—on the floor, over her clothing, over Vivienne. She had just killed another human being and felt...completely empty. Worse, no rescue party stormed the door. Abandoned, they were on their own to escape this frozen prison surrounded by a hostile force and environment.

But who shot the guard and blew up Martel's car? Was it possible there could be an enemy of Martel who could help them?

It didn't matter. Maybe other guards weren't incapacitated. If she and Vivienne stayed indoors, death would eventually find them. If they could make it outside and to her car, they might have a chance.

"We have to get out of here before the guards discover Martel is dead," Blade said.

"I can't. Just go," Vivienne said through clenched teeth. "Someone is bound to see the fire and call for help."

"I'm not leaving you," Blade said, trying to lift her.

Vivienne screamed in pain.

"I'll drag you out," Blade said, grabbing a throw from the sofa. She laid it flat, allowing Vivienne to scoot onto the soft fabric. Blade pulled on one end of the throw, straining for the front door. Just as they'd crossed the threshold, another explosion erupted, sending her flying twenty feet into the air.

Blade landed facedown in a snowdrift, gasping for air. Lifting her head, she saw a figure in white camouflage standing yards away, backlit by a wall of fire. She closed her eyes to the welcoming blackness.

CHAPTER
FORTY

November 30, 1:44 a.m.
Gstaad, Switzerland

Alec weighed his options as he observed Blade through the whirling smoke and snow flurries. The bobbies and emergency personnel would be arriving soon. He closed the distance between them, turned her over, removed a glove, and placed his hand on her chest. It rose and fell gently. Her upper arm bled, but it wasn't life-threatening. No noticeable broken bones, but the possibility of a head injury or internal bleeding still remained. Better to take her out now. He aimed a Beretta at her chest, but he couldn't bring himself to pull the trigger. *Shite.*

The heat from the fire became intense, even through the frigid cold. He dragged Blade well away from danger to an open area near the drive. Emergency personnel would see her immediately. If the storm persisted, the concern would be frostbite and hypothermia. He considered removing his jacket and draping it over her, but his DNA and fingerprints were all over it.

Fight to live another day.

Using a torch, he scanned the area, searching for Vivienne. Bloody hell, if she wasn't dead already, he *would* need to finish the job.

Something glinted in the torch's beam about forty feet away. He plodded through the snow to investigate.

Vivienne resembled a statue, posed on her side, impaled by a three-foot piece of wood to the frozen ground. Her blood seemed to freeze on contact with the packed snow. Alec drew closer, pointing the torch to her body, heedful for any sign of life.

Her breath came in short gasps.

If he fired a shot, the police would open a murder investigation rather than rule this an accident. Sirens were getting closer. Removing his jacket, he donned his snowshoes and walked backwards toward the tree line, using his coat to erase his tracks, although the steady snowfall would obliterate his presence in minutes.

Red emergency lights glistened through the snow-covered trees. No time to make it to cover. He eased onto his stomach and threw his jacket over him, effectively making him invisible in these conditions.

It was damn cold as he shivered in the darkness. He kept his Beretta close. These yokels might venture from the chalet looking for other survivors.

He heard the muffled sounds of car doors opening and closing, shouts, and radio traffic. From the timbre of voices, they must have found Blade. The disruption offered a chance to make a run—well, a clumsy snowshoe-trudge—for the trees before this area became a full-on circus.

As he struggled through the storm, he thought of Blade. She was free from Martel and the thought was exhilarating. Although that freedom had come at a high price—Vivienne's life in exchange for hers. Rather than agree to such terms, his own mum most likely would have tried to negotiate a deal. The world would be a better place with Genevieve "Blade" Broussard in it. And if she decided to follow in her mother's footsteps, he would deal with the consequences. But first, he needed to get the hell out of here.

Earlier in the day, one of his team had left a car at a vacant chalet about a half-mile from Martel's. A manageable distance to cover. His man had reported he'd also disabled the security system.

A lamp shone bright in the modest chalet's front window. Alec opened the unlocked door, gratefully shed the accursed snowshoes, and padded in stocking feet into a blissfully warm great room. He removed his bulky jacket and sat on one of the leather sofas. The wind howled outside, but he found the quaint room idyllic with its family pictures and cuckoo clock, a quilt neatly folded on the ottoman, and lace curtains on every window. Not his style, but he could really use a few hours of kip.

He took the cell phone from a zippered pocket and punched in the number.

"*Si?*" Teresa Escobar answered on the second ring.

"It's done. Arrange a meeting of investors—in two days. And Teresa, make no mistake who is in charge."

"*Mi amor*, of course, you are in charge. I have no interest in your daily operations. My board of directors is delighted with our profits, all made possible by my arrangement with René. There is no reason for change."

"Be at the rendezvous point as planned. And be punctual," he said.

"Of course. It would be gauche to keep you waiting."

He disconnected the call, congratulating himself on a well-timed performance. Of course, the daft cow would believe she and the other investors were indispensable. Teresa operated in an environment where sex equated to dividends, relationships forged from mutual gratification. She wasn't calculating enough to play this game and win. One by one, Martel's original investors would meet with an accident today, and he would be free to carve out his own empire.

Settling more deeply into the sofa and giving his weighted eyes permission to close, Alec drowsed and contemplated his relationship with Martel over the years. The man had rescued him from poverty and clearly recognized a bit of himself in the teenager. No expense was spared to educate and train Alec. In return, Alec gladly handled the more distasteful aspects of the Spaniard's enterprises. Gradually, Martel had relinquished control of his vast empire to his protégé. Alec felt sorry for the mentor he respected, but the chuffed bastard had lost his edge. Alec would never be so careless.

His mother, a heroin addict willing to do anything for a score, knew the human condition better than most. If she said it once, she said it a hundred times: *Never trust anyone but yourself.* The lessons had almost broken him, but she'd taught him well. He'd learned to never trust his own mother, her johns, social do-gooders, or anyone else on the street.

Leaving Blade alive might well bite him in the arse, but he could live with that decision. If his survival ever depended upon a choice between them, he would kill her in an instant, with no regrets.

As he drew the quilt over him and closed his eyes, he wished Blade would return to the States. With money in the bank and the talent she possessed, nothing would be impossible for her. As he drifted to sleep, he placed his hand on his chest, aware of his breath echoing Blade's as she lay on the snow.

He would see her again.

CHAPTER
FORTY-ONE

November 30, 1:48 a.m.
Gstaad, Switzerland

Fire licked the skeleton of the house, the flames gorging on the contents of the chalet. Orange ribbons of light reflected off the white carpet of snow. The sensation of light penetrated Blade's closed eyes, and she became dimly aware of sirens disturbing the sound of a crackling fire. A sharp pain penetrated her skull, and every part of her throbbed—her eyes, limbs, body. At least there were no broken bones.

Chunks of burning wood and metal lay all around her. Intense heat warmed her, although a blustery wind scattered snow through the wreckage.

Then she remembered pulling Vivienne to safety until...

Headlights blinded her as a police car braked ten feet from her. She tried to shield her eyes with her right arm, but found it wouldn't move past a few inches. Panic seized her then, a terror so deep she scrambled to the police officer who bounded from the driver's seat.

"*Ist da noch jemand drin?*" the officer yelled in German. "Is there anyone else inside?"

"My mother!" she screamed above the wind. "Find my mother!"

"*Bist du verletzt?* Are you hurt?" The officer helped her stand and led her to the passenger side of his vehicle.

Even through her haze, she considered his question ridiculous. She touched the wound on her shoulder with a shaking hand, broke off a piece of the frozen blood on her turtleneck sweater, and handed it to the police officer.

"An ambulance is on its way," the officer said, dropping the frozen blood to the ground and wiping his hand on his blue trouser leg. "Sit. You'll be warm in here."

He removed his jacket and drew it around her before running to his fellow officers, shouting in German. She barely made it out of the car before retching. In a matter of seconds, she had taken someone's life, even if that someone was Martel. She had experienced the aftermath of death, but never like this. The incredulous look on the man's face as he realized there were only moments to live. The vain, panicked attempts to stop the inevitable. His eyes, searching for something beyond anything anyone could give.

Blood stained her hands. She grabbed fists full of snow, the ice biting into her skin painfully. Uncaring, she furiously rubbed her hands together. The throbbing burning sensation in her shoulder intensified, keeping beat to the storm. If they didn't find Vivienne soon, she would die from hypothermia.

"*Ich habe sie gefunden!*" a shout echoed through the darkness. "I found her!"

Blade whirled at the sound. Staggering forward, she couldn't see fifteen feet in front of her. Fighting through the darkness, she finally came upon something illuminated by flashlights.

Vivienne.

She sucked in a breath of bitter cold air before taking two halting steps and falling to her knees, taking her mother's hand in hers. It felt like a block of ice.

A wooden stake protruded from Vivienne's side, impaling her at an odd angle to the ground. Her waxen skin and stringy wet hair, once luxurious and dark, reminded Blade of a porcelain doll she'd abandoned as a child.

Blade's hands shook uncontrollably as she tried to wipe the

snowflakes from Vivienne's face with her left hand, but the storm's steady barrage made it virtually impossible. The second officer removed his jacket and held it above Vivienne, like a makeshift umbrella. Blade looked up at the man, grateful for this small gesture of compassion.

The first officer on the scene drove the police cruiser closer, allowing its headlights to bathe Vivienne in light. The sharp beams vividly displayed her mother lying still, as if asleep in a white satin-lined coffin. Blade closed her eyes, unwilling to let this be the last image of her mother.

Other sirens could be heard in the distance. A female officer brought a blanket to cover Vivienne, and Blade gently tucked it under her.

Vivienne's eyes fluttered open, recognition immediate. Blade wanted to cradle the woman in her arms, to feel her mother against her own body, to give her the warmth she so clearly needed. Instead, she rested her forehead on Vivienne's shoulder.

"Mom," she breathed, a sob catching in her throat. There were only a few precious minutes to convey emotions that she didn't understand herself.

"So much to explain," Vivienne said feebly.

"Shhh, the ambulance is almost here. Just hang on." Feeling completely ineffectual, all she could think to do was hold Vivienne's cold hand, willing her to live through this. Never in her entire life had she prayed to God or any higher power, but it was never too late to hope for a miracle. That somehow God would intervene and let her mother live. Surely a God would not allow her to lose two mothers in a lifetime.

"I've always loved you," Vivienne wheezed through the pain and freezing cold. With one final burst of energy, she squeezed Blade's hand. "Serum. Find Alec Quinn." And with her last breath, Vivienne's body surrendered. Before Blade's eyes, the woman who had lived and breathed was reduced to an empty shell, robbed of the ability to feel love, joy, desire, or anything good that had constituted the unique personality of Vivienne Martel. Blade wept, regretting her decision to leave the Soldati headquarters without having a heartfelt conversation with her biological mother. What a waste of destiny.

A police officer pulled the blanket over Vivienne's head while the second officer drew Blade to her feet. These past few days, she'd fought hard for survival. Perhaps her mother would still be alive if Blade had kept her pride in check and stayed with her.

Emergency personnel scurried about while curious onlookers were kept back by people wearing reflective jackets. As the fire blazed, the stench of burnt bodies permeated the air.

"The ambulance is here, but first we need a statement," the first officer said, his breath condensing in the frigid air. "We have found surveillance equipment in your car. What happened here?" His tone no longer sympathetic.

Serum. Find Alec Quinn.

Vivienne, with her last words, had targeted Alec with a laser. How had the two known each other? Scenes of the past few days' events flashed through her mind, like scrutinizing an old silent movie frame by frame. To her knowledge, the two had never met, yet Vivienne's last thoughts were of Alec.

Blade shook her head. The officer was waiting for a response. Of course, they would look inside her car. And without anyone else to blame, she would be their prime suspect for arson. Once they found the remains of other bodies, she'd also be suspected of murder. No time for explanations.

Alec must be found.

With the extent of Martel's wealth and apparent illegal operations, his death would not stop the threat to the UN. On the contrary, Martel's demise provided his associates with a flawless endgame that would eventually indict a dead man. She didn't understand men like Martel or Alec in any depth, but she knew one truth: she could not find Alec without help. Blade focused inward, quieting the distractions of the waiting officer's gaze, the sirens, the smoke, and the brutal cold.

Alec would have everything to gain by Martel's death.

Bury…the…emotions. It would do no good to dwell on Vivienne's death or reconcile her own actions in killing Martel. Time for that later. What she needed was a plan.

If she could make it to the hospital…

She did what any stage performer could do on a moment's notice —faint.

Emergency personnel placed her on a stretcher and carried her to an

ambulance. As the paramedics transported her, she analyzed every interaction with Alec. Could he have been the man in the snowsuit? If so, he
would regret leaving her alive.

I will find you and make you pay, in full.

Forgiveness was not part of her vocabulary. But pursuing the truth
about Vivienne's involvement with him might be able to still the seething
in her heart. Somehow, she would break free at the hospital. Maybe
Vivienne could put in a good word for a miracle.

CHAPTER
FORTY-TWO

November 30, 3:46 a.m.
Gstaad, Switzerland

Dr. Catherine Rochat leaned over Blade's outstretched arm, methodically suturing her wound. The thirty-something woman wore thick black glasses perched low on her nose. Her delicate hands moved with precision. Blade observed the procedure with a certain detachment, numb from the shock of killing another human being—even if that human happened to be Martel—and witnessing Vivienne's death. The doctor said little about the injury, and Blade was thankful for the lack of conversation.

Behind the curtain, the emergency room buzzed with activity. Footfalls, equipment being moved, and occasional moans filled the space. She thought about how most of those patients had been brought in by a loved one. Work and ambition had kept her too busy for any meaningful relationship—romantic or otherwise. Until this moment, aloneness never bothered her. But as she listened to their conversations, the walls she'd built around her were all too evident.

Next to her bed, a mother railed against a doctor for his slow diagnosis of her young son's appendicitis. Blade wanted to applaud the young mother's wrath. *There's nothing like a mother's love.* How she ached for Marie. And Vivienne.

Blade checked the clock in the emergency room. Thirty minutes until Chase met her at the helipad. She needed to get this *done*, and get out of here.

Before arriving at the chalet, she had memorized the phone number on the smartphone given to her at the airport by the millennial executive. Presumably, the police had possession of everything left in the car, including her new passport and phone. Under the pretext of contacting a family member, she'd borrowed a phone from a young nurse and punched in the number.

Chase answered on the first ring. He was here, in Gstaad, and currently planning a rescue operation. He already knew about Vivienne and the explosion at the chalet. Thomas had made it out of Florence, but given the urgency of the situation, had made his way to Switzerland rather than reconnoiter in Rome. Thomas, working with the Ecumenical Council of Churches, tried to convince the United Nations security force to postpone the Human Rights Council meeting. Without concrete intel, the security force, presently on high alert, refused to listen to unsubstantiated hearsay. The President's address would commence on schedule.

"You are a lucky young lady," Dr. Rochat said. "The bullet passed through your arm without hitting the bone. A few inches to the left, and you would be in surgery. Your inability to move your wrist is temporary and you should regain total use of your arm with physical therapy."

They heard some sort of commotion before a short, portly man pulled open the privacy curtain. Water dripped from his black overcoat, creating small puddles all around him. The sleeves of his coat ended at the knuckles, giving him the appearance of a boy wearing his Father's Sunday best. Thin, graying hair was plastered to his head.

"Genevieve Broussard, you are wanted for questioning," he said without waiting for a reply. "You left the scene without giving a statement."

Blade almost laughed. The man reminded her of Danny DeVito, all bluster and attitude.

"I was brought here by ambulance before I could give a statement. There's a difference. I'm a victim, not a suspect."

Dr. Rochat drew herself up to her full height. "You are contaminating our emergency room, Detective Mettler. Get out before I call security." Her eyes traveled to the growing puddle on the floor.

"This woman is a suspect in a murder investigation," he said in a booming baritone, loud enough for the entire emergency room to hear.

Irritated and pressed for time, Blade shifted on the hospital bed, ready to challenge the detective. But the doctor stayed her with a hand.

"*This woman* is my patient."

The detective's dark eyes bored into her. "I'll be waiting right outside the door."

After making certain he had gone, Dr. Rochat shook her head in disgust. "*Polizei*, he thinks he can come into my emergency room and bark orders."

"You've run into him before?"

"Yes. Many times, unfortunately. Gstaad attracts tourists, which Detective Mettler loves to bully—when he can."

Fifteen minutes to showtime.

"There," the doctor said. "Once the wound heals, I don't believe anyone will ever notice the scar. I must admit I do excellent work." She smiled warmly at Blade, expecting agreement.

Blade examined her swollen arm and recalled the same being said about the scar on her face. A reminder of survival.

"What happens now?"

The doctor frowned. "You heard Detective Mettler. He will take you into custody, and the legal process begins." She cleared her throat, detaching herself from the situation. "My work here is finished. Technically, after you are released, you are no longer my patient."

Blade smiled. "Technically, I haven't received my discharge paper-work yet. You do have discharge orders in Switzerland?"

"Of course we do. This is not a third-world country."

"Then I would like to review my discharge orders with you before I'm released. I assume you will prescribe an antibiotic?" She pivoted. "I need to use the facilities. Where is the nearest restroom?"

"The lavatory is to your right."

While Dr. Rochat stepped into an adjoining room with a couple of computers and printer, Blade alighted from the hospital bed and peeked around the curtain. No one glanced her way. She grabbed the plastic bag that held her clothes.

Only one restricted access door led in and out of the emergency room. Earlier, she had noticed one of the nurses return through it from outdoors, snow still clinging to her curly hair. Smokers would endure any foul weather for a cigarette. Now that same nurse was wheeling an IV stand to one of the patients. She sidled out from behind the curtain, casually bumping into the startled nurse and apologizing before continuing to the lavatory, palming the woman's lighter in her left hand.

Once inside the lavatory, she threw on her clothes, grabbed the trash can, and removed the lid. Dumping the damp paper towels on the floor, she threw dry paper towels and unraveled a roll of toilet paper into the can.

She cracked the door open. Medical professionals rushed about, focused on their patients. Taking the lighter, she lit the edge of a paper towel and threw it into the trash can before quietly placing it just outside the lavatory behind a linen hamper. She casually stepped to the emergency room fire alarm and pulled the lever. Immediately, an alarm blared throughout the hospital.

"Fire!" she screamed.

The room erupted into pandemonium. Doctors and nurses barked orders as orderlies threw themselves into evacuating the injured. Smoke billowed from the trash can. In the panic, no one thought to grab a fire extinguisher.

Blade wedged herself under the nearest gurney and gently pulled on the top blanket to partially cover her presence. A middle-aged woman on the gurney, evidently heavily sedated, didn't notice. An orderly bashed into it, cursed, and wheeled the gurney ahead of him into the heart of the building. Peering out from between the orderly's legs, Blade saw the detective muscle his way into the emergency room before the orderly wheeled the gurney around a corner to another set of double doors. He stopped to use his key-card to deactivate the locking mechanism.

Just as the doors were closing after them, Blade saw Detective Mettler round the same corner. His beady eyes scoured the hallway until they fastened on her peeking out from behind the blanket. Their eyes locked. He made a run for the door, but his rotund body made it difficult. The doors fell shut, and the lock automatically engaged.

She scooted from her hiding place and stood, facing a surprised orderly. "Where is the helipad?"

The orderly shrank away from her, confused and rattled by the disruption. But he inadvertently glanced down the hallway to another set of doors.

Blade hoped she'd read the nonverbal signal right. "Give me your key-card," she ordered before grabbing it, then ran to what she hoped was the exit.

Somehow, the detective had managed to open the locked doors behind her. With only ten feet to freedom, Blade heard the man shout, "*Halt. Arrêt.* Stop."

She charged ahead, and not seeing a key reader, hit the push bar at a full run. Blade found herself, to her great relief, in the frigid night air within sprinting distance of a helipad where a copter was making its descent. She squinted through the driving sheets of rain that had replaced the earlier snowstorm to see Chase leaning against the chopper's cargo door frame with a rifle pointed at the exit she'd just hurtled through.

Blade rallied every bit of energy she had on reserve to run for the helicopter.

She heard a shot fired and chanced a glance behind her shoulder. Detective Mettler stood, legs braced a shoulder width apart, his arms extended with a gun firmly held in his hand. Damn, he was actually shooting at her.

Chase reached for her hand and hauled her into the cabin as a bullet hit the fuselage.

"Damn idiot," Chase said. He carefully aimed as the helicopter lifted upward. He pulled the trigger, hitting the pavement inches from the detective's foot. He leaped into the air, then barreled behind a wood column for protection.

"That got his attention."

The chopper banked hard left. Blade could see by the dim lights from the instrument panel that this was an EMS helicopter, room for three personnel and a stretcher, and every inch of space used for medical equipment. "A jet is waiting for us at the airport," Chase shouted above the noise of the blades.

Vivienne was right. The Soldati family were committed to one another and connected by a cause. She'd been a fool to think Chase would ever abandon her. Clearly, there were circumstances that took precedence over any individual. Vivienne had just given her dying breath as a testimony to her oath.

Chase's expression was a mixture of tenderness and sorrow. Without thinking, she unbuckled her safety harness, threw herself into his arms, and wept.

Wrapped in his strong arms, she had never felt so safe.

CHAPTER
FORTY-THREE

Blade swallowed hard, trying to control the rage that threatened to spill over like a pot of boiling water, bubbling and rolling to the surface. She wanted to scream at the injustice of meeting Vivienne, only to then have her snatched away in a split second.

She stopped at the threshold to the conference room, girding herself against the expected platitudes of people who would insist Vivienne was in a better place. When Marie had died, she had been disgusted by the lack of sincerity people showered on her. As an adult, she was no more prepared than she'd been at sixteen.

But there was nothing for it but to move on into the room.

"You look like hell," Thomas said, crossing to her in a few swift strides and wrapping his arms around her. Blade's breath caught in her throat before her own arms encircled him. His embrace felt like a cocoon, warm and protective. The room stilled as if it, too, grieved for Vivienne.

She pulled back, examining his face. "An injury from Florence?"

A six-inch line of stitches ran from brow to ear. "I've experienced worse."

Yes, she knew his wound ran as deep as hers. Judging from the scar around his neck, Thomas had placed his life on the line and paid a heavy price. And this morning he'd lost another beloved soldier.

"We will catch the bastard," Thomas promised. "Thanks to your briefing from the plane, Xiu has a head start on locating Alec Quinn. I've also recruited an old friend, the Reverend Grigori Lazarescu, with the Ecumenical Council of Churches. Thanks to him, we're using this conference room as our war room."

Of average height, Grigori was in his midfifties, with a mass of steel-gray hair combed back from his forehead, more hip movie star than man of God. He wore black slacks and a burgundy clerical shirt with a white tab at his Adam's apple. His radiant smile warmed her from the inside out, and she couldn't help but smile back.

"I knew your mother," he said, taking her hand in his and squeezing it gently. "I see her beauty and fire in you."

Blade reddened at the compliment, not trusting herself to speak about Vivienne.

Xiu rolled between two laptops, not bothering to look up. Some things never changed.

A blueprint of the United Nations building was spread among papers strewn over the surface of an eight-foot table.

"Where are Finn and Luc?" Blade asked, gingerly lowering herself into an empty chair near Xiu. Every muscle ached. She tried to stretch her right arm, but the stabbing pain made her wonder if she'd ever have full use of it again.

"Both in the hospital," Thomas said. "Luc hasn't heard about Vivienne. And we plan to keep both men in the dark until this is over."

Blade nodded. "Alec is here in Geneva."

"Tell me something I don't know already," Xiu snapped.

Blade's fingers curled into fists. *Keep a lid on your temper.*

"Is there anything we can do while we wait?" Chase asked, brushing aside Xiu's impatience. "What about CCTV cameras and facial recognition software to find him?"

Xiu sighed. "Switzerland uses a limited number of CCTV cameras. And, of course, I'm monitoring them. I'll tell you if and when I find him."

"Thomas, I think we have a problem," Grigori said as he looked out a second-story window. "We have company."

They all rushed to the windows. A dozen police cars surrounded the building.

"That is an understatement," Thomas said.

"Why are the police here?" Grigori asked.

"Someone doesn't like our interest in global security," Thomas said. "I'm afraid you and I are expendable at the moment. Perhaps if we're in custody, someone will listen." He checked his watch. "Just over three hours before the Human Rights Council meeting commences. Chase, you are in command. If we cannot make them listen, use any means necessary to stop this catastrophe."

"Yes, sir."

"One last order of business. Genevieve, I'm afraid you will sit this one out. I owe my friend this much. And I'm sure Xiu could use the help."

"No way are you sidelining me. I *need* to finish this. And besides, I got us here, if you'll remember. You wouldn't have any lead if not for me."

"True. But you aren't a soldier. You were shot once and almost shot again escaping the hospital. My word is final."

"Alec won't kill me. Surely we can use this to our advantage. I may not be a soldier, but I can hold my own."

"How can you be so sure?" Chase said.

"He could have killed me at the chalet but didn't."

"You're trusting a liar and murderer?" Chase said, a muscle twitching in the corner of his jaw. "What, you think he has a *crush* on you, so he won't—"

"I understand, it sounds naïve," she interrupted. "I can't explain it, but I'm a weapon to use against him."

Xiu all but rammed into Blade as she rose abruptly from her chair. "If anyone is going to have Chase's back, it's me."

"Thomas, please, I can do this."

"There is no time to argue," Thomas said, putting up a hand. "I could never win against Vivienne. You're just like your mother: impetuous, determined, and impossible. Perhaps this is for the best. At least we can keep eyes on you."

Blade couldn't help but smile.

Thomas bowed his head. "Grace be with you all."

Chase locked the door behind Thomas and Grigori and turned to Xiu and Blade.

"We need to formulate contingency plans—fast. Not that anything's leaping to mind. Gaining access into the UN building is pretty much a non-starter. Security is ridiculously tight. Posing as a repairman won't cut it."

Blade peered out the window. The trees, absent their foliage, looked naked and barren in the pre-dawn light. Police cars formed a convoy to deliver Thomas and Grigori to some mid-level official who would discount their information until everyone was dead. The snow-covered ground glistened under the streetlights. Lights…votive candles…churches.

"Father McCann," Blade said to herself. Then, with a whoop, she repeated, "Father Sean McCann."

"Who the hell is Father Sean McCann?" Chase said.

"A new friend who resides at the Vatican and may work for someone who has the juice to get us into the UN building."

CHAPTER
FORTY-FOUR

November 30, 7:10 a.m. CET
Geneva, Switzerland

Alec leaned against the French door of the posh Hotel des Bergues overlooking Lake Geneva, sipping a cup of Swiss hot chocolate. He felt like a new man after a few hours of sleep and a hearty breakfast. The gray morning promised a day filled with intermittent sunshine and a long-overdue reckoning. He planned to pull up a chair to the small balcony and watch the sunrise—something he hadn't done in ages.

Taking a deep breath, the air smelled fresh and clean after last night's storm. The streets, on the other hand, were hazardous after the snow and rain. Commuters cautiously drove on Quai des Bergues, slowly churning the snow into dirty slush.

Plans to eliminate loose ends would be executed within the hour, except for Blade and the Soldati.

November 30, 9:15 a.m. AST
Riyadh, Saudi Arabia

Muhammed Faheem swung the pheasant lure over his head, studying *Najila*, his prized peregrine falcon, as she flew in fast and straight, only to be deprived of her prey. He would subject her to a few more rounds of this training exercise, then allow her to capture the lure as a reward.

This year, he would win the falcon 400-meter race at the King Abdul Aziz Falconry Festival. Tired of being the butt of jokes for not even placing, he had paid over five hundred thousand riyals for the magnificent raptor. *Najila* circled above and stooped to the lure. Once again, Muhammed pulled the lure away at the last moment.

On the eastern horizon, a cloud of dust rolled upward. He squinted against the morning light. A black SUV was approaching him. Most likely a competitor. Falconers used this stretch of desert in Ha'il because of its wide-open space.

This time, he would allow *Najila* to capture the lure to boost her confidence. He swung the pheasant lure once again. The black SUV braked hard, directly in the line of the raptor's approach.

"What are you doing?" Muhammed yelled.

The driver should have better manners. Muhammed disliked rude and unsportsmanlike behavior. This was, after all, the sport of kings. Stalking to the driver's door, he yanked it open. Without hesitation, the driver lunged, knocking Muhammed off balance. He felt a needle penetrate his neck. He recoiled in fear and within seconds he lay on his back on the warm, bronze sand as the SUV sped away.

Through the dust, he could barely spot the outline of *Najila*, soaring above on a thermal, her wingspan distant in the sky. With deliberate effort, he lifted his left arm, protected by a leather gauntlet. As he closed his eyes, he could hear the wind blowing, sense grains of sand caress his skin, feel the soft brush of his *ghutra* on his face. A weight landed on his arm. *Alhamdulillah.* Praise be to God. He would not die alone.

***

November 30, 2:05 p.m. CST
Dongcheng District, Beijing, China

A man of his age and stature should not have to endure a mother who was such a pain in his ass. Jack Han had long ago tired of his role of tour guide—cursed because he spoke and understood the English language. Ever since his father died twenty-one years ago, his mother had welcomed family from the United States and England. Proud of her successful son, she would have them stay for weeks, sucking up his every free waking moment.

So it was with his cousin, Feng Han, who had arrived in China two days ago. Jack disliked the spoiled and entitled young man, who did not think twice about making demands on *his* time. Feng, accepted into Berkeley, had insisted on discovering the "real" China, although he did not speak one word of Chinese. This life experience would enhance his résumé, making him more desirable for prestigious internships. Yesterday, they spent the day visiting street markets. Jack's feet ached from walking for miles in uncomfortable shoes.

Today was certain to bring another rich helping of familial annoyance.

The two had arrived at the Temple of Heaven complex early to join the locals in Tai Chi among the ancient cypress trees in the park. With Feng's incessant questions, it had proven impossible to achieve the inner peace Jack sought.

After trudging through The Hall of Prayer for Good Harvests and the Circular Mount Altar, Feng swore he heard the voices of ancestors at the echo wall that surrounded the Vault of Heaven. Jack rolled his eyes. Feng wasn't the first relative to have a head-on collision with his ancestral spirits. And Jack knew he would not be the last.

"I have a conference call to take," Jack said. "I shouldn't be long. No need to hurry. I'll meet you in the park." They fist-bumped, and Jack pulled his phone from his pocket.

He ambled to a copse of trees, immersed in conversation, when a group of disruptive teenagers caught his attention. The three girls and two boys jostled each other, quickly overtaking an elderly woman. Laughing, one of the girls shoved the old woman aside, causing her to fall to one knee.

"Hey! Have some respect," Jack said, disconnecting the call to help the old woman regain her footing.

"Mind your own business," the taller boy said.

They all laughed at an inside joke. The other teenage boy hung back, openly glaring at him. Jack didn't have to take this disrespect from these hoodlums. Before he could rebuke the boy, the young man rushed forward and bashed against him, holding him close with surprising strength.

Jack felt a sting in his chest, a slight pressure, before dropping to his knees and keeling over. The teenager winked at him before running away.

This made no sense. In the last moment of his life, he thought about the great Jack Han dying on a dirty sidewalk as the old woman limped away.

November 30, 3:03 p.m. KST
Pyongyang, North Korea

Pak Yong-Chun removed his ski jacket in the warm sitting area of their suite and shouted for his mistress. The vacation at the Masikryong Ski Resort was compliments of the Workers' Party of Korea. Known for his skill in taking care of Supreme Leader's problems *before* they became problems, he had been welcomed into the family's inner circle and treated like royalty.

Upon their arrival yesterday, he and Kwan were escorted to a luxurious room. For dinner, the staff presented them with *Pansangi*, twelve dishes served in traditional bronze bowls fit for personages of his prominence. Afterward, in the privacy of their room, Kwan had served him dessert—naked.

"Kwan!" She should be waiting for him with a vodka tonic on ice. His mistress was beautiful but insolent. Her delicate exterior hid the ferociousness of her true nature. As with any feral animal, a master must prove his dominance. He generally disliked the use of force on a woman, but in some cases, he made exceptions.

He stormed into the bathroom to see a tub filled with water, rose petals drifting on the steamy surface. Lighted candles reflected off the mirror. His robe and slippers draped on a chair. A handwritten note rested on the vanity.

He smiled as he read the note out loud. "I will be with you shortly, *tongji*." Kwan's behavior demonstrated her respect for him. This is what he deserved after a day of skiing. He removed his clothes and left them in a heap. She could take care of them later. He carefully stepped into the tub. The hot water felt soothing against his legs. A chill ran through him. He sank lower in the tub, closing his eyes, fantasizing about the pleasure she would give him.

Something touched his leg. He brushed the flower petals away and scooped out a small octopus, no larger than the palm of his hand. He threw the brown-speckled creature on the floor, then grabbed a bar of soap and washed his hands. Kwan would pay for this impertinence. A disturbing prickling sensation around his mouth and lips intensified until it sent him into a panic. Standing abruptly in the tub, his legs shook until giving way, sending him bouncing roughly against one side of the tub. He eventually succeeded in hauling himself out of the water by using his arms, hitting the cold tile floor hard.

He heard the hotel room door open and close. Help had arrived.

Kwan breezed into the room and stood motionless.

"Call a doctor," he choked. He couldn't move. Paralyzed. He tried to crawl to the door, but she stopped him with her foot.

"You met my friend, a blue-ringed octopus," she said. "They are small, like me. Yet deadly, like me."

He could hear her move about in the next room. She returned with a container for the octopus.

"You will vanish as if you never existed," she said. "I will disappear as well."

After scooping the octopus into the plastic container, she closed the bathroom door behind her.

The paralysis intensified.

So many enemies, so few friends.

November 30, 8:15 a.m. CET

Geneva, Switzerland

Alec's smartphone pinged, notifying him of incoming messages. Smiling smugly, he read all three in succession. Three pawns taken off the board in less than an hour. Only one more pawn to capture. He would be king, with the queen still in play.

His eyes roved to the aluminum briefcase sitting innocently on the desk. Time to celebrate.

He called room service. "Send a chilled bottle of your best champagne to my suite."

Bloody hell, he was brilliant.

CHAPTER
FORTY-FIVE

November 30, 8:36 a.m.
Geneva, Switzerland

It's Baltic freezin'.

Alec pulled the collar of his wool coat up around his ears, hunched his shoulders, and started the short trek to the Hôtel Du Lac. The rich aroma of coffee and fresh bread wafted on the morning breeze. He crossed the street to tear along Lake Geneva. Fresh snow covered the benches, sidewalks, and boats moored at the marina.

A lone white swan glided over the ice-cold water of the lake. It reminded him of Blade, an independent woman swimming against the current. He couldn't forget the image of her lying unconscious through the smoke and fire. Vulnerable and lost in that moment. He had turned his back on her, abandoned her to allow fate to decide whether she lived or died.

A few tourists paused to admire the Brunswick Monument on the Quai du Mont-Blanc. *Tossers.* It was the bloody tomb of a duke of no notable feat except his excessive wealth, which he didn't earn. By this evening, Alec would be home in Barcelona, strumming his guitar on his terrace overlooking the Mediterranean Sea. He'd worked damn hard for his money, and he'd damn well enjoy it.

With Martel and his inner circle dead, he would manufacture a fresh start for himself. Thanks to his investment banker in London, he possessed a diversified portfolio. Gold, real estate, stocks. He could retire as the Spaniard—with no one being left alive to refute the claim—and live like a king anywhere on the planet. But first, Teresa must be sacrificed to win the game.

The dismal morning mirrored Alec's mood as he barged through the glass doors into the hotel lobby. Pretending to succumb to Teresa's charms during the past six months had made his skin crawl. She reminded him of his mum—a needy, clawing, cunning scrubber. Without a wealthy family supporting her, Teresa would probably be running an expensive escort service. She'd reserved a suite, which she'd described in detail as they made final plans over their smartphones.

Alec skirted around hotel guests as he made his way to the lift. A family of five waited for the lift door to open. Their twin boys played tug-o-war with a ball. The tallest used his weight to pull the ball from his brother's grasp, knocking into Alec. Not saying a word, he scowled at the parents. The mother smiled apologetically, obviously embarrassed. She spoke to him in a Scandinavian language, but Alec did not respond.

The lift door opened. Alec sauntered past them and turned. The father held his family back, obviously willing to wait for the next lift. Alec smiled at the family and pressed the button to the fourth floor.

"Hey, I've got something," Xiu said. Chase and Blade gathered around the monitor. "Here." Xiu pointed to a man walking past the lake.

"It's Alec," Blade said.

They moved closer to get a better look as he entered the Hôtel Du Lac with an aluminum briefcase in his right hand.

"Xiu, find out anything you can about the registered guests," Chase said. "Flag anyone who might have ties with a UN delegate or other related individuals."

Blade paced around the room while Xiu's fingers danced over the keyboard. Chase remained utterly still near the window, studying the street below, reminding her of a taut spring waiting impatiently for release.

"We don't have time to wait." Chase pulled out his smartphone from his jeans pocket.

"What are you doing?" Blade asked.

"Calling an Uber. It's about a ten-minute drive from here. If I can secure the briefcase, then we've neutralized the threat."

"Where would you begin to look? Maybe this is some sort of counter-surveillance trick. What are Xiu and I supposed to do?"

"I'll be wearing a wireless earpiece. Keep me advised."

"I'm in," Xiu said, her excitement sparking the room. "There are numerous dignitaries, as I feared."

"Get me likely conspirators," Chase said, starting for the door. "You have ten minutes."

"Wait, you can't possibly contact every lead," Xiu said worriedly.

"Watch me."

The door slammed behind him.

Alec knocked, and within seconds Teresa opened the door, dressed in a black pantsuit with a cream silk blouse underneath. A string of demure pearls hung around her neck. She'd taken great care to impress. A shame she'd be dead soon.

"Like what you see?" She snuggled in close and wrapped her arms around his neck.

"You're a beautiful woman, but business before pleasure." He extricated himself to set the aluminum briefcase on the glass coffee table.

"Not what I wanted to hear," she said, taking a seat on the sofa.

By God, she's high-maintenance. Good thing he planned on offing her after the meeting.

For a minute, the sun broke through the gray blanket of clouds, a sliver of sunlight targeting the brunette. She paled in comparison to Blade. He wondered if he would forever compare women to her.

"We have a little over an hour before the meeting begins," Alec said. "Let's run through the plan again."

She rolled her eyes. "I'm not an imbecile."

He waited expectantly.

"Fine. I find my seat, remove my shoes, set them by my chair, put on my comfortable shoes, and leave. How simple is that?"

Alec opened the case and carefully removed the black suede high heels with the iconic red sole. He held them to the light for inspection. Excellent work. The heels appeared untouched, but the inside had been hollowed out and replaced with a titanium core to keep the serum stable. With a mere press of a button, the nerve agent would be released, causing cardiac arrest or apnea, but always resulting in death.

She moved to the far end of the sofa. "Are you sure this is safe?"

"Would I be standing here if there was any danger?" He pulled her up and drew her to him. "Trust me. There is no danger. I've taken every precaution. You'll be far from the contamination zone when I blow these beauties."

She took the high heels from him and held them warily for a moment at arm's length, then sighed, gingerly slipping them on. A perfect fit. Taking an uneven breath, she began walking around the room as if a gang of pirates were forcing her to walk the plank.

"Be natural, would you?" Alec teased. "You're strutting in the most expensive high heels in the world. Show some attitude." Responding to his playfulness, Teresa straightened and high-stepped her way to him. All the while he thought of Blade commanding the stage in a black leather jumpsuit and boots.

"You're sure this will work?" she said, admiring herself in a mirror.

"No worries, luv. After today, the world will be a much different place."

"The serum will kill everyone in the room?"

"It will kill anyone within one hundred feet in thirty seconds. You like?" he asked.

"I love."

"Chase, where are you?" Blade said into the mic.

"Running," he panted. "Long story. I should be there in four minutes."

Xiu interrupted. "I think we found our man…or woman, in this case. Teresa Escobar, a Venezuelan banker and a member of the President's delegation. She recently traveled to Mallorca."

"What room?" Chase said.

"Room 405 on the fourth floor."

Blade glanced at the monitor and rapidly spoke into her mic. "Alec just left the hotel minus the briefcase."

The two women viewed the monitor as Alec rounded the corner and disappeared from view.

"We can't lose Alec," Blade hissed. He was the one person who could possibly give her answers into Vivienne and the events of the last twenty-four hours.

"We have a bigger problem," Xiu said, looking over Blade's shoulder. "That is Teresa Escobar getting into the black limo. She is on the move—without the briefcase."

CHAPTER
FORTY-SIX

November 30, 8:55 a.m.
Geneva, Switzerland

"I'm headed for the UN. Escobar must be smuggling the serum in some other way." Blade grabbed a set of tactical earbuds and a smartphone from the table.

"I will continue to monitor both the hotel and UN," Xiu said. "Quinn may have handed the briefcase to someone else."

Blade inserted the earbuds while Xiu connected the three of them via smartphone. She skidded to a stop on the sidewalk, frustrated to see commuter traffic still clogging the streets. No taxis in sight. "I may have a problem in finding a ride to the UN," Blade reported over the smartphone.

"What the hell are you doing?" Chase immediately responded.

"No time to explain."

Blade ran into the street, waving her arms for drivers to stop. Some shouted obscenities as they steered to avoid her. In the confusion, a motorcyclist braked and swerved to miss her.

Instantaneously, Blade yanked the driver off the motorcycle, mounted the bike without a word, and shot into traffic like a bullet. The young man shouted after her. Chancing a glance back, she saw he'd torn off his helmet and thrown it after her. It was still bouncing when a delivery truck struck it, propelling the helmet into traffic like a ball inside a pinball machine.

The slush on the street made it difficult for Blade to navigate the bike, and listening to Xiu through the earbud made it worse. It was still difficult to believe that Alec, the man she had met at Gators, could be the mastermind behind all this deception and murder. She would not rest until he was captured—alive. Alec held all the answers, but she had only one question: what was his connection to her mother?

Traffic ahead had slowed to a crawl. A long line of limos waited to pass through the UN security gate. Blade easily moved between cars with tinted windows, making it impossible to see the occupants.

"Xiu, which limo is Teresa Escobar in?"

"She isn't using the main entrance. There is no chance you'll intercept her. Go to Plan B."

"What the hell is Plan B? Chase, what should I do?"

"Get into the building. I'll try to head Escobar off on the grounds."

"The meeting is being held in the Council Chamber, Building C, First Floor," Xiu added.

Blade ditched the motorcycle on a side street between two cars and jogged toward the entrance. Despite the bitter cold, onlookers had gathered to gawk at a wooden sculpture of a giant chair, nearly forty feet tall, with one splintered leg. Her own body felt battered and splintered as she slowed her jog to a walk. She couldn't allow the pain to cloud her concentration.

It appeared the UN was undergoing a major renovation. Construction workers operated cranes as others busied themselves on scaffolding. The noise carried for blocks, and she wondered how the UN held meetings amid the chaos.

None of this appeared to be distracting the security team from screening visitors, leading German Shepherds through the grounds, and patrolling the perimeter with assault rifles. Blade could only assume surveillance cameras blanketed the compound inside and out.

Nervously, she fingered the credentials and badge arranged by Father McCann. He had been so humble when she met him at Il Duomo. But after making the initial phone call asking for his assistance, she discovered he worked in the office of the Cardinal Secretary of State. Within an hour of her request, Blade and Chase were cleared for observing the meeting on behalf of the Pope.

"I'm going through the security checkpoint," Blade said. She felt herself flush as she showed her badge to one of the guards. He studied her for a long minute before gesturing her to a screening area much like an airline's. She sailed through the walk-through metal detector since there had been no time to grab a knife, or any weapon for that matter.

Her black jeans, black puffer jacket, and boots drew unwanted attention from men and women obviously from other nations—delegates—gathering around the Council Chamber. She steadied her pace, willing herself to exhibit not even slightly suspicious behavior.

"I'm in," she said. "No sign of Escobar. Do you see her?"

"I missed her. She'll be with the Venezuelan President. Remember, you're only here to surveil her," Chase warned. "They just closed the door. Once you locate her, don't take your eyes off her. I'll join you as soon as I clear security at the main entrance."

Men and women in black suits patrolled the interior. Blade tried to look inconspicuous by striking up a conversation with the nearest person available. The stately woman, obviously important, stood erect, her shiny black hair worn in a French twist. Her violet sari was rich in texture, its silver sheen luminescent under the lights.

"Are you one of the delegates?" Blade asked, hoping her tone was conversational.

"Obviously," the woman said, giving her the once-over. "Are you some sort of undercover officer?"

"I'm trying to blend in, but *obviously* not doing a very good job." Blade gave the woman a self-deprecating smile. "Will you play a part in the debate?"

"No, I sometimes find debates tedious. Too much talk, not enough action," the woman said. "I should have chosen law enforcement or the military rather than law and diplomacy."

They both laughed. It felt *normal* to engage in small talk.

A man of medium build with slicked-back hair entered the room. He reminded her of a mafia don with a deeply lined face from years in the sun. Teresa kept a few paces behind him carrying a Louis Vuitton tote.

Blade excused herself and reported out of earshot. "I just spotted her carrying only a handbag. What should I do?"

"Do not approach her," Chase said. "She's already gone through security and a metal detector. We may be wrong."

"We're not wrong," Blade argued, moving to get a better view. "Fifteen minutes before the meeting begins. We can't just stand here."

"Keep surveilling."

Frustrated, she observed Teresa Escobar take a seat in an assigned chair behind the Venezuelan President. After a minute, Teresa dug into the tote.

"You won't believe this," Blade said, "but she is replacing her heels for a pair of athletic shoes."

The woman wore an expensive pant suit with a strand of pearls around her neck. She would never make this fashion faux pas. If comfort was a consideration, then patent leather flats would have been a better choice than these.

"Xiu," Blade said, "how much serum would be needed to kill everyone here?"

"Unsure, but if it's more potent than Novichok, maybe two ounces."

"I'm in the building." Chase sounded as though he were fighting to control his breathing. "We have to assume the serum is somewhere in the Council Chamber."

Blade scrutinized every inch of Teresa Escobar, looking for anything that might hold two ounces of serum. Teresa stood and walked to the Venezuelan President. Leaning over, she whispered into his ear. He nodded, then turned his attention to China's Foreign Minister. She turned, picked up her handbag, and headed for the door.

"She's on the move," Blade said in a hushed tone. "Without her heels. It has to be her shoes! We need to evacuate the building."

"I'll alert security to start an evacuation and call in a hazmat team," Chase said. "Blade, follow her. We need her as a witness."

It's about time.

She slid through the door and stepped into the corridor. Escobar moved briskly in the direction of the main lobby. There were several pockets of delegates lining the corridor, but none took notice of Escobar. Blade quickened her pace.

Escobar glanced behind her, and their eyes met. In a flash, Blade saw recognition dawn in the woman's eyes, like a wild animal caught in a snare. She did the only thing she could do—run.

Blade turned on the speed, only fifteen feet away. Escobar threw her handbag aside to allow the use of both arms to increase her speed, but she couldn't outpace Blade.

The door to the main entrance lay just ahead, and still no security team in sight.

Damn.

Blade leaped through the air and delivered a resounding kick to her back before landing solidly on both feet. Escobar's outstretched arms absorbed the fall before her body slid over the carpeted floor. Chase and a five-person security team surrounded the inert woman, guns drawn.

"Put your hands to your sides, palms up!" Chase commanded.

Escobar remained motionless.

Blade considered whether she hid a weapon on her person and was just waiting to attack.

Chase moved in, grabbing one of her arms and cuffing one wrist, and repeated the motion for the other arm. Once both arms were cuffed, Chase rolled her over onto her back.

Escobar's body convulsed, then stilled.

Chase quickly uncuffed her while one of the security team started CPR.

Emergency responders, already on high alert, made their way through the lobby. From the corner of her eye, she saw an EMT shake his head over Escobar. *Our only witness, dead.*

Blade leaned her back against the wall, slowly allowing herself down to a sitting position. Chase slumped beside her.

"The shoes are contained, but I'm afraid Alec has disappeared," Chase said.

The news did not surprise her. The Great Mancini would have applauded this masterpiece of misdirection. While they were occupied in containing the serum, Alec had vanished into his shadow world. He hadn't left her alive because of a connection between them, but to ensure the serum would be recovered and contained. She should be relieved, yet the thought of his flagrant self-preservation disturbed her.

Blade closed her eyes, exhausted and emotionally spent. "Did she commit suicide or was she poisoned? Escobar could have made a deal, possibly even escaped a prison sentence."

Chase shrugged and clasped his hands together, using his thumbs to massage his brow. "I've given up trying to explain why people do horrible things to themselves and others. Teresa Escobar and others like her live without hope or faith in anything but themselves. Sometimes that isn't enough to keep living."

CHAPTER
FORTY-SEVEN

December 15, 3:35 p.m.
Siena, Italy

The castle rested on a high hill overlooking acres of vineyards and olive groves. Over the centuries, the Soldati had used this bastion as a final resting place for their fallen soldiers and for the recuperation of wounded ones.

Vivienne's ashes rested in an engraved copper urn on a heavy wooden table amid a feast of lavender, hyacinth, white roses, and lilacs. Blade imagined the oak table had been used many times over the centuries for the same purpose: giving homage to the dead. The courtyard, as large as a football field, seemed sorrowful with only a solitary olive tree and a sliver of grass to soften the dull brown earth.

Blade could not decide which was worse: Marie's casket being lowered into the ground or Vivienne's vibrant life and warrior spirit condensed into this small container. Holding her biological mother while she died in her arms had changed Blade in ways she couldn't compre-hend—not yet. She'd *felt* the moment Vivienne's spirit left her body. How could she explain the unexplainable?

Thomas, Chase, Finn, Xiu, and Father McCann—the newest member of the Soldati— stood in a semicircle facing the table. The sweet subtle aroma of the flowers filled the air. "Your mother loved the color purple and the scent of lavender," Luc said under his breath as Blade stood stoically near the makeshift altar. This detail was one more nugget to tuck away in her growing knowledge of Vivienne.

Each member of the team, in turn, told a story about their comrade and friend. Some hilarious, others genuine and authentic, but the most heart-wrenching was Luc's simple statement—"I should have asked her to be my wife."

Thomas cleared his throat before turning misty eyes to Blade as he prepared to deliver the final scripture. "Vivienne was more than my friend and confidante," he said, his voice husky with emotion. "I loved her. She asked me to read this today, in the event that she…" he paused to steady himself, "that she went home before me. In Romans 8:37-39, Paul writes:

"No, in all these things we are more than conquerors through him who loved us. For I am convinced that neither death nor life, neither angels nor demons, neither the present nor the future, nor any powers, neither height nor depth, nor anything else in all creation, will be able to separate us from the love of God that is in Christ Jesus our Lord."

A stiff, chill wind blew through the courtyard, as if Vivienne had breathed one last gasp on them all.

The next morning, Blade stood like a lone sentry on the castle turret, surveying the land before her. Wisps of fog still lifted from the gently rolling hills revealing acres of vineyards, green open fields, and tall cypress trees in the far distance. On a clear day, one could see the cities of Florence, San Gimignano, and Pisa. Like the men and women who had traversed these smooth stones in centuries past, she searched for signs of an enemy's attack, of Alec or his mercenaries, but she noted nothing peculiar in this lush countryside.

She burrowed into her wool coat, a clear signal the onset of winter and the Christmas season were upon them. This was Marie's favorite time of year. Blade wondered what Marie would think about the past colliding with the present, and the ramifications of secrets pierced in darkness now revealed in the light.

Joining her, Chase whistled low. "You have the best seat in the house."

"It's breathtaking. No wonder the Soldati di Cristo chose this place as their sanctuary."

"Some of us call this home."

Indeed, Thomas had shown her the catacombs under the castle yesterday. A thankful nobleman, centuries before, had bequeathed this estate to the Soldati. The catacombs were converted to hold vaults of their valiant brothers-in-arms. Vivienne would rest with hundreds of fellow soldiers, including Shen. A fitting place for a warrior.

"Tell me more about Vivienne," she said softly.

Chase chuckled. "Vivienne was one tough woman. Always had my six. Committed. Private. Willing to compromise her principles in order to protect you."

Blade touched his hand and slowly entwined her fingers in his. Never looking at him, but keeping her eyes on the Chianti Mountains on the distant horizon.

"I can tell you she has no regrets. And she'd want you to live a full life." He squeezed her hand. "Believe me, survivor's guilt can eat at your soul. Vivienne helped me through the worst of my self-punishment."

"Those last few minutes in the chalet. If I'd been smarter, attacked sooner, we both could have made it out alive," Blade said. She swallowed her tears, nearly choking on the memory of Vivienne impaled in the snow.

"That's exactly the kind of thinking that will keep you from living the life God meant you to live." He gently turned Blade by her shoulders to face him. "The brotherhood teaches us to rely on each other and gives us a purpose greater than ourselves." Chase drew her close and wrapped his arms around her. "Join us. Be a part of our family of misfits."

"How could I be a soldier of Christ when I'm not sure there is a God? I'm more confused than ever."

Chase pressed on. "We all feel that way at one time or another. After Cheyenne was murdered, I turned to drinking myself into oblivion. But then, your mother stood shoulder to shoulder with me and helped me fight my guilt and shame—my demons. I want to stand with you. Help in any way I can. What do you say?"

After a few moments, she said, "I need to go home, maybe get a dose of normal. Maybe even meet with my father and clear the air—be honest with each other—for once." She rested her hand on his chest. "I've never met anyone like you, and that's a compliment."

He reddened at the praise.

"I want to get to know you better, Mr. Chase Maserati. I'll be back. That's a promise." Lifting on the tips of her toes, she kissed him lightly on the cheek.

But she had some unfinished business—find Alec Quinn and make him pay.

Reluctantly, Blade pulled away, looking into his bright blue eyes that never missed a detail.

"You can contact me, day or night," Chase reminded her.

As she returned to her bedroom, she knew this moment must sustain her for the next few months. Chase was exactly the man he portrayed— she valued the strength he exuded, applauded his character and integrity, and he was easy on the eyes. This felt more like a death march than the next chapter in her life. Why couldn't she stay right here and leave well enough alone? Let Alec Quinn live his life.

Marie had encouraged her to think for herself, believe that she was capable of anything in life, and stay the course. Unwittingly, Vivienne's death had given her purpose, a future beyond throwing knives and making a mediocre living.

She closed the bedroom door and sat on the edge of her bed. One solitary black rose lay on the white pillowcase.

Hesitantly, she picked up the rose and brought it to her nose, its aroma sweet and heady. She remembered a tattoo of a black rose on Alec's forearm. He'd claimed it symbolized power and strength. A thorn pricked her thumb. Blade pressed around the wound until a droplet of blood hit the floor.

Alec had thrown down the gauntlet.

How did he make it through the Soldati defenses? She hurried to the window. No smoke, no sound of shots being fired, no explosions. Only the rush of wind past the hillside.

Opening a window, she snapped the bud from the stem and squeezed, allowing her restrained anger to roll over and through her. Hoping Alec was watching through binoculars, she stretched out her arm through the window and opened her fist. Mangled rose petals scattered on the breeze, lifting and swirling in every direction.

She accepted the challenge in the sure knowledge that both mothers would have done nothing less.

ACKNOWLEDGMENTS

Thank you, dear reader, for making it to "the end." I sincerely hope you enjoyed the book as much as I loved writing it! The time spent with my characters has been an absolute joy, and I anticipate the second Blade Broussard book will be just as thrilling.

Forever and always—many thanks and love to Mark, my husband, who has supported me through the ups and downs of my creative process, the challenges of COVID, and the loss of loved ones during the past six years. He has been a rock and the voice of reason on so many occasions. He is truly the best man I know.

Monica, my daughter, has been a constant surprise in my life. Since the beginning of my writing journey, she has been a trusted partner in crime. Someone who I've come to rely on for her sharp intuition and invaluable advice. Her husband, Jeff, is my resident expert in all things that go bang in the night. I am forever grateful to you both!

I extend my heartfelt thanks to all the unsung heroes who have helped improve this novel. I would like to give a special shout-out to Jacob and Amy (www.thejustices.co), who have been in my corner for years. I will always be your cheerleader and friend. Last but not least, Twyla and Diana. Thank you for being part of my posse of first readers. It is no little commitment to give your time and invaluable feedback.

ABOUT THE AUTHOR

An adventuress at heart, Nannette Potter lives vicariously through her fearless and impetuous characters, inventing lives balanced on a knife's edge. PIERCE THE DARKNESS, her debut international thriller, inspired by her Christian faith, was a 2022 Claymore Award finalist. Beyond writing, she loves spending time with family and traveling the globe, where she dreams up future novels while sipping mango margaritas. An active member of Sisters in Crime, she lives with her soulmate and husband, Mark, in California's Central Valley.